CECE RIOS
and the
KING OF FEARS

Also by Kaela Rivera:
Cece Rios and the Desert of Souls

CECE RIOS

and the
KING OF FEARS

KAELA RIVERA

HARPER

An Imprint of HarperCollins*Publishers*

Library of Congress Control Number: 2022940755
ISBN 978-0-06-321389-0

Typography by Catherine Lee
22 23 24 25 26   PC/LSCH   10 9 8 7 6 5 4 3 2 1
❖
First Edition

For my younger self. Don't be afraid. I promise you: life will sprout from the ashes.

Prologue

When Juana and I walked into our home together, our casa was too quiet.

The kitchen was empty. Two plates of cold food sat untouched and forgotten on the tabletop. Juana squeezed my hand. Off to the right, the curtain sectioning off Mamá and Papá's bed was pulled back, but the bed was made, and no one was in it. Beside it, Papá's boots, clothes, and bags were gone.

My heart clenched, and I gripped Juana's hand tighter. Together, we turned to the fireplace.

Mamá sat there alone.

She knelt near the flames, her hands covering her face. She looked small there, in a way Mamá never had before. I realized after only a few moments that her shoulders were shaking, and the sound of sobs twisted up from her slumped form.

For the first time ever, my mamá was crying during the criatura months.

Tears filled my eyes immediately. Mamá was *crying*. She must have thought she'd lost both of her daughters forever. I stumbled forward.

"Mamá," I called out.

She shifted around. Her eyelids were puffy and reddened, her wide face streaked with tears where I'd normally only seen nocheztli war paint. She glanced from me to Juana, back and forth. Her eyes widened. They grew so large, it seemed like they would engulf us both.

"Cece?" She hesitated and looked to Juana again. "J-Juana?"

Mamá had never said our names that way before. Like she wasn't sure if we were real. And the way her gaze reached for us—like she thought we might fade away. Because it was loco, impossible, to think that we were here, wasn't it? The daughter who'd been stolen by El Sombrerón. The daughter who'd left to become a bruja right after.

I smiled. Mamá covered her mouth in disbelief. "I brought Juana back, Mamá. Just like I said I would!" I wiggled my and Juana's joined hands. A smile finally spread on Juana's face.

"No puedo creerlo," Mamá said to herself, shaking her head. I couldn't blame her. It *was* hard to believe.

But Juana, as always, seemed to know exactly what to do. She let go of my hand, charged across the room, and launched herself into Mamá.

"I missed you!" she burst out, throwing her arms around Mamá's frame. "¡Te quiero! ¡Te quiero, Mamá!"

She repeated so many *I love yous* that she could barely breathe. And Mamá pulled back to stare at her, to run her fingers through her hair, to say her name. My heart swelled big and wide. This was exactly what I'd hoped for. And when Mamá's face collapsed into tears again, I knew she finally believed what she was seeing. She kissed every inch of Juana's face she could reach. She squeezed her close. I held myself and watched, still smiling.

My familia was finally back together. Tears of joy filled my eyes.

After a moment, Mamá looked up at me as she clasped Juana to her chest. She reached a hand out. I held my breath.

"Cece." Her voice shook. "You—you really brought your hermana back. H-how?" The edges of a smile hovered around her trembling mouth.

Her question gave me the courage I needed to approach her. "You're not mad that I'm a bruja?" I whispered.

Mamá kept her hand extended. "Cece, I don't understand it. But this—bringing familias together, saving hermanas—is not what brujas do. And you are mi hija. In a moment, I will listen to your whole story. Everything you've wanted to tell me. Right now, just let me hold you."

My toes tingled with the same hope I saw swimming in her gaze. Mamá wanted to listen. I reached for her. She immediately pulled me close and wrapped her large, warm arms around me and Juana, her tears dotting my scalp.

"Oh, Mis hijas," she wailed. She caressed my head as I pressed my face into her collarbone and cried in relief. Juana's hand gripped the back of my shirt. Mamá rocked us in her hold. "mis hijas, you're back. Everything can be okay now. Everything."

For that long, beautiful moment, I forgot about Papá's missing shoes and clothes. I pushed them to the back of my mind and let myself believe that everything was okay, that I'd put our whole family back together, the way I'd promised myself I would. Mamá's and Juana's hugs were so warm, and I wanted to bathe in that comfort for as long as possible.

We didn't sleep that night. We were all absolute wrecks—Juana's shoulder-length hair frizzed at the ends, Mamá had cried so hard that her face swelled up, and the black eye Papá had given me probably looked even worse than it felt. But there was too much to talk about. Too much to finally laugh about. We cuddled up together on a bed of pillows and blankets in front of the fireplace, holding each other, sharing with each other, in awe of each other. And as morning light filled our house, I finally realized Papá wasn't coming home.

1
Feliz cumpleaños, Cece Rios
About two months later

My birthday was always during Semana de la Cosecha—
the Week of the Reaping. And this year, I had to make
sure it didn't steal away my new criatura friends.

Dominga del Sol carefully teased out a few jade beads
from her hair and let them drop like dew into my palms.
We stood together in the laundry room of the Sun Sanctuary, with the low evening light trickling in through the
one window. I kept glancing between the jade beads and
the delicate book propped open on the counter on my
right, *Cantos de Curanderas II*.

"Okay," I said. "I think that's enough. I only needed
a few more to finish the jade ring around my house." I
pocketed the jade with a shaky smile. "Muchas gracias,
Dominga del Sol."

"I'm happy to help," she said, and eased the book shut
carefully, like it was made of glass.

I couldn't blame her—as one of the last books remaining

from the curanderas, it was so old some of its pages were crumbling into dust. Dominga del Sol had been nice enough to let me read it even though it was part of her secret collection.

"Is there anything else you need to finish this spell, mija?" She smiled up at me.

"I don't think so." I ran through the list in my head again. "Mamá came home early to help place the basil, moonstone, water jars, and fire opal inside the house. So I just need to finish the circle, and, hopefully, the hunting parties won't even notice my house is there, let alone any of us inside it." I swallowed and squeezed the jade beads tight in my pocket. "The only thing I need for the spell now is . . . a curandera to activate it."

Dominga del Sol's brows pulled together. "Is it getting worse?"

I shuffled my feet and tried not to meet her eyes. Dominga del Sol was the only person who knew that my powers had been slowly flickering away over the past couple of months. Neither of us knew why. It's not like they'd *disappeared* exactly, but it was getting harder to use them every day. It was as if every time I tried to call out to the water, something shouted over me and drowned out my voice.

I sighed. That was the whole reason I was using this

curandera spell. The book said items from nature, from the four gods, could bolster a curandera's powers and allow them to accomplish more intricate magical effects. It didn't explain *why* it worked like that, but I hoped the power-strengthening parts of the spell would make up for what I lacked.

"I see." Dominga del Sol cocked her head so her long black-and-gray braids swished across her sunny robes. "There is much about your powers we still do not understand. You have no teacher, and what the curanderas left behind is—incomplete." She patted the worn *Cantos de Curanderas II.* "But be patient, mija. You will grow with time. And the people you love will surely support you."

The urge to cry rose in my chest. But I called up a smile to push it back. "Mamá and Juana are working so hard in the fields now that Papá is gone. They've sacrificed so much. I can't let them down tonight." I nodded harder, like that would help courage stick to my ribs.

Dominga del Sol's brows pulled together. But she smiled after a moment and pushed my hair away from my forehead. It had grown back a few inches, so it curled around my ears now.

"It is good you want to help your familia," she said. "But there are better ways to love someone, Cecelia, than to carry all their pain for them." Her gaze dropped to my neck.

I tried to soak in her words, but they slipped off me like rain on tile. What did she mean? I felt the necklaces at my collarbone, hidden beneath my shirt. There were five—one for each of the five souls I bore. Coyote, whose soul was filled with worried gray and kind pink. Little Lion, with his stormy, hot feelings. Kit Fox, cool and sunshiny all at once. And Ocelot, with the steadiness of confident orange. And, of course, mine. Shaped like a tear and dangling on an old, crumbly leather strap, the bright turquoise reminded me I was supposed to be a better curandera than I was right now.

I looked over at *Cantos de Curanderas II* again. It sometimes referred to the extensive training curanderas were supposed to go through in the sanctuary belonging to their god. I wondered, for about the thousandth time, whether it would be worth trying to find the mysterious Ocean Sanctuary. Maybe it would help fix my powers. Then I could protect my familia better, and they wouldn't have pain for anyone to carry.

Across the room, a knock sounded at the door.

"Oh," Dominga del Sol said. "Cece, could you get that?" She turned back to her laundry.

"Sure," I said and ran across the room to pull the door open.

My older hermana, Juana, stood just outside.

Her hands sat on her hips, her hair waving around her

face and framing her black almond-shaped eyes. She used to keep her hair longer, but it had been shoulder-length since our battle with El Sombrerón. She wore a long black-and-red dress today, her hem covered in dirt from working in the fields. And for the first time in weeks, she wasn't scowling.

"Cece!" she said. "Why weren't you at home, birthday girl?" Juana smiled, but the expression didn't reach her eyes. "I got home, and Mamá said you'd run off here." She reached out and squished my cheeks. "What? You that scared to be thirteen?"

I beamed between her warm hands. Juana had been in a bad mood basically since she'd come home. But she seemed extra nice today. Birthdays were the best.

"No!" I laughed. "I just had to grab more jade for"—I leaned in to her and dropped my voice—"the preparations for Semana de la Cosecha."

Juana's face tightened. "Eh. Right. Better get going, then." She dropped her hands from my cheeks, grabbed my wrist, and tugged me out of the building. "Adiós, Dominga del Sol!" she called back as she pulled me down the stairs.

Dominga appeared in the doorway. "Adiós, chiquitas. Hurry home and be safe!" She gazed up at the burning sky. "Semana de la Cosecha will soon be upon us."

Juana's face tensed as she dragged me away. "And so will the hunting parties."

The sun was lowering fast, so Juana walked faster. She scanned the adobe houses on either side of the road as we went, with every turn and every step. She did that a lot now. Like she expected something to leap out from the shadows of our neighbors' roofs.

Semana de la Cosecha wasn't usually dangerous for humans. Most people in Tierra del Sol even looked forward to it, since it meant El Cucuy's hunting parties took every criatura they could find back home to Devil's Alley. The secret entrance would seal shut after that for another nine months, and most of my people could finally relax. But most of them didn't have four criatura friends stowed away in their house. And none of them had beaten El Cucuy's Dark Saints to rescue their sister either.

Juana and I turned onto our street. There was a quiet hustle and bustle as a few of our neighbors were still out chatting about the end of the criatura months. But the moment we came into view, heads turned Juana's way. And her scowl deepened as their whispers changed.

"That's her, isn't it? I haven't seen her in a while." I heard someone say to their friend as we passed.

The other one nodded. "Juana Rios, the Sun-Heart."

"They say she burned her way out of Devil's Alley,

slaying every criatura and bruja in her way. The only Bride of El Sombrerón to ever return from his clutches."

Juana gritted her teeth. People had been talking a lot about her since she'd come back—even more than they used to. Before she'd gotten stolen by El Sombrerón, they'd respected her, sure. But now, the townspeople treated my fiery hermana like a demigod. A miracle. But Juana didn't smile and chat with them the way she used to. Now, as I looked up at her, her mouth was flat and hard, and small dots of sweat traced her jaw, like she was overheating from the inside.

I squeezed her hand. "Are you okay?" I whispered.

She gripped me tightly. "Let's just hurry," she mumbled, and dragged me to our front door.

Juana went inside immediately and called out to Mamá. But I stooped down by the side of our door and knelt to finish the jade ring I'd been making earlier. I'd run out with only about two feet to go. I let out a relieved sigh as I placed the jade beads like seeds into the thin trench Coyote and Little Lion had dug the night before. Once I finished, I hesitated and laid my hands over the last one. Maybe I should run a quick test and see if the stones would even respond to my weakened powers. Just in case. I closed my eyes. *Please help me do this*, I called out in my mind. My throat tightened as I tried to reach out to the stones. *Por favor. I have to be able to do this for my familia and friends.*

The jade stones didn't react. My soul dimmed, and I pulled my hands to my chest, biting my lip.

"Psst. Cece."

I lifted my head. Our front door was propped open, just an inch, and a pair of golden eyes and a curl of white hair peeked out at me. Coyote winked.

I stood up to block him from view of our neighbors. "What is it?"

"Come inside," he said. "We got you a present."

A present? I bit my lip again. We had been really tight on money since Papá left. Why had they gotten me something? He backed away from the door so I could slip inside. I shut the door behind me quickly so no one got a peek of my—uh—unique familia.

Inside, colorful red ropes tied with knots of basil hung over every window and door. Mamá must have lit a dozen candles all around the room, and colorful jars of water sat beside the front door. It looked like everything was ready for the spell. But more important, Coyote, Ocelot, Little Lion, Mamá, and Juana stood together in front of me, smiling.

"Feliz cumpleaños, Cece!" they said in unison.

A rush of feeling nearly turned to tears in my eyes. Everything had felt harder since I'd returned home with

Juana. But seeing Mamá smiling, even when she was clearly tired, and my friends standing with her, and even Juana trying *not* to be mad—it warmed me from my toes to my head.

Coyote stretched out his arms, holding a small package. "It's from all of us."

I glanced down at the package, which was wrapped in a piece of white paper that had clearly been ripped out from one of my schoolbooks. I'd worry about that later. I peeled the paper back, and bright colors came into view.

I gasped and pulled the dainty present free of the confines. It was a necklace. It had a strong thick leather strand as a base, with bright blue and green threads wrapped around it to strengthen it. The pattern of colors mimicked my turquoise soul stone perfectly.

"For your soul," Coyote said. His smile wavered, and a snake of gray feelings moved in his soul. "I may not be able to put your soul stone back inside your chest yet, but this should make things more comfortable in the meantime." He cleared his throat. His soul pulsed with a brief, bleak gray.

Oh. I clasped the gift to my chest. Ever since Rodrigo, the Soul Stealer, had taken my soul out of my body, Coyote had watched me more carefully, like he was afraid someone would try to steal it, the way brujas did with criaturas.

"Muchas gracias. It's beautiful!" I slipped my soul stone necklace off my neck and switched the old strap out for the new one. Coyote grinned. When I put on the new one, I caught Juana watching my teardrop of turquoise. Her face was blank, completely unreadable. But there was a heaviness in the air around her.

Sometimes, I wished I could touch Juana's soul stone. Maybe then I'd understand what she was feeling.

"Later, we'll celebrate your birthday properly!" Mamá came over and kissed the top of my head, so I giggled. Then she straightened up, eyeing the door as a familiar, gut-flipping sound rumbled outside. "But it's time, Cece."

My insides went cold. The hunting parties. They were already on their way.

Mamá squeezed my shoulders. "You can do this, mija."

I'd longed for Mamá to believe in me like this for years. And I wasn't going to let her down now. With a shaky breath, I knelt by the door and took my soul out of my shirt. Coyote picked up a jar of water. We'd rehearsed this at least five times already. But now that the moment was here, my hands were shaking. Come on, me. We'd done everything right. This would work. The distant sound of feet pounding against the desert dirt shook the ground. Shrieks and moans built from far down the street. I closed my eyes and prayed one last time.

"You got this, Cece." Coyote knelt beside me. "Don't be scared. After this, we can finally relax." He smiled. "¿Sí?"

Relax. Yeah. Coyote held the jar aloft, ready to pour, and I held my soul just a couple of inches above the door's threshold. The noise outside grew closer, so I could make out the beat of marching feet. Mamá and Juana stood nearby. Ocelot, Little Lion, and Kit Fox crouched behind me, listening, waiting—ready to defend. I nodded to Coyote just as the sound of feet, growls, and prowls avalanched toward our home.

Coyote poured the water over my hands. It trickled down my soul, through my fingers, and ran out the space beneath the door to fill the small jade-dotted trench outside, just like the *Cantos de Curanderas II* said it should. I grabbed hold of the warmth I'd felt earlier, seeing my familia, and imagined my love wrapping around us like a shield. The water began to glow. My heart leaped. The air hummed, and my senses stretched wide.

Through the crack between the door and the wall, I saw the mob of criaturas and brujas fly past. I held my breath and waited. None of them noticed my house. The water continued to glow. ¡Qué bueno! I just had to hold this until they left—

Suddenly, a criatura stopped right in front of the house.

He was clearly a dark criatura—one of the destructive

spirits that Coyote had made to take vengeance on Naked Man for its brujas. He was nearly seven feet tall, with a skeletal build, his ribs protruding, his arms so long and bony that his hands scraped the ground. I froze and gripped my soul tight. The water's light flickered for just a second. The dark criatura turned his head in our direction. I forced my fear back and waited, holding my breath. He—couldn't see us, right? For a moment, there was nothing but distant rumbling and suffocating silence. Then, a bruja stepped into view, and I realized he'd been looking at her all along.

"You will have to take care of Tierra del Sol from here," the dark criatura said. I could hear him, somehow, like my senses had stretched outside with the water. "El Cucuy wants me to retrieve Cecelia Rios before the door to Devil's Alley closes."

Coyote, Kit, Lion, and Ocelot stiffened. A roar of feelings—my own and my friends'—crowded the stone in my hand and echoed in my chest. El Cucuy was after me? The water's light flickered again, and I struggled to hang on to the warm feelings that kept it flowing.

The bruja sighed. "You know how hard that'll be without El Sombrerón? Ay, this is so unfair. Unloading all the work on me. Shouldn't the third Dark Saint help at least?"

"She has her own orders to attend to," the dark criatura's voice was electric, deep, scratchy. "As do I. Now, stop complaining"—he raised his needly fingers toward her, and she flinched—"or do you want me to show you the power of the new form El Cucuy has given me?"

The bruja lifted her chin but took a subtle step back. "Never mind, El Silbón," she spat. "I get it."

A gasp stuck in my throat. I scanned the dark criatura's spidery height, his long, clawed hands, and the white holes for eyes that occasionally disappeared under the brim of his hat. That was *El Silbón*? What exactly had El Cucuy done to him? He didn't look anything like the squat announcer who'd run the Bruja Fights. Except for—I spotted the bag he still had slung over his shoulder—the bones he carried. I gulped.

"Go on, then. I'll handle the reaping. You hunt the curandera." Beyond the door, the bruja waved El Silbón away. "We'll meet back up at sunrise."

The bruja strode out of view and called for her criatura. There was a rush of feet, and a roar shuddered through the air and settled on my skin in prickles. El Silbón watched her for a moment—then, in a movement like the slash of a knife, he sprinted forward and disappeared from sight.

My body tingled with sharp, confused feelings. I waited a whole minute before breathing again. Another five minutes until the rumbling of the hunting party vanished from earshot completely. Ten minutes until Coyote stopped pouring the water, and I slowly rose from the ground. My mind whirled with El Silbón's new, frightening form and far more frightening words. El Cucuy was after me. I checked Mamá's and Juana's expressions—they didn't seem to have heard. But one glance at Coyote's hard face, and I knew he had.

What was I going to do? I struggled to keep the fear from sinking its hard teeth into my friends' souls. If El Cucuy was after me, and my power was barely even working—my chest squeezed—would I be able to protect my familia? Why did he want me in the first place?

That was a dumb question, I guess. I'd defeated El Sombrerón and Rodrigo, his second and third Dark Saints. He probably wanted revenge. I tucked my soul into my shirt as questions and panic stung my skin. How long could I stay ahead of El Silbón if he was hunting me? What—what if he caught me? Would he really drag me all the way to Devil's Alley?

I tried not to let the fear crush my or my friends' souls. But Devil's Alley was a place so terrible that my powerful friends shuddered at its very name. What would a place like that do to me? Especially now that my curandera power—the only thing that made me strong—was barely working?

"This is stupid!" Juana threw down the basil she'd been holding and crushed it into the floor with her heel. "We're risking *our* lives so Cece can keep her little criatura *friends* around," she yelled, and, distancing herself across the room, glared at Coyote, Kit, Lion, and Ocelot.

I stumbled around to look at her. For a second, heat flushed up my chest and rattled with panic. But I shook my head. Juana's eyes were on fire. Right now, she needed me. I'd worry about the rest later.

"Juana," I approached her softly. "Please don't say that."

"Why not?" she barked.

I jumped.

Her eyes glowed with the burning orange of the fireplace, and her hands knotted into fists. "They should go back to Devil's Alley where they belong!"

The words shook the room. Mamá's face tightened. Coyote glared but didn't speak. Ocelot held still and calm, as always. Kit Fox edged toward me, the way he usually did when he was nervous around Juana.

But it was Lion who decided to speak. "I would think you, of all humans, would know why no one should be in Devil's Alley against their will." His gaze matched hers, burning for burning.

A pulse moved through the room. Like a skipped heartbeat, or a sharp intake of breath. Juana never talked about Devil's Alley. I gripped my shirt and peeked at her.

"Juana . . . ?" I started.

She screamed and lunged at Lion. I yelped. But Lion

didn't retreat, even as she grabbed the front of his shirt and shook him.

"How would you know what it was like?" she roared. Lion was strong enough that she didn't actually move him much, and he held his ground with a terrible calm. "You think you have any idea how trapped and broken I— *No!* You have no idea what I went through!"

Coyote and Mamá dove for them. I joined them late, reaching for Juana's mud-splattered dress as her nails left red half-moons on Lion's bare arms.

"You think I *don't* know?" he hollered back, just as loud. Coyote tried to drag him away, but Lion resisted. "You think I don't know exactly what it's like to be you?" Moisture caught in his crimson eyes.

"Juana, stop!" I grabbed the edge of her skirt.

Coyote yanked on Lion again. "She's hurting you! Step back!"

Mamá looped her arms around Juana's waist from behind and pulled her back. "¡Mija! Shh! We don't know how far away the hunting party is."

But Juana still kicked and slashed her nails at him like they were claws. Lion finally caught her wrist to stop an oncoming blow, and a flash of surprise stirred his soul at my throat. His hand tightened on Juana's wrist.

Mamá got a better hold on her and dragged her back. Lion finally released her, but his stare remained glued to the wrist he'd held. Juana swung her fists, even as Mamá dragged her into the kitchen.

"Are you okay?" I turned to Lion. Juana's nails had left red lines on his shoulders.

He fixed his stare on her. "Cece, something's wrong with Juana."

My stomach wrapped around itself. Across the room, Juana's fight dissolved into panting. Her thick black hair hung over her face, so I could see only one raging eye glaring out from the wild waves.

Mamá rocked Juana side to side. "Shh, shh, shh," Mamá said. Slowly, she stroked Juana's hair. "It's okay." Mamá embraced her. "No more fighting. You're safe, mija."

Juana's eyes closed. Her chin dimpled and started shaking. The room bloated with the silence of my sister trying not to cry.

I squeezed my hands together. Lion was right. Something was wrong. "I know," I whispered to him. "I just—don't know how to fix it for her."

And I was afraid it was my fault.

"No, Cece." The scratches on Lion's face had faded to pale brown lines already, but they still must've hurt. "I mean *really* wrong." I went to ask more, but he took a few steps forward, eyeing Mamá. "Señora Rios, check Juana's heartbeat."

Mamá's brows tugged together. I straightened. What

kind of request was that?

Still looking bewildered, Mamá slowly lowered her ear to Juana's chest. Juana tried to pull away, glaring at Lion the whole time, but Mamá's grip would not be resisted.

After a few moments, Mamá released Juana and gasped.

"Juana," she said, her voice aghast. "You have no heart-beat!"

2
The Heart of Juana Rios

I sat in my bed, my favorite blanket pulled tight around me. Mamá had made it for me for my tenth birthday, stitched together with brilliant reds and oranges, yellows and sharp pinks. My favorite colors—colors that burned bright as the sun.

Mamá and Cece sat on Cece's bed across from mine, ogling me. I sighed out my nose and glared at my bare feet. The mud between my toes was uncomfortable, but nowhere as bad as Mamá's and Cece's gawking.

"Can you stop looking at me like I'm going to fall apart?" I snapped.

Heat burned inside my chest. When I'd first come home a little over two months ago, it had been only a light throb of heat, just on occasion. But it had grown hotter, more painful, as each week went by. Like a sunburn from hours in the desert. Except this sunburn was on the inside, and as it had gotten stronger, my heartbeat had gotten weaker.

Until, a week ago, it disappeared completely.

"How is it possible?" Mamá asked quietly.

I threw my hands out. "I don't know, okay?" This was why I hadn't told them. I knew it would freak them out. Cece already watched me like she thought I'd crumble any second. And Mamá examined me whenever I got even a little mad, like she was searching for something toxic growing inside me. But I didn't know why this was happening either. I'd just hoped it would go away if I ignored it long enough.

I scraped the mud off my feet. "All I know is I'm fine. Kind of. I'm not dead. I'm just . . ."

"Without a heartbeat," Mamá said, and her voice was hard. Clearly, she thought it *wasn't* fine.

I already knew that. But I didn't know what else to say because it was just how my life was now. It had been since I'd come home. Since Cece had had to rescue me.

I'd been avoiding looking at Cece since her pet Little Lion blurted out my secret, but I finally turned and faced my little sister.

Cece's eyes had always been dark and shiny, like two river stones. But her new, short haircut made them rounder and gentler than ever. And it made the slight sheen of tears on the edge of her thick lashes more obvious, too. I averted my gaze again. Lately, she always seemed on the verge of crying.

"It must have to do with El Sombrerón and Devil's Alley," Mamá said. The sunburn heat inside me kicked up a notch just at the mention. "What could it be? A curse? I have never heard of a curse that steals a heartbeat and leaves a life behind." She lifted her head. "Is there anything else, Juana? Other symptoms?"

There was so much more. I couldn't sleep anymore, for one. And my hair hadn't grown a single centimeter since I had come back—like it was frozen at the length El Sombrerón had cut it, when I was stuck inside his prison, cornered in the castle of the terrible El Cucuy.

The sunburn grew hotter inside me, and I shuddered. Flashes of El Sombrerón's hands, his sharp claws, and his towering glare, scraped my insides.

"Isn't a missing heartbeat enough?" I forced out. I knew I should tell them more. But—the words always seemed to bury themselves inside me before I got the chance.

"I have an idea," Cece said.

Mamá and I both turned to her. Cece was staring out the window with her shiny eyes, like she could see something we couldn't. Her small hands gripped the front of her shirt. The movement pulled the fabric away from her neck, so I could see the necklaces lining her throat. Five souls. Four criaturas souls, and her own, outside of her chest.

I nearly shivered. Seeing her soul stones always gave me

the creeps. I didn't know how she could stand it. No one should get to carry someone else's soul like that. It was wrong.

I knew from experience.

"Mamá." Cece shifted toward her. "I know you've never liked curandera stuff, but . . . Dominga del Sol let me study some of their books she found." Cece sounded worried, but Mamá's hard expression melted. She hadn't seemed to mind criatura or curandera stuff lately. I gripped my knees. Mamá had softened so much since we'd both come home. Sometimes, that scared me more than anything. "Some of them mention the Ocean Sanctuary. If I went there, I might be able to fix my—I mean, find answers about your heart, Juana. Maybe I can even discover a way to heal it for you."

My skin crawled at Cece's sincerity, like my body didn't know how to handle gentle feelings anymore. She wanted to help me so much.

How did I tell her that I wasn't sure I could be helped?

"You know where the Ocean Sanctuary is, Cece?" Mamá asked.

Cece hesitated. "Um, not exactly . . ." She bit her bottom lip. That wasn't a good sign. "But I know from Dominga del Sol's books that it's supposed to be on the east coast of Antiguo Amanecer, around Costa de los Sueños, apparently." Mamá's brows drew in concern. Cece's voice withered a little: "It may be a stretch, but I think it could help us fix Juana."

Fix Juana. The words creaked against my ribs, heavy enough to break. I ran a hand back through my too-short hair and tried not to breathe fire. Since I'd gotten back, Cece was always trying to do this—protect me from everything, do everything for me. Moon above, *I* was the older sister. I squeezed my hands into fists. My nails dug into my palms.

"It's dangerous to travel so far, Cece," Mamá said. "Semana de la Cosecha just began."

"I know," Cece said, "But—we don't know how long Juana can live without a heartbeat."

Mamá and Cece both turned to me again. My insides burned.

"I'm fine," I insisted. "It's been a week already. It can't get much worse than this."

At that, Mamá and Cece looked even more nervous.

"Okay." Mamá patted Cece's shoulder. "Let's talk it over with your friends. Maybe we can find a way to make it work."

They both stood up and made for the loft hatch. I gaped after them. "Are you serious?"

"Rest up, Juana," Mamá insisted as Cece pulled up the

hatch. "Don't worry—we'll make a plan."

"*Mamá*," I said, with all the venom boiling up inside. "You can't really be considering this. Cece will get hurt. And doesn't she want to protect her *precious* criaturas?"

Cece's chin dimpled. Mamá sent me a look—hard and tender and loving all at once. It nearly turned my stomach. That happened a lot lately. The love I wanted to receive the most—it was like I'd become allergic to it.

"Go on downstairs, Cece," Mamá said, and ushered her down the ladder. "Un momento. I want to speak to your sister."

Cece's face crumpled with worry—did she even have another expression lately?—before disappearing obediently down the ladder. Mamá shut the hatch and turned to face me. I frowned up at her, crossing my legs on the bed.

"I'm not pathetic, you know." I set my jaw and picked at a thread in my blanket. "I work nine hours a day, just like you, to help support us now that Papá's gone." I gestured hard down at the floorboards. "You're really considering sending tiny Cece and her criaturas off to go unbury secrets that *might* help me?" I scoffed. "I thought you hated all that stuff! You always *said*—"

"I know what I said. And I was *wrong*." Mamá's voice came down like a mountain. I stiffened as her stare hardened, and she sat down at the end of Cece's small bed.

"Criaturas brought you home, Juana. And they did so because tu hermana saw them for what they are—people, creations—when the rest of us had grown blind in our fear disguised as fire." She laid a hand on my knee. "Yes, they can be frightening. But if nothing else, I have learned from your father that human beings have the same potential for cruelty and kindness as criaturas." She reached up and cupped my cheek. "You must decide now which *you* will choose to nurture."

For a moment, the burning inside me quieted. On the first morning after we'd come home, Mamá had told us what had happened with Papá. After he'd hit Cece (the thought still burned through me like lightning), she had given him an ultimatum. Either he stayed at the oil refinery's shared accommodations until he got his life back on track, until he stopped drinking, until he made things up to us, until he proved he could be trusted again—or he had to leave our home permanently.

Papá had chosen the last option.

Mamá had answered as many of our questions about it as she could that day. But after that, she hadn't spoken of him. We hadn't really either. We'd just reweaved our lives into a shape that fit around the hole he'd left behind.

Mamá's face softened at my silence. She ran her hand over my cheek. "You are so much like me, Juana," Mamá said. "Fiery and strong, you have always fought to survive. You have burned deep and burned hard and burned long. I am not surprised you are hurt and angry after being stolen. None of us can know what it was like." She tucked my shoulder-length hair behind my ear. I remembered when it used to be so long that she'd get her fingers tangled in it. "But after all this time, I can tell you—to be fiery is not always to burn, and not only to survive. It is also to comfort. It is also to thrive."

"I'm tired, Mamá." I pulled away, turned my back, and lay down. "I'm going to sleep."

It was true that I was tired. But I wasn't going to sleep. Mamá waited for a long, hurt minute before going downstairs. I listened to her and the others discuss Cece's mission through the floorboards and set my jaw.

Cece shouldn't be going off on any more quests to save me. I wanted to save myself. I tightened my fists as the thought filled the place my heartbeat used to be. My familia might have forgotten, but I was powerful. I was the one who'd performed the Amenazante dance. I was the one who'd defended Cece from bullies growing up. I was the bright and burning Juana Rios. It was about time I reminded everyone, including myself, exactly what I was capable of.

The plans hardened in my mind. I gripped my sheets

in my hands. Sí. Tomorrow, I would leave. Tomorrow, I would take my life back.

And I dared anyone to stop me.

I didn't say goodbye to Cece the next morning, when she left with her criatura friends before the sun rose. I pretended to be asleep when she whispered, "I love you, Juana" before she went. The words left a wedge where my heart used to beat.

Mamá and I ate breakfast together in the hour that followed. I barely listened as she told me how brave Cece had been when she left early that morning, how she had a plan to avoid the hunting parties. After a while of me not responding, Mamá finally left for the fields alone.

The moment the front door closed behind her, I went for our family knives.

Mamá kept them hidden at the bottom of our familia's history trunk. I lugged out the giant box from under Mamá's bed and yanked it open to dig through the papers. Books from my childhood, papers with our birthdates, Mamá and Papá's marriage certificate—I stared at that for a second too long before throwing it on the ground—until I touched a cold, heavy box toward the bottom. I dragged it up from the dark recesses and yanked it open.

The Rios family knives.

They were a set of three, their fine, sharp blades all inset with crushed fire opal. I picked up the largest one in the center, and it gleamed iridescent orange in the low morning light. This was the hunter's knife, with serrated metal teeth on one side and a smooth, sharp edge on the other. The next two were twins—small throwing knives, with a hole in the middle of each, where I could hook my fingers to send them flying.

Mamá had made me promise not to tell Cece about the family knives. I'd been nine years old when she'd first shown them to me. She'd pried them out of the trunk in the dim light of a single ocher candle, after Cece had gone to bed. Earlier that night, Cece had set Tzitzimitl—the Criatura of Stars and Devouring—free from execution. It was the first time I'd seen Mamá truly scared. I'd watched her hands shake as she set the knives out before me.

"If anything happens to Cece," she'd said, "if criaturas come into our home and I cannot protect you both—you must use these to defend yourself and tu hermana." The low candlelight had burned across her wide face, coating her in oranges and yellows and the sharpest of fears. "I used these to defend our home from the criaturas who came seeking revenge against your tía, Catrina. They are not to be wielded lightly. You use them only when you are certain something stands between you and your life. You only use them when you are prepared to protect—and to kill. That is what these knives were forged for, Juana. Protecting our familia."

I ran a finger down the hunting knife's fire opal blade. I'd grown up waiting for the right time to use these. The one night I'd actually needed them, I'd been unprepared.

I wouldn't be this time.

I stripped the knives out of the box, pulling the small leather belt with sheathes out alongside them, and buckled the belt and knives around my hips. The weight of the weapons was comforting as I yanked on a jacket over my red dress and pulled a bag filled with equipment onto my shoulder. I left home without looking back, already eyeing the southwest.

Envidia was that way. Cece had said so. And if anyone in Tierra del Sol knew where my heartbeat had gone after living in Devil's Alley, it would be the maker of brujas, Grimmer Mother.

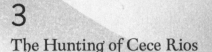

3
The Hunting of Cece Rios

"We're making really good time!" I said as the moon rose overhead.

Coyote had carried me on his back most of the way. Over the past few hours, the dry, open desert had faded into stretches of long grasses and the beginnings of full, leafy trees. I knew that meant we were getting closer to the coast. My heart soared at the thought.

"Your mamá's map said the city should be just on the other side of this peak!" Coyote gestured toward the one large cerro that blocked our way. It rose over our head as we crossed into its shadow, readying to climb its rugged slope. "Hey, why don't we race to the top?" He flashed a grin. "Huh, Ocelot?"

I turned to Ocelot, where she jogged beside us, but she didn't answer. She was staring back at Kit Fox, where he ran behind us.

Kit's large fox ears flopped down on either side of his

head, and his arms dangled as he struggled to make each flying step. My heart ached, and Ocelot's eyebrows pulled together as she slowed. How had I not noticed he was so tired? But then, his soul was so quiet. Like he was purposefully hiding his weary, brick-red feelings away from me. Kit had never done that before.

The moment Coyote spotted him, he winced and halted. Ocelot did too. Kit peered up at us, blinking and dazed.

"Hey, Kit." Coyote walked us over to him. "Are you okay?"

"Huh? Sí, I'm fine!" He made a big show of smiling.

I didn't believe it for a moment. "Maybe we should rest for a while. Dawn is almost here anyway, and then we can climb the cerro in the daylight—"

"No, no! We promised Señora Rios we'd run the whole way so we wouldn't get caught." His face dropped, and he played with his fingers. "What if El Silbón finds us?"

My stomach flipped. I'd been trying to focus on getting where we were going as fast as possible, but that same fear had been waiting, curled up, in the back of my mind too. I checked the sky as I debated between Kit's exhaustion and what El Silbón would do if he caught me—or, I guess, what El Cucuy would do.

Daylight would be coming soon, if the gray sky was any indication. Semana de la Cosecha's hunting parties moved only at night. We should be fine, right? I bit my lip. I couldn't let Kit wear himself down like this.

"We can just take a few minutes, then," I said, as confidently as I could, but Kit's face tightened. I rushed to console him. "I mean, Coyote, Ocelot, you're probably tired too, right?"

They nodded, but Kit's eyes flashed green in panic as they darted from my face to Coyote's.

"We can't!" he squeaked. "The hunting parties—if they find me, I'll have to go back, and then I'll be given to another bruja. I can't do it—I can't face that again—"

His soul screamed with clashing mustard yellows. I stuttered, trying to figure out what to say. But Ocelot interrupted by swooping down and picking him up.

Kit was my height, but in Ocelot's long arms, he looked like a little kid. She cradled him to her chest so his legs dangled on either side of her hips, and she folded her arms under him to support his weight.

"We'll never let a bruja have you again, Kit Fox," she said in her softest voice. "You're safe with us."

She strode forward and gestured for us to follow. Coyote, after a moment's hesitation, kept moving too. Kit pressed his face into her shoulder as she stroked his hair. A swell of white and blue—fear and sadness—rushed through his soul. But beneath it all, there was a small but powerful center of sunny-yellow gratitude.

Sometimes I forgot exactly how much Kit Fox had gone through. He was so cheerful and warm most of the time now that it surprised me to find how close to the surface his fear still lived. Slowly, he relaxed in Ocelot's arms. My chest ached. His reaction reminded me of Juana's the night before, only less angry. As I watched, Kit's head lolled to one side on Ocelot's shoulder. Oh. He'd fallen asleep.

"This is the first life where he hasn't had a bruja, isn't it?" Coyote said quietly. His brows yanked down, and he shook his head. "I'll *never* let that happen to him again." Something dark—and determined—rolled through his soul as he started forward again.

Ocelot nodded to the statement, careful to balance Kit's weight as she trekked up toward the last cerro. She wasn't one for long speeches or unnecessary facial expressions, but she held Kit like he was her own child. I couldn't help smiling.

"What is it?" Ocelot asked.

"Oh, uh—" I giggled. "I was just thinking you look like you could be Kit's mom right now."

Coyote snorted too. We looked at each other and laughed harder. But slowly, Ocelot's tawny eyes warmed, and her mouth actually moved when she smiled.

"I was a mother once," she said. "A very long time ago."

My mouth dropped open. Coyote straightened.

"Really?" I asked. "But—how?"

Criaturas didn't, as far as I knew, have kids the way Naked Man did. They each had nine lives and could regrow, so it was kind of unnecessary. She just brushed a hand over Kit's hair and quickened her pace, so we reached the bottom of the mountain. It was a steep slope, but she pushed up its angle easily.

"I fell in love with a human man two lifetimes ago," Ocelot said as Coyote joined her. I held on tight to his shoulders. "We had the most beautiful daughter this land had ever known." A burgundy color filled her normally cool stone, and with it, a fond and distant memory. It was so powerful, her stone began to buzz against my skin, and images entered my mind in flashes.

A child with long, silky black hair and a birthmark on her left cheek. A man laughing as he herded goats. Ocelot telling her familia to stay inside their home, protecting them from a pack of angry men with weapons waiting outside.

I gasped as I vaulted back out of the memories. Ocelot paused. The fading night was quiet, the desert listening.

Then Ocelot chuckled. It was a quiet, fragile sound. "That was the past," she said. "Let's keep moving."

Coyote stepped forward to do just that—before halting so suddenly I rocked sideways. I scrambled to right myself and scanned the bushy landscape.

"What is it?" I whispered.

Coyote's soul flashed with confused, scattered colors. A distant, scratchy whistle echoed across the landscape. I stiffened. The fact that there was more foliage here actually made me nervous. I was used to the desert's broad and open landscape, but this area was dense with places to hide. Coyote squeezed my legs. Ocelot locked her arms around Kit, and a sharp sneer curled around her mouth.

"Hang on, Cece," Coyote said.

"What? Why?" I asked.

Right before a mangled skeleton leaped at us from a nearby cluster of trees.

El Silbón carved his long, needly fingers toward my face. "There you are!"

I screamed. Coyote dove back, keeping his front between me and the long, spidery shape of the dark criatura. El Silbón's white eyeholes didn't blink, didn't waver, as Coyote kept dodging back, keeping me out of reach.

"I'm warning you!" Coyote roared. "If you lay a single finger on her, I'll—"

"Do what?" El Silbón struck forward, so quickly that Coyote didn't have a chance to move before he was suddenly looming over us, his fingers poised like knives. "You already made me a dark criatura. What punishment could be worse, Great Renamer?"

Coyote's breath caught as his legs locked up. Bursts of roiling red and ugly blue filled his soul until no other color had room to breathe. I nearly choked on it, and his body froze, paralyzed.

I tugged on his shirt. "Coyote!" I yanked harder as El Silbón reached for our faces. "Coyote, you have to move!"

"*You.*" El Silbón clasped my cheek.

I grabbed at his sharp fingers, struggling to pull them off my tender skin.

"You will undo the seal the curanderas placed on the head of our king." His other hand closed down over Coyote's mouth like a cage. "You will heed the order of El Cucuy." He gripped us harder, leaning in.

Ocelot leaped in from our right and, with a smooth kick, sent El Silbón crashing into the nearest tree.

I let out a gasp as my cheek throbbed. Ocelot grabbed Coyote's shoulder with her free hand. Kit, now very much awake, held on to her back like a monkey as she shook Coyote.

"You don't have time to drown in regret," she said, sharp and hard. "Move. *Fight.*"

Coyote jolted to life just as El Silbón recovered and swung his head our way.

"We need to reach the daylight," Coyote blurted. Ugly, dark colors streaked his soul, but his muscles were focused and ready. I gripped his shirt. He turned with Ocelot, ground his feet into the dirt, and raced up the cerro.

"It doesn't matter where you run!" El Silbón called after us, following step for step. He kept his free hand with its needly, clawed fingers outstretched toward me, his other gripping the bag filled with the clattering bones of his dead father. "El Cucuy will rule the surface as he does Devil's Alley, and you will help him do it!"

We were nearly at the top now. El Silbón's holes widened, and he sprang forward in a wild, deranged leap, wielding a rib bone directed right for my face. I shrieked.

Coyote suddenly turned to face him—and threw me backward, so I flipped in the air, cresting the top of the cerro. I yelped as my stomach flew around in my gut. For a moment, I was weightless there in the sky, wind rushing through my clothes.

"I wish I'd just killed you all those years ago!" Coyote lunged forward and punched El Silbón in the ribs. A terrible cracking resounded from the impact.

El Silbón loomed over him, dark and terrible. "So do I."

Coyote's soul curdled with sour, vicious purple. Gravity grabbed me by the legs and pulled me down again. Coyote grappled and shoved El Silbón back. I screamed as the ground rushed up to meet me.

Ocelot dove and caught me, just as dawn crowned the horizon.

I cringed into Ocelot's arm, and Kit helped steady my

landing. Coyote had his teeth bared, facing the dark criatura where they still fought on the peak of the cerro. El Silbón lifted his head—and shrieked the moment the sunlight brushed over him.

El Silbón's new long, spidery body crumpled inward under the touch of day. The joints in his spine and arms started to snap and crack, shrinking back into the smaller limbs I remembered. My mouth dropped open as he cried out, his skin smoking wherever the sun touched him. His white, glowing eyeholes vanished into the shadow-disguised face I remembered, and he finally collapsed on the ground.

Short and quivering, gasping in pain, El Silbón scuttled back into the shadows on the other side of the cerro. He moved like an animal with a broken leg. I should have been grateful. Relieved too, probably. But despite everything— my soul ached at the agony in his retreat.

"This is not the end, Cecelia Rios!" El Silbón squeezed out. I scrunched into myself as he disappeared over the other side of the cerro. "El Cucuy will have his freedom! The sun cannot protect you forever."

4

Juana Rios and the Mother of Brujas

About an hour into the ruins around Tierra del Sol, I picked out a light trail of footsteps between the scrub and cacti left behind by brujas. I followed them, weaving my way through the outskirts, until I stopped between two abandoned adobe houses and raised my head to the horizon. Just fifty feet away, nine buildings jutted out of the desert landscape. Crammed together, scrunched, like rotten leftovers. Envidia.

"You shouldn't go in there."

I ripped the hunter's knife out and whirled around. My blade stopped just a few inches from Little Lion's nose.

I froze. His eyes crossed as he stared at the point of the knife.

"What are *you* doing here?" I snapped.

His surprise faded into a frown quicker than I liked. "Fire opal knives," he grumbled, and stepped back to put some space between him and the glowing metal. "I'm here to protect you," he said.

"You've got to be kidding me." I shoved the knife back into its sheath on my right hip. "Cece left you behind to *babysit* me? How pathetic does she think I am?"

He blinked. "That's *one* way of saying that your sister loves you enough to ask me to watch out for you. Specifically, the *worst* way of saying that." He pulled a necklace from his shirt and flashed his soul stone at me, like proof of how much Cece cared. I kept my face flat, but I'd be lying if I said I wasn't surprised. Cece'd really let him go with his soul? I thought she was obsessed with protecting them.

After a second, Little Lion tucked it back into his shirt and huffed at Envidia. "I don't know what your plan is, but nothing good comes out of that place. You should turn back."

"Oh no, *no, no, no, no.* You are not messing this up for me." I stabbed a finger at him, then at the ground. "Sit. *Stay.*" I set off toward the haven of brujas.

"I'm a black lion, not a lap dog," he snapped as he caught up with me easily.

"Could have fooled me." I gripped the knife hilt at my hip. "If you're a black lion, why does everyone call you 'Little Lion?' Real black lions were, like, six feet tall on all fours. Bigger than a grown man."

He scowled. "It's a long story."

We stopped in front of Envidia's entrance. Above our heads, a paper banner covered with ancient writing fluttered in the low breeze. Warnings were scratched onto the surrounding walls with charcoal. I gave them all a cursory glance, then scoffed and charged in. I wasn't scared of brujas anymore.

"I'm telling you . . ." Little Lion tailed me through the narrow pathway. I rolled my eyes. He really wasn't going to leave me alone, was he? "Working with Grimmer Mother isn't a good idea. How do you think she'll help? Offer you another heart? She'll probably be jealous that yours isn't beating," he grumbled.

"She's an expert on all the disgusting things about brujas and criaturas and Devil's Alley. If anyone will know what's happening to me"—I came out of the other side of the entrance—"she will."

The nine buildings opened around us into a small enclosure, almost like Tierra del Sol's town square—if it had been ugly and filled with nasty brujas and brujos. The few standing around stared at me like they'd never seen a normal human before.

I scowled back. Lion stopped beside me as I turned to face the house Cece had once described. The one with tendrils of smoke pouring from its front door.

Standing in the doorframe, shrouded in the gray, was Grimmer Mother.

She looked exactly the way Cece had described, with long black hair streaked with iron gray. It must have recently been set free from a braid, since it tumbled down her shoulders in kinky waves. She grinned, and her leathery skin twisted with wrinkles. Moth tattoos painted her hands—mysterious and dark, with glowing streaks and white eyes that moved to watch me.

"Juana Rios," Grimmer Mother said, like she'd been expecting me. "The girl who returned. Sun-Heart of Tierra del Sol, blood of a bruja, sister of a traitor."

I gripped my hands into fists. She didn't seem intimidated. But she would be.

"That's right," I said, voice hard and burning at the edges. "You taught my tía, Catrina. You showed Cece how to fight in the Bruja Fights. But now you're facing me, and I'm not like either of them. I want answers, or else."

"You want to know why your heartbeat is gone?" she asked.

I stiffened. Her grin widened. So she did know something I didn't. And she loved holding it just out of reach.

My glare darkened. She was exactly the kind of person I despised.

"This is indeed an interesting chapter in the Rios family story," she said, taking a single step back toward her doorway. Her gaze cut from me to Little Lion. "It's nice to see you again, Little Lion. I didn't think you'd be drawn to another Rios chica so easily after Catrina. I suppose you can't help yourself, eh?"

Lion stood close enough that I felt his breath catch. I knew a bit about Lion's story and how he'd been my tía's criatura in his last life, but I forced myself not to check his face. I didn't want this bruja to think I cared about him or something.

"Come." Grimmer Mother swung inside her house and gestured for me to follow.

I glanced back at Little Lion as I entered the building. He stood at the end of the stairs, waiting. A sticky, dark feeling hung around him that reminded me of the sunburn in my chest.

The inside of Grimmer Mother's house was dense with the smell of charcoal and herbs. But I refused to clear my throat. I sat down in front of her, a small table piled with animal skulls between us.

"Well?" I snapped.

Her nail dug black filth from between one of the skull's fangs. "Your heart's not beating because it still belongs to El Sombrerón."

I straightened with something hot and sharp. "My heart *never* belonged to him," I belted.

She just grinned beneath hooded eyes.

"Anyway, El Sombrerón is dead. I watched Cece kill him."

The woman laughed with her full body. "That's right!"

she crowed and dropped the skull. "I heard how little Cecelia Rios slayed the second Dark Saint." Her smile curled wider, despite discussing the death of her ally. "But he will regrow. You, on the other hand?" She pressed a single finger to my chest, right over my heart. "A piece of your soul is *missing*."

A piece of my soul? I stared her down.

"Did you think a being as powerful as El Sombrerón would risk losing his bride after he'd taken her?" She picked at her teeth. "When he first takes a girl hostage, El Sombrerón snaps her soul in two. Anytime he leaves El Cucuy's castle, he takes the larger piece with him and transforms it into a braid. You remember that, hmm?"

My body was shaking. But I felt detached from it. Angry and hot.

"Sí," I ground out begrudgingly.

"You've forgotten the splitting though, ah?" She wiped gunk from her teeth onto her dress. "Maybe you were too frightened. Maybe you fainted. But that first night, he would have broken your soul and shelved the smaller piece in his collection."

I may not have remembered the splitting of my soul—as I tried, all I could summon was screams and darkness—but I could still picture the collection. It was the thing El Sombrerón was proudest of. An entire wall in his castle suite was dedicated to a polished wooden shelf with individual compartments, each tiny square showcasing a soul stone. I used to stare at it from where I was chained. I knew that after a year, my soul stone would join them. Inanimate, frozen—an object for him to admire. Sometimes, he'd take one out and turn it into a braid, stroking the long hair, before turning it back and replacing it.

That's all those past brides were now. An amusement for a monster.

I found my nails digging into my palms and mechanically released my grip.

"So you're saying," I said carefully, "that part of my soul is still in Devil's Alley?"

"Exactamente." She nodded. "That's why your heartbeat is missing. It's why you can't sleep."

I hadn't told her that, but her smile widened with surety when I stiffened.

"And the longer you're separated from your soul, the more things will disappear. Your patience. Your laughter." She tilted her head, so her half-hooded gaze pinned me. "Your ability to love."

The heat scratched inside me. I kept my face hard, stony, cold.

"Maybe it's already gone," she said. Then she straightened and lit a candle. "But it won't kill you. Half a soul is enough to live on. Just not enough to thrive."

So I wasn't going to die. But I would have to live like *this* forever, with a burning in my chest that would get worse week by week, without sleep or dreams, and without the ability to feel Cece's and Mamá's love. I would just lose—myself.

I uncrossed my legs and stood. "Thanks for your time. I hope you die here in this disgusting hovel."

The woman only laughed. "Cece may have gotten Catrina's power, but you have her tongue."

I strode out of the house. Little Lion was waiting for me just outside the door. One glance, and I knew he'd heard everything. He cocked his eyebrow, almost like he was asking if I was okay. But I didn't answer; I was busy making a plan.

My soul was broken. Part of it was in my chest, and the other was in Devil's Alley, probably sitting on that tiny shelf where El Sombrerón could admire it as he regrew. I wondered if he'd turn it into a braid. Would I be able to feel it if he did? Would he get to just sit there in his room, playing with something that didn't belong to him?

I marched out of Envidia, Little Lion stubbornly at my side. My soul didn't belong to El Sombrerón. I wasn't going to let him make me live like this—angry, blistering, with emptiness instead of a heartbeat.

Little Lion eyed me as we crossed the desert. "What are you thinking?"

I glared out at nothing. "I'm going to Devil's Alley." He looked at me like I was crazy. "I'm going to raid El Cucuy's castle. I'm going to steal back my soul. And when El Sombrerón tries to stop me, I'm going to shatter *his* soul completely, so he never comes back."

Let him try to own me then. Let anyone try to hurt me again.

I'd show them exactly how brightly Juana Rios could *burn*.

"So run back to your little bruja, before you get yourself in trouble." I glanced at Little Lion over my shoulder.

He was staring off into the desert, to the south, where the volcano Iztacpopo—the entrance to Devil's Alley this year—was just a shadow creasing the horizon. His eyes narrowed.

"I'll go with you," he said.

I stopped. "What?"

He faced me with a resolve that could puncture metal. "I'll go with you to Devil's Alley."

I scoffed, but he went on. "You know those fire opal knives aren't enough to get past the entrance, right? And there are less than two days now before the entrance seals shut. You'll need my help to get in and out in time."

I squeezed the hilt of my hunter's knife. Of course I knew they weren't enough. But I wanted to believe they were. Knowing they were forged by my ancestors, to protect our familia, to protect me—it made me feel stronger.

"I don't want a criatura's help," I snapped. "I told you, I'm not just getting my soul back. I'm going to burn your home to the ground."

He lifted his chin. "That's why I want to help."

I paused. He stepped closer.

"That place isn't a home, not with El Cucuy ruling it. If it takes burning the place down to set my siblings free from him, I'll do it. Let me help, and I'll make sure you get your soul back from the wreckage." He stopped in front of me and held out his hand. "Deal?"

I stared at his offering: his open palm, the way the sun streaked over his shoulder and left the rest of him to darkness. A deal with a criatura? To get into Devil's Alley of all things? I'd been taught better than that.

But I'd had different priorities ever since I'd been taken by El Sombrerón.

I took his hand. "Deal," I said.

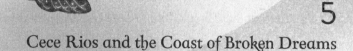

5

Cece Rios and the Coast of Broken Dreams

My friends and I stood at the highest point of Costa de los Sueños. The city descended before us in a long, steep slope stacked with colorful buildings and decorated with thick, leafy palm trees, all the way to the rough cliff and sandy beach edges. But beyond the bright white seashore, I finally, for the first time in my life, saw it—

The ocean.

It took my breath away. For as far as the eye could see, that's all there was—blue-green stretches of magnificent sea. It rolled out like the most expensive cloth, shimmering in the sun, clear and turquoise and frothy as it stretched onto the shore. The wind flooded up the hill, pushing my short hair back and turning the air salty, sharp, clean.

A massive crowd of people passed my friends and me on either side. Coyote, Kit, and Ocelot were disguised with clothes we'd nabbed from washing lines earlier. Coyote stood close beside me, a straw hat perched on top of his head that was so big it covered his hair and eyes.

"Mother Ocean," I said, breathless and tingling.

"She's so much prettier than I thought," Kit breathed. He was absolutely drowning in his orange poncho and sombrero, but he'd been excited to pretend to be human anyway.

Ocelot tilted her hat down and offered me a real smile. "Do you want to go meet her, Cece?"

My body flooded with cool, joyful certainty. *Yes*, was the first word that filled me. The sensation spilled over, untamed and raw. I could already imagine what the water would feel like. It would be cold down near the sea floor. But warm at the surface, kissed by the sun, carrying stories and life and happiness.

I didn't just want to meet the Ocean. I wanted to *run* to her.

"Sí," I said out loud, with my whole soul. "But we don't have time—we need to find the Ocean Sanctuary."

That had to be my priority. Juana needed me, and I had to stay out of El Silbón's clutches long enough that I could save her and the rest of my familia. Figuring out what was going on with my powers was key to that. So I tried to turn away. I really did. But my eyes dragged themselves back to the ocean's endless blue.

For the first time since this morning, Coyote smiled. It

was stiff, and distant blues and grays still stained his soul, but he was trying. "How about you and I check the coast-line for the sanctuary?"

"Sí, that would be useful." Ocelot pointed down the long, steep cobblestone road, which ended at the beach. "Kit and I will search the city and meet up with you two later."

"That does sound like a good plan . . ." I could barely stop myself from grinning.

A flicker of pink pushed into Coyote's soul as he took off. "Then vamos!"

We flew down the path. I squealed as we went, and the ocean breeze blew my old jacket out behind me, so it filled like a ship's sail. Coyote held on to his hat with one hand, trying to tilt it down so the wind didn't blow it off. We careened all the way down the path, giggling as we swerved around various annoyed pedestrians, stumbled all the way across the soft, warm sand—and reached the mighty, rolling waves.

My breath caught when I stopped near the water. A single wave reached up toward me, and cool, calm peace filled my chest. I stepped forward, and the water flooded over my feet, warming my skin.

I laughed and stumbled as it pushed and pulled me with each wave. "It's so strong!" I awkwardly waded deeper, closed my eyes, and spread my arms. The sunshine mingled with the water's spray, and I was filled with the ocean's breath.

Suddenly, a huge splash of water crashed over my head. I coughed and rubbed the salt out of my eyes to find Coyote grinning mischievously.

"Taste as good as you thought?" He winked.

"Ugh, you!" I giggled and splashed him back.

For just a moment, the dark colors in Coyote's soul faded. He grinned, and we screamed and laughed as we poured the ocean over each other. I caught some salt water in my mouth and coughed, but even that briny gulp made me smile.

The sound of distant talking and grown-up laughter broke into ours. I turned, still dripping, to the beach. A group of fishermen walked together, pointing at us and smiling. They'd probably never seen kids so excited to be in the ocean. I was about to turn away, to face a sniggering Coyote—when I noticed someone on the edge of the group.

A jolt ran through my body. He looked exactly like Papá.

I rubbed my eyes and checked again. The man had his back to me now, walking slowly with the others, his hat hiding his face. No, it couldn't be Papá. I slowly turned back to the ocean. That man was too thin anyway. Right? I tried to calm my newly racing heart. If any of us had to meet Papá again, it would be better if it wasn't me. Juana could handle it, I was sure. He'd probably even regret not coming home, not picking us, if it was her. But me? I waded further into the waves, so they came up to my hip, to try to distract myself. If he saw me, he'd probably just remember why he hadn't wanted us. Or more likely . . . me.

"Cece, look out!" Coyote leaped over and yanked me out of the water.

I spluttered as he lifted me—*bridal style*—in the air. My cheeks flushed. Wow, we were so close. But he frowned at me, all the pink in his soul gone.

"You have to be careful, Cece." He gestured his head back at the waves. I checked over his shoulder and spotted a silky blue fin sinking away into the froth. A gasp caught in my throat. Coyote frowned. "That thing almost caught you. There are dark criaturas in the ocean too, you know. You can't let your guard down."

"Wait, *that* was a dark criatura?" It really had been too close for comfort.

"Probably La Sirena." He nodded, scowling. "She's known for drowning people."

My heart raced, and my mind darted back to early this morning. "Do you think she's . . . working with El Silbón?"

"Don't know," he said, and let me down on the sand. I wrung out my jacket, and my stomach squeezed itself even tighter. "But you can't trust *any* dark criatura, so you should stay out of the ocean for now." He frowned at the waves.

"Well, that can't be all true. Tzitzimitl is good. Right?" I said. Coyote's face stayed hard, scanning the ocean's surface. "She saved me twice."

The thought sent me back to this morning, facing El Silbón's crazed, frightening form and his absolute determination to steal me. I shuddered. He wasn't at all like Tzitzimitl—except . . . My heart cramped as I remembered the way he'd cried out as the sun's touch had forced him to return to his original form. As I remembered the way he'd said he wished Coyote had just killed him all those years ago.

I frowned to myself. What had he meant by that, anyway? Coyote had confessed to me months ago that he'd Named the dark criaturas like El Sombrerón, El Cucuy, and El Silbón the same way he'd formed the animal criaturas. Only, instead of dust, he told me he'd made them from nothing, and instead of making them to fill the desert, they were designed specifically to punish Naked Man. So why did El Silbón make it sound like he'd had a life before he'd been Named?

"Coyote, can I ask you something?" I turned to look at him, but he was already walking away, shoulders slumped, toward the cliffs. I started after him. "Wait! Coyote, I had a question about El Silbón—"

"Let's just search for the sanctuary, okay?" Coyote flashed me the fakest grin I'd ever seen in my life and turned his back. "We need to find answers for Juana and get you somewhere safe before nightfall."

"Well, that's true. But—hey, Coyote, are you okay?" I slowed as I caught up to him. "Did . . . did I do something wrong?"

The way he looked at me made me feel like I had. My insides shivered. Maybe it was just because I'd been thinking about Papá, but, for just a second, Coyote's dark gaze reminded me of him. I shook my head.

Coyote evaded my gaze. "No," he said, a little too fast.

I hesitated. "You can tell me, you know," I whispered, and leaned closer. "Is it because you froze in front of El Silbón?"

Coyote's shoulders hiked up around his ears, and his jaw tightened. Coyote hated not being able to protect people.

I tried to smile. "Don't be so hard on yourself. You did—"

"I said don't worry about it!" he snapped.

I flinched back. His eyes burned like gold coins, and

a throb of navy blue and ashamed purple splattered up in his soul. It lasted only a second. But it burned into my mind, even as he stepped back and softened his expression. He pulled all the dreadful grays and blues in his soul away from mine—but I could still only shrink beneath how they'd felt.

"Sorry, Cece," he mumbled.

I tried to smile again, but I couldn't speak yet. Something wasn't right. He wasn't telling me something. And I was starting to worry it really *was* my fault, if he was trying this hard to hide it.

Coyote looked away again. "Let's just go." He headed up the beach.

About three hours later, Coyote and I had bothered basically every fisherman on the beach to ask about any legends or ancient buildings that could match the description of the Ocean Sanctuary. They told us lots of old stories about magical women who used to haunt the seashore—but nothing about a meeting place.

"Lo siento, chica," said the last one. He tipped his hat and climbed aboard his boat. "Pero, be careful asking questions like that. Someone might think you're a bruja or something!" He hooted and cackled at his own joke as he set out on the sea.

I laughed awkwardly while he drifted away before

slumping over in defeat. Great. Another dead end.

"Cece!" a voice picked up behind us.

Coyote and I turned to find Kit Fox dashing across the sand toward us. He held on to his poncho and hat to stop both from slipping off his thin frame, and I laughed as I ran to meet him.

"What is it?" I asked. "Did you find it? Please tell me you found it!"

Kit's grin suddenly wavered. I held my breath. Coyote had been distant and sharp during our search, and everything depended on us finding the sanctuary. I wasn't sure my bruised heart could take any more bad news.

"Um," Kit said, grinning hesitantly. "I think so. But it's not exactly—"

"¡Qué bueno!" I clapped. "Lead the way! Come on!"

Kit hesitated, but he led me and Coyote down to the beach and past a cliff edge that hid more sandy shore from sight. He helped me onto a tall rock, and my stomach fluttered in anticipation. As we crowned its top, I searched breathlessly for the building I was sure would be looming on the other side.

But it never appeared. I straightened—and tilted my head down to take in a patch of ruins.

There were only pieces of wall left, outlining a large circle in blues and greens. I eased myself down to stand among the rubble. Kit followed, his steps awkward and hesitant. Stained glass shards peeked through the sand in a few places, and the far wall had shed chunks of forgotten coyamito agate. I stopped in the center of the evidence, my insides rumbling with a distant, muffled sort of pain.

"Is this . . . ?" I couldn't bring myself to finish the question.

Kit's soul squirmed with greenish hesitant yellow. He stepped up beside me, playing with his fingers. "I asked one of the fishermen about it. He said they have a legend about this place. It was an outpost for magic women hundreds of years ago. But when the women disappeared, storms and high tide and angry people destroyed it over time." He glanced toward me slowly, like he was scared to see my expression.

"The Ocean Sanctuary," I breathed. "It's gone."

6

Juana Rios and the Dark Saint's Skull

I stood on the edge of the canyon that led to Iztacpopo. The volcano loomed over it, nearly blotting out the low sun. Mamá would be heading home from work soon. I had to be gone from this world by then.

"What are we doing?" Lion huffed as he came up beside me.

"*I'm* finding my way into Devil's Alley. *You're* being a nuisance." I stepped into the canyon and scanned the ground. There was one last thing I needed for this plan to work, and it was in here somewhere.

"We're too close to the entrance," Lion said, and dropped his voice as we went. My dress skimmed over the dust and sand blowing down the canyon. "The guards will catch our scent soon if we're not careful."

"Don't be a baby." I slowed when I spotted scratches on the canyon wall. "The wind's blowing in the wrong direction. You'll smell them before they smell you." I knelt and ran my hands over the scratch marks. They weren't deep, not like claws. They looked more like they'd been left behind by humans fighting. I smirked.

Little Lion paced beside me, clearly on edge. "What's your plan to get in, anyway? The entrance is heavily guarded this time of year."

I followed the scratches down and started scooping dirt away from the base of the wall. It had to be here.

"Not to mention you're just a human," Lion said, a little louder. "You can't get into Devil's Alley without—"

"The Mark of the Binding," I said, as I found something hard waiting beneath the sand.

Lion squatted next to me. "What's that?"

"An old friend of yours." I gripped the circular object with both hands and, slowly, pried it out of the dirt. It was a skull. Lion started at the blackened bone cupped between my fingers.

I'd never met Rodrigo the Soul Stealer during my time in Devil's Alley. I hadn't met *anyone*, locked up alone in El Sombrerón's suite. But I'd demanded Cece tell me the story of how she rescued me again and again. I listened until her voice went hoarse, obsessed with how she'd succeeded—and I'd failed. She'd told me how she'd killed the third Dark Saint by setting his criaturas free. His flesh had crumbled into ash and sand. And his bones, I remembered, she'd left to the desert.

I tapped the dead man's skull. After a moment, a pale line shimmered out of the bone.

"There," I breathed.

"The Mark of the Binding." Lion leaned forward. "El Cucuy owns him even now."

"And I'm guessing the portal to Devil's Alley can't tell who the mark belongs to . . ." I grabbed the nearest rock and slammed it against the back of the skull. The top half of the face—including the mark on the forehead—broke off the rest of the head. I lifted it and placed it over my eyes like a mask. "If I wear it like *this*."

I whirled around, and Lion jolted back, horrified. I snorted. Hilarious—a criatura being uncomfortable with violence, of all things. I nodded to myself and lowered Rodrigo's skull to my lap.

"This'll work," I said. The wind changed direction, stirring my hair, as I sorted through my bag.

"It doesn't bother you at all?" Lion asked.

"What?" I pulled some cord loose from my bag.

"That you'll be wearing someone else's face?"

"Why should it?" I knotted the string through the eye sockets and around the temples on each side. "This guy tried to kill my sister and worked for El Cucuy. At least now that he's dead, he's good for something."

I placed the skull over my face again, tying the cord around the back of my head, and stood to face the rest of the canyon with a mask made from the skull of a Dark Saint.

"There." I slipped out my fire opal hunting knife. The wind picked up, and sand blew against my back, scattering through the canyon. The looming shadow of Iztacpopo lay dead ahead. I narrowed my eyes behind the mask. The last time I'd gone up that mountain, I'd been over El Sombrerón's shoulder, completely helpless. This time, I was on a mission, and I'd make sure Devil's Alley regretted my return.

I charged ahead, up the craggy, windswept canyon.

Little Lion was by my side in moments. "Hey, don't just charge in. There's probably triple the usual number of brujas and criaturas guarding the entrance, since El Sombrerón is out of commission. We need a plan."

The canyon split ahead of us. The tip of Iztacpopo, where the entrance waited for me. Lion dropped his voice as we left the comforting shadows.

"At the very least we shouldn't be walking up in plain sight!" Little Lion checked the edge of the canyon far above us. His pace slowed. "They could spot us before we even get close."

"This is the only way to reach Iztacpopo," I said. A stream of dust fell from the nearest canyon wall. I kept moving but traced the place where the orange stone walls blotted out the lowering sun. "What? Do you want me to fly?" I squinted at the ledges overhead.

Little Lion suddenly grabbed my arm. I ripped out of his grip and turned around, knife raised, but he wasn't facing me. Over his head, descending out of the shadows of the canyon, eight long legs descended the canyon wall. My skin turned to fire. Down came a giant spider, its red hourglass mark glinting on its bulbous abdomen, as it hit the ground in front of us.

"Criatura of the Black Widow," I breathed.

"Trespassers!" someone above us yelled.

Ten brujas and brujos stepped into sight and glared down at us from atop the canyon walls. More crept out from the end of the canyon, blocking our way to Iztacpopo. The giant spider moved toward us, its fangs glinting.

"Kill them!" a bruja cried.

Little Lion and I ran. Black Widow scuttled behind us, hissing, her giant eight legs looming over our heads. As we fled, animal criaturas in a variety of forms dropped down on either side of us from above. Criatura of the Cantil Snake's jaws opened wide. I dodged his blow and kept running. Next, Criatura of the Vulture transformed so her mighty wings and talons were out. A rain of dangerous animal criaturas sent sand spraying as I twisted and danced around their bodies, eyes set on the canyon's exit. Criatura of the Bobcat pounced for me, and I dodged to the side with a quick two-step move from the Amenazante dance after slashing her ear. But a mass of dark criaturas and their brujas waited at the end of the canyon. I ripped out my throwing knife. Fine. They wanted a war? I'd give it to them.

Little Lion leaped in front of me. "Get on my back!"

"What?" I tried to pull away, but the other criaturas jumped toward me. Lion's hold tightened, and out of nowhere, he flipped me high, high in the air.

My skin screamed with heat and rage as the world spiraled. He'd *thrown* me? How dare he—I was going to—

My vision righted. Far below, Little Lion faced the oncoming storm of animal criaturas, pinned between Black Widow's dripping fangs and the wall of brujas waiting behind him. ¡Gato estúpido! I readied my throwing knife. This kid was going to get himself killed. And so was I, probably, when I landed. But I had to do something.

I was about to let the knife loose when Little Lion's form began to change.

I'd never seen an animal criatura's transformation before. As if all the lines of Little Lion's body smeared into charcoal, he swept his shape into something larger. In a single moment, he shed his human form and rose—throwing off the criaturas who had just landed on him—in the body of a towering, vicious black lion.

Black lions had died off years ago, so I wasn't the only one shaken by how huge the animal looked in real life. Knowing something is six feet is one thing—seeing it is another. And the moment Lion's transformation finished, the brujas and criaturas around him stumbled back. And I landed on his massive back, instinctively clinging to his thick black fur.

Lion roared. The earth shook, and the canyon made it echo twice as loud. I shuddered and slipped my knife into its sheath. Lion threw his head back to give me one sharp glance of his red eye.

My stomach flipped in disgust. He was giant. Powerful. Stronger than me. I hated it.

Lion charged the still-reeling brujas at the end of the canyon. I had to grab his fur to hang on, my guts still knotted. The brujas screamed. Their criaturas pulled them out of the way as Lion broke through the line and carried us up the sharp slope of Iztacpopo.

The armies of Devil's Alley were quick on our heels.

"Why didn't you just do this before?" I asked when I got my voice back. It was in tatters, and I hated how weak it sounded. So I glared and tightened my hold on his fur, focusing on the top of the volcano. "It would have been faster!"

"You think you can outrun us?" a brujo screamed out behind us. Cantil Snake carried him on his back, but they lagged behind. Little Lion was apparently faster. "There's no stopping El Cucuy's will!"

I smirked. We'd see about that.

Lion crowned the volcano—and the entrance at its center came into view. It was just the way I remembered it: a wide, open pit throbbing in the ground, now just ten feet away. Creepy, gray veins spread from its edges into the stones and earth. So close. Finally. One leap and Lion and I would finally be back in Devil's Alley and one step closer to my soul. Little Lion crouched as the thunder of footsteps and raging outcries built behind us. Black Widow was at the head of the pack, so close I could see the venom dripping from her fangs.

Little Lion leaped into the air, aimed perfectly for the entrance. I sucked in a breath and braced myself as we soared through the air.

But something was wrong.

The fur beneath my hands disappeared. Little Lion and I separated in midair as his body smeared again into waves of charcoal and graphite. The colors bundled smaller and smaller, reassembling into the short kid I knew. As we spiraled through the air, his red eyes rolled back into his head. Had he just passed out?

That *idiota*.

The transformation threw off his trajectory. He was going to hit the ground instead of the portal now, but I'd just make it in. Everything slowed as we descended. The cold prickle of the portal swam up my calves as I watched Lion crash into the dust beside the entrance. I had to get into Devil's Alley. That was all. I should just leave him.

I caught myself on the edge of the portal entrance, slamming into it so hard the impact rang through my teeth. I pulled myself up, shoulders burning, and caught a fistful of Lion's shirt. He'd better appreciate this later.

I yanked him back into me, knocking us both into the cold entrance, just before Black Widow could take a bite of him.

The portal swallowed us whole. I clasped Little Lion close as the faces of the brujas and brujos disappeared in the distance. The Mark of the Binding glowed on the skull I wore, and familiar, heady whispers roamed the darkness as we plummeted.

I held my breath to suffocate the fear in my hot chest. I could do this. I *would* do this. Even if it meant going back into the cold world I hated. Because this time, I'd get my revenge—and make things right.

7

Cece Rios and the Father Killer

When I woke up, it was the dead of night. Kit curled against me in fox form, his fluffy tail laid over his body. We were in a wooden shed filled with old tackles, fishing line, oars, and the sound of waves crashing nearby. Coyote and Ocelot slept facing the moon-touched window that overlooked the ocean, but Coyote's back was to me.

It had felt like that all day yesterday too. I wished I understood why. If I knew what I was doing wrong, why he wouldn't trust me with his feelings, I could fix it. I swallowed hard and curled into Kit's warm, comforting fur. Maybe Coyote was mad that he had to keep protecting me from dark criaturas. Maybe he was upset I'd put them all in danger only to find the Ocean Sanctuary in ruins.

Speaking of—what was I going to do now? I plastered my hands over my face and fought to keep my feelings back from my friends' souls. Mamá had trusted me. Juana needed me. How would I face them now? Thoughts of the broken Ocean Sanctuary, confusion, and fear roared through my veins. Finally, I sat up. I couldn't just sit here. I had to try to find some clue that would help me with my powers and figure out whatever Juana was going through.

I stood and headed for the door. I knew it was a bad— no, terrible—idea to go out alone at night. El Silbón could find me again. But right then, I didn't care. It was more important that I find some possible way to save my sister. I was the one who'd gotten her into this heartbeat-less mess, after all. It was the least I could do.

I left the small fishing shed and wound my way to the ruins of the Ocean Sanctuary, hugging the cliff face to stay in the shadows for protection. The wind was stronger in that direction, and it widened the holes in Papá's old jacket. I crouched under one of the slanted pieces of leftover wall, just to stay out of sight, and checked every piece of stone for any sign, clue, or helpful piece of information—anything that could direct me. It was hard to see in the dark, and I had to examine a few chunks of stone in the moonlight.

A thump reverberated through the ground behind me. I muffled a gasp and dropped the rock. Heavy footsteps vibrated toward me. I crawled deeper into the shadows, my heart jogging in my chest. Please let it be a stray animal. Or maybe a stone fell from the cliff. Or—

"The last curandera." El Silbón's voice prowled around my hiding place. "I heard you, scuffling around like an insect in the sand. There is nowhere to run, nowhere to hide."

A scream stuck like a ball of ice at the back of my throat. I flattened myself to my belly, melding into the darkness as much as possible. Creaking knees passed on my right. I watched every long, gruesome step of El Silbón as he wandered past my hiding place. I fished out Coyote's soul. Should I wake him up? No, wait. If something went wrong, El Silbón would take Coyote, Kit, or Ocelot back to Devil's Alley too. I couldn't let that happen.

El Silbón's feet disappeared from view. I closed my eyes and let out a thin, wavering breath. Maybe I could wait him out.

The wall above my head crunched. I screamed as El Silbón tore it free from the ground, and crumbs and dust poured down on my jacket. He tossed the stone away, then turned to loom over me, his hat blotting out the moon, his hollow white eyes crinkled as he sneered, his laugh grainy and electric.

"Pathetic chiquita!" he crowed. "You're unworthy to hold the power of the ancient curanderas."

He lunged for me. I scooped up a handful of sand and pitched it into his eyes.

El Silbón let out a shrill whistle. I scrambled backward, trying to gain my feet, but the rubble sent me stumbling and rolling onto the shore. El Silbón's head vibrated with an electric, violent buzz as he followed every move I made. He reached for my neck. My heart pounded, but I slapped a hand down over the four necklaces at my throat.

"No!" I reached my spare hand up to block him. "Stop!"

His went to smack my hand out of the way—but the moment his skin touched mine, a powerful, blue ripple erupted from my soul, and a current of light sent him stumbling back.

El Silbón shivered and panted, cradling his hand to his chest. The aftereffects of the light tingled through me. Just a few feet away, the surf reached closer to me. The sound of the wind and the steady waves wrapped around me—and started to curl into words. I stared at El Silbón, as he shook out his fingers like he'd been burned. The steady beating of the ocean formed a few impossible words: *Look for the child of Naked Man. See where he waits?*

I had no idea where the voice had come from. It seemed stitched from the night air and the brine, crocheted from the steady crashing of the waves against the sand. But I listened as it had said to. And for the first time, I noticed that El Silbón's face wasn't completely hidden in darkness in this tall, twisted form. He lifted his head and stepped closer again. And I saw a human face beneath the shadows of his wide hat.

He had cheekbones, barely visible, that reminded me of my abuelo's. His hollow white eyeholes started to fade, and he seemed confused, like he'd lost focus, as they transformed into two warm brown eyes. My heart hammered. Wait a second. I craned my head up toward him. How did El Silbón suddenly look so . . . human?

El Silbón flinched at my stare and tried to hide his face, like he'd felt the change in himself as well. But I'd already seen that El Silbón was something else—someone else— other than the dark criatura he appeared to be. My mind churned, and El Silbón's and Coyote's words from the other night came flying back. El Silbón had called him the Great Renamer. When had I heard that term before?

I nearly gasped. That's right, back when Coyote had confronted Bruja Bullring after she hurt me—Lion had said Coyote was trying to Rename her. My stomach tightened. No, it couldn't be.

"Wait . . . " I whispered. "Did Coyote Rename dark criaturas from . . . *human beings?*"

El Silbón peeked at me through his long spidery fingers. My stomach twisted and knotted until I was nearly sick.

"Aah." Slowly, El Silbón dropped his hands again and tilted his head down at me. "He didn't tell you, Cecelia

Rios? He didn't mention how he took the humans who disappointed him"—he creaked closer—"and made them like *this*?"

I scanned him, from his toes to his hat. My heart fluttered like a frightened bird. El Silbón nodded, letting out a rusty, pained laugh. The white hollow holes tried to replace his eyes again.

"But, then, who were you, El Silbón?" I asked.

He froze. I swallowed and mustered up the courage to keep speaking.

"The legends call you the Father Killer. Is that why you said Coyote punished you?" I peeked at his bag of bones. He flinched, but his eyes stayed human. "Because you hurt your papá?"

El Silbón brought his needly hands over his skeletal chest and groaned. It came out like a painful animal whistle, and he bowed his head under the weight of old and tattered memories.

"My father . . . took my wife's life," he said. The bones in his bag clinked. "He tried to do the same to my daughter. I came home to find the horror of it. I had to stop him, once and for all." His head bowed lower. "It was the only way to be sure my daughter would not suffer as my wife had."

My heart broke open instantly. Slowly, I reached out— and this time, El Silbón let me rest my hands on the brim of his hat. He winced a little—as if a lifetime without gentleness now made it burn.

"That's terrible," I said through my tight throat. "How—how did Coyote—"

"I didn't know he was watching me until he stepped in front of the grave I was digging," he said. "He was ancient then. I knew who he was without a word. But he didn't know why I'd done what I'd done. He didn't know my daughter was waiting for me in the house. He'd only seen me carrying my father's body out. He was angry. He was disappointed." He lifted his head as I touched his skeletal arm. "And he Renamed me *this*."

My chin trembled. A bone-deep ache pressed through my chest. I got up and stepped under his hat, until I could place both my hands on El Silbón's cheeks, the way Mamá did when she comforted me.

"I'm sorry," I said, through a knot of tears. He must have suffered so much. "Lo siento, El Silbón."

His eyes closed. "Alejo." The grainy electric tone completely vanished from his voice. "My name was Alejo," he said again.

The way he said it, I could feel how badly he missed being human. My heart ached for his grief. There had to be a way to give El Silbón back his name. A way to transform him back into the person he'd been. I knew not all dark criaturas would want to be human again, but what if they could choose? What if they had the chance to be who they'd been before Coyote Renamed them?

My hands shook on El Silbón's cold cheeks. I had to talk to Coyote. I wasn't sure if he'd lied about how he'd made the dark criaturas on purpose, or he hadn't remembered at the time, or what. But he'd been trying to make up for a lot of the mistakes he'd made in his last life. Surely he'd be willing to redeem this one too. Right?

El Silbón took my hands in his long, spidery fingers. I tried not to shudder as he loosened my grip from his face.

"Cecelia Rios," he said, with new urgency. "Listen, before I lose the war with myself." His voice wrestled with spots of grainy noise. "El Cucuy wants the last curandera's power to undo the seal placed on him by your forebears two hundred years ago." He squeezed my fingers gently. "He will not rest until you either break his seal and free him from Devil's Alley—or he kills you, so you can't finish what the curanderas started." He grunted in pain. "If you want to live and save the people you love—you must defeat him first."

I did shudder this time, and the shadows under El Silbón's hat seemed colder. Me? Fight *El Cucuy*? "But El Cucuy is the most powerful criatura in the world. How the sunset could I—"

"*Finish* the seal, Cecelia, instead of breaking it," he said. "It keeps El Cucuy captive to Devil's Alley, where the curanderas meant to turn him to stone." He pulled his other hand free and cringed. He was fighting, hard, somewhere on the inside. "The seal was meant to take four curanderas to complete, but only three could. You must be the fourth. You could seal him away—and—rescue—us—" the electric tinge of his voice crackled back into place.

El Silbón's entire body trembled like a beast was waking up inside him. Hunched over his long arms, a shudder moved through him, and a whistle—sharp and piercing—split the air. Oh no. I stepped back, so the edge of the sea licked my feet. The dark criatura turned away, buzzing with that electric sound.

"Alejo?" I asked.

El Silbón rounded on me, clawed hands raised. I gasped and stumbled into the ocean's waves.

"You had better hope your Ocean goddess is with you, Cecelia Rios." His glowing, empty white eyeholes were back. "It may be the only way you survive this night."

The surf washed up my ankles with agitated urgency. El Silbón's needle-sharp fingertips swiped for my face. I screamed and threw my arms up to block the blow—but something grabbed me from behind.

I twisted around. All I spotted was a fin poking out of

the water and a blue webbed hand gripping my belt loop. My stomach dropped. A scream jangled between my ribs.

La Sirena, the Criatura of the Deep and the Drowned, tightened her hold on my pants—and yanked me backward. I looked up to see El Silbón frozen on the shore just before the ocean waves crashed over my head.

8

Juana Rios and the False City

Lion and I fell through the sky into the disgusting world of Devil's Alley.

Okay, I could admit it looked beautiful at first glance. The streets below were paved with gems instead of cobblestones, and the adobe houses were painted gold and spotted with stained glass windows that reflected the perpetual, hazy sunset. Papel picado banners strung from one side of each of the mazelike streets to the other, so bright pinks, oranges, purples, blues, yellows, and reds fluttered below like lost butterflies.

But that's why I hated this place. Because it disguised itself as a paradise.

The city came up fast beneath us. The wind shoved my hair back and tugged at my skull mask. I would've lost my hat during the fall if it weren't for the strings tying it around my neck. Little Lion dangled, still unconscious, in my arms. Ugh.

A few feet from the ground, a rush of hot air plumed upward and softened our descent. Slowly, gently, my feet touched down on the gem-dotted street. My bag fell back against my hip, and Little Lion's body collapsed against me once gravity was working. I dragged him to the nearest adobe house and leaned him against the silver-embossed door. Híjole. Had transforming really knocked that much out of him?

I slipped out my fire opal knife and checked our surroundings. Far in the distance, looming over the rest of the city at its northern center, rose a tall, dark castle tower, glinting with dots of fire opal on its exterior to protect it from rebellious criaturas' invasion attempts. El Cucuy's castle, waiting at the heart of this false city.

There were no brujas or criaturas living in the glamorous houses set all around us. Like the rest of Devil's Alley, these homes were part of an elaborate game of pretend. El Cucuy made almost every criatura and bruja live inside his castle, under his thumb.

Lion finally jerked awake, coughing as he clutched his chest.

"About time you woke up," I said. "You're welcome for saving you after you fainted."

Lion spat and grimaced. "Ugh. I forgot how gross the air tastes here."

He wasn't wrong. I'd been trying to take shallow breaths to avoid the rotten flavor hitting my tongue.

"We need to get to the castle before those patrols follow us through the entrance." I checked the skies and hitched up my skirts. No falling bodies yet. That gave us some time. Lion struggled to get up, and I cocked an eyebrow at him. "Unless you're going to slow me down again?"

He folded his arm and growled. "It's harder for me to transform into my full-grown animal form than most criaturas, okay?" He wiped sweat from his brow and panted. "My human form is still young, and a full-grown black lion is a lot bigger and more powerful than, say, a full-grown *coyote*." He mimed the height difference between the two animals.

I almost snorted. That was clearly a sore spot. "How long is it going to take you to recover, then? I don't want the patrols to catch up—"

Lion and I froze as a seam spread open in the sky high above us, cleaving the dull clouds. Never mind—they were hot on our heels already. I whirled around, checking every door nearby for a hiding place, but they were all sealed shut. Just another reason to hate this place. But I spotted a nearby gold-and-red house with one of its stained glass windows barely cracked open.

I pointed at it just as bodies started descending from the

crack in the sky. "There!" I sprinted for it. "Come on!"

I forced open the window, and together, we scrambled inside. The house's interior was barren. No one had lived here since Devil's Alley was Named, by all appearances. I slammed the window closed just in time for the sound of feet hitting the cobblestone road outside.

Lion and I crouched in a corner, near an old fireplace.

"Great," I grumbled, keeping my voice low. "They're going to slow me down even more." I ran the numbers through my head; if I had the time straight, we had only another thirty-six hours before the door to Devil's Alley closed. That wasn't much time to break into El Cucuy's castle, steal back my soul, and get my revenge on El Sombrerón.

Beside me, Little Lion laid his head back against the wall. Sweat trickled down his temple. "I need at least ten minutes . . . to recover," he wheezed. "Let's just . . . hide."

"Hide? Like *cowards*?" The hole in my chest burned.

"No, like smart people," he snapped back.

The sounds of patrols calling to each other and crawling around the front street had my skin prickling. I bet they thought they were so scary. I traced the skull mask I wore. Hmph. I'd show them. I went to stand, but Lion grabbed my dress. I glared at him.

"Come on," Little Lion whispered with a flash of his

fangs. "Just wait the patrols out. You need to fill me in on your plan anyway."

For the first time, I hesitated. I hadn't really made a plan past this point. I just wanted to do as much damage as possible on my way through Devil's Alley to get my soul back.

"*Obviously* I have a plan," I said, with all the fake confidence I could muster. "We sneak into the first floor of the castle, fight everyone in our way, get up to El Sombrerón's room, and steal my soul back." I sat down in front of him again.

Little Lion's eyes widened. "That's your *plan*?"

"Yes," I hissed. "Want me to dumb it down?"

"It's dumb enough as it is!" He scowled harder. "It's not even a plan! El Cucuy's castle is the most heavily guarded part of Devil's Alley! Its gates are made of fire opal so that no criaturas can climb it, and a whole team of brujas and their criaturas guard the front doors. There are lava pits around it too. And then it's even *more* impossible on the inside." He wrinkled his nose. "We'll be executed if we rush in, or worse—get put in the dungeon." I squinted. How was that worse? But he went on: "Don't you remember anything about the place? You lived there."

Fire flooded through my body. "I didn't exactly get to *wander* around the castle with a tour guide," I spat. "I was kept in a single room with a chain around my waist, where the only thing I could see was the shelf filled with the souls of past brides, knowing that next year *I was going to join them*—" I bit my tongue as the memories loomed in my mind. I didn't want to go back there. I wanted to stay here, where my anger felt like a weapon, and where the burning in my chest was so loud I couldn't think about what was hiding beneath it.

Little Lion stared at the dirt floor.

"Sorry," he said.

I folded my arms. "Whatever. Since you seem to know so much about it, why don't you make a plan?"

He frowned at me. "I haven't lived in Devil's Alley for two lifetimes. I'm running on really old memories here." He started drawing a rough picture of the tower in the dirt floor. "All I remember is that each floor has its own group of brujas and criaturas who live on it. The more powerful ones live near the top." He drew lines across the tower to indicate floors, tapping the second floor from the top. "This is where you would have been."

My empty chest squeezed, but I kept my face stony as Lion tapped the topmost floor.

"And this"—he tapped again—"this is where El Cucuy lives and reigns. His throne room."

The big bad king of Devil's Alley himself.

I pointed to the third floor from the top, beneath the

one where I'd been held prisoner. "So I guess this is the third Dark Saint's?"

Little Lion nodded. "It used to be Brujo Rodrigo's suite, but with him gone, they'll have replaced him with whoever was ranked right beneath him. We'll have to watch out for them since we don't know who they are or what criaturas they have." He rubbed his chin.

"The third Dark Saint wouldn't be another dark criatura?" I didn't see why they wouldn't keep things in the criatura familia.

But Lion smeared the drawing of the tower back into powder. "The third Dark Saint is always a bruja or brujo. It's part of what keeps them all under El Cucuy's control. They know they can hit the upper ranks and get the power they've dreamed of, as long as they obey." His face curled.

"That's awful," I muttered. Little Lion met my eyes with a question in his. "Keeping someone's soul captive for your own power," I said. "It's disgusting. Souls shouldn't be treated that way."

I would know. I'd felt it firsthand.

"Sí." Little Lion's tone softened. "That's exactly what it feels like to be a criatura."

My stomach squirmed. I didn't like thinking that I shared something with criaturas now, even if it was true. Little Lion's face gentled, the way it usually only did when he was around Cece. He had a rounder face when he didn't frown, with a jaw that would probably get squarer as he grew up. His red eyes lost the heat they usually carried.

Right then, he was just a boy, not a monster.

It made me uncomfortable.

So I flicked his forehead.

"Ow!" He pulled back and rubbed his forehead, growling. "What in Desert's voices was that for?"

"Stay focused." I crawled over to the window and flattened my ear to the wall. It was a convenient excuse to not make eye contact with him and check on the patrol at the same time.

The sounds of wings and claws sounded farther away. Bien. We could start moving.

"If you're done resting—" I started.

"I'm not. We've been here for, like, five minutes."

"—then we need to get going." I peeked out through a transparent piece of the window. Everything looked clear outside.

"Like I said, I need to—"

A sound scuffled through the air. I froze. Lion and I both twisted toward the fireplace. Crumbs of stone and ash fell down the flue, scattering on the ground.

Something had found us.

My blood raced. My skin prickled with hot and sharp

sweat. But I wore the bones of a Dark Saint and weapons forged to protect my familia. I ripped out my throwing knife and slipped into the first pose of the Amenazante dance, ready to face off. The dance was not just a performance, after all. First and foremost, it was a martial art. One I was practiced in. I lifted my knife as the intruder's approach grew louder and louder. Little Lion gestured for me to run. But I planted my feet.

"I'm not recovered enough to protect you!" he hissed.

"Then you better hide." My dress whipped around my ankles.

A body landed, perfectly crouched, on the empty fireplace stones. I didn't even pause to take in the creature—I flung my dagger, aimed right for the eyes. Lion cried out.

The criatura turned its head just enough to dodge the blade—and caught it in their teeth, by the golden hilt. I froze. Slowly, they turned their dark head to meet me. Everything stilled. Without a word, I knew the importance of the shadow staring at me across the dusk and distance.

"Jaguar," Lion said, as he forced himself to stand.

In our legends, there were a few animals that my people revered. The coyote was a complicated symbol of wisdom and creation, but also mischief and trickery. The black lion, though the species was now extinct, was honored for its indominable strength and power. And then there was the last of the three great creatures Mother Desert had particularly blessed—the jaguar.

Legend said Jaguar was the first criatura Coyote ever made. And her animal wasn't just a symbol of power, like the black lion was, but of the authority of kings and queens— the right to rule. Early tribal royalty in the south of Isla del Antiguo Amanecer even used to hunt the mighty jungle cat, just to prove they were worthy to ascend the throne.

Jaguar slunk forward into the room, still holding my knife in her teeth. Its orange glow outlined her deep ebony skin and strong, muscular shoulders. I yanked my hunter's knife out next and went to charge, but Little Lion ran over and skidded into a protective stance in front of me. The small action confused the heat in my chest. I wanted to show him I could take Jaguar on myself. But I also knew I was at a disadvantage with one fewer knife, and in cramped quarters.

"You looking for a fight?" I demanded, glaring at Jaguar instead.

Jaguar spat my knife to the ground in front of us. Its orange light went out as her light brown eyes lifted to meet Lion's. She nodded to him, so her long, black hair fell over her shoulder. It was combed back in a thousand tight braids, all strung together into a single thick one. Brightly colored ribbons—red, gold, magenta, and orange—weaved through it all the way down.

"You're on a dangerous path, Little Lion," she said. Her

voice was softer and higher pitched than I'd expected—the way Cece sounded when she'd just woken up from a nap. "Returning here when you were free. And with a girl who has no heartbeat."

Lion shifted to cover more of me with his arm. "Did a bruja send you?"

Jaguar scanned his face. Her gaze was a bit filmy, the way criaturas looked when they were being controlled by a bruja. But she pulled a necklace free from her shirt—a gray-black andesite soul stone, carved with the elegant lines of a predatory jaguar.

Lion's shoulders relaxed.

I pointed my knife at her. "So what? She might report us herself."

"And what would you do if I tried?" she asked, her voice soft and dangerous.

"Fight you," Lion said, with no hesitation. He flexed his claws. "Even you."

Jaguar's head tilted. The response didn't seem to bother her. "Something matters to you more, then." In one smooth movement, she turned and prowled toward a nearby door. "Follow me. I know where you're going, and I know the way. The patrol will circle back and find you if we don't leave soon."

Everything in my body screamed not to trust her. Something was off. I couldn't put my finger on it—was it the way she spoke, or her bleary expression?—but my gut told me to find another way.

I shook my head. "No way! I'm not going anywhere with a criatura—"

"Juana." Little Lion turned to me. "She knows Devil's Alley better than I do." His voice softened, and more sweat trickled down his forehead. "If she's managed to stay out of a bruja's hands, she might even know a secret way in and out of El Cucuy's castle. She's our best bet."

"I don't like the look in her eyes," I hissed. "Why would she want to help us overturn the Dark Saints?"

"Why wouldn't I?"

We looked Jaguar's way. She stood near a window, so just a slant of orange light fell over her distant eyes.

"El Sombrerón and El Cucuy are a plague," she said, lifting her chin. "I want them gone. But El Cucuy is powerful. And because El Sombrerón is now mortal, he's been locked away inside his room to keep him safe, behind a special door with a puzzle combination only you, besides El Cucuy himself, knows. You are the one bride who has gone inside his suite, seen him enter the combination—and left again." She folded her arms. "I'm assuming you want to get your soul back. Which means you'll have to kill him, no question. That is an opportunity I won't let slide."

So she was in it for the same reason Lion was, huh?

Revenge against the Dark Saints. Guess we had that much in common.

But I still didn't like it.

I grabbed Lion by the shirt and yanked him around, so we huddled away from her. "She could still be lying," I whispered in a hurry. "She could betray us."

A calm strength filled Little Lion's expression. "If she does," he said, "I'll fight her with you. Por favor—let's go."

Something about the way he phrased that moved my insides. Like my organs were rearranging themselves to fit his sentence inside me. Fight her with me. Fight her *with* me. He was saying I wouldn't have to fight by myself. And I wouldn't have to be fought *for*.

Slowly, we turned back to face her. A distant, stony shriek filled the air. I scooped up my throwing knife and sheathed it. I worked my jaw. I didn't want to work with any criaturas. I could barely stand Lion. But—I glanced at his tired red eyes, and Jaguar's soul stone. I had to try to think clearly. Getting my soul back and punishing El Sombrerón were my top priorities. If that meant another deal with a criatura, so be it.

"Fine," I said. "But I don't like it." I charged toward the door. "Vamos."

The ocean was so cold it almost burned as La Sirena dragged me into its depths. I tried to kick my way free, but her grip was too strong. My lungs begged for air. My inner ears rumbled, and I fought the urge to gasp.

Suddenly, the hand on my belt loop released me.

I drifted free in the water. My lungs burned as darkness surrounded me. I thought I'd known silence in the desert cerros back home, but the quiet of the ocean was like a blanket. It wrapped around me in a blissful, rich hush as I floated gently into a wall.

It was cool to the touch and smooth. I looked for La Sirena in the darkness, but beneath my hands, stones twinkled to life with a turquoise glow. They lit up the figure of Mother Ocean, just like the one in the mural at the Sun Sanctuary. My lungs squeezed tight. What? How was this here? The light traveled out, and from the darkness, the images of the other three gods lit up to complete the mural

I'd memorized. They were a perfect match.

Suddenly, turquoise light shot out from the mural, and I started as it raced around me, lighting up a circular room with stained glass windows. La Sirena had dragged me into a building? Why was there a building underwater? Behind me, the front entrance had two open silver doors—and they slammed shut the moment the turquoise light reached them. I jumped. Wait, how was I going to breathe?

A thump echoed through the room, and the water level began to drop overhead. Air! I swam upward and gasped in a huge, bright breath.

"Ah!" I coughed and spat out salt water.

I waited for the sea to finally drain away, and the soles of my soaking shoes met the tiled floor. The whole room glowed with large turquoise stones embedded in the ceiling above, like little lamps. Wow. I turned in a circle, head craned up, and took the place in. My soul thrummed as I stared at the mural of the four gods. As Mother Ocean's depiction filled with light. And I smiled. Laughter filled my mouth. This was it, wasn't it?

This was the real Ocean Sanctuary.

"You are the one the Ocean has waited for," came a silky, slinking voice.

I whirled around. La Sirena stared at me across the room from a gigantic bowl filled with leftover water. I blinked.

It was too large to have any other use—had someone made it for her? She patted the painted pot fondly with webbed fingers and eyed me through streaks of her long black hair. Her skin was silky and smooth, but patterned with blue scales like a sea serpent's. Her tail made waves in the water of her cistern, and she smiled over at me with razor-sharp teeth.

"I am La Sirena," she said. "I am the one who was snatched and turned. I am the Criatura of the Deep and the Drowned."

"I saw you this morning. Were you trying to bring me here all along?" I drifted closer to her tub.

"Sí." She watched me as I neared. "It is my duty. As one of the Court of Fears, I am an ally of the curanderas. And you are the only one who still hears, who listens. Who soon will know."

Well, that would have been nice to know a couple of minutes ago. "Wait! You knew the curanderas?" I gasped and ran up to her, beaming. She pulled back a bit as if surprised. "But they lived hundreds of years ago. Before Tierra del Sol was nearly destroyed." I scanned La Sirena's face. She looked like a young adult. I was surprised she could remember that long ago.

"I am seven hundred years old in this, my third lifetime," she said. "Dark criaturas do not age the way animal criaturas do, curanderita. Coyote did not Rename us to have lives. We were made to be *monsters*." She placed her clammy, webbed hands on my cheeks. They were cold, and her breath in my face was even colder.

A chill scampered down my back. I smiled awkwardly as La Sirena withdrew and sank back into her pot of seawater, up to her chin.

"But the curanderas did not mind. I knew them well," she said, smiling with her sharp teeth. "Consuelo made this for me." She patted the pot again.

"Who's Consuelo?"

"The last ocean curandera," she said. "Before you. But Consuelo was not the last curandera to be in this sacred place, chiquita." La Sirena flicked a single webbed finger toward the mural. "Another curandera has waited centuries for the one who can speak the language of souls."

Language of souls? I followed Sirena's finger back to the mural, where a small box sat inside the wall beneath it. It looked like a brick had been removed to make space for it. I approached it, my shoes sloshing, and carefully pulled the box from the wall. Before I even opened it, I could feel a distant sort of noise calling from inside it. It was almost like—a voice. But it was so quiet, it was hard to tell. Was I imagining things?

I glanced at La Sirena. "You said *she's* been waiting?"

"She is waiting." La Sirena pointed at the box again.

My soul filled with a restless pulse. The noise vibrated through the box, into my hands, up to my soul. And it was getting louder. Slowly, I pulled the box open. Inside sat a big chunk of raw, iridescent moonstone.

"She is speaking," La Sirena said, as I touched my fingers to its smooth surface. The strange noise pulsated up my skin. "Can you hear her?"

The noise rushed up my bones, raced across my chest, and resonated in my soul with colors like cream and sky blue. My soul stone lit up. I'd felt something like this before, hadn't I? It was so familiar. My mind flashed back to my fight with El Sombrerón, and the way Juana's soul, in braid form, had burned in my hand.

This wasn't just moonstone, was it? This was someone's transformed soul.

My heart beat faster. "Curandera?" I called.

Ayúdame. The fully formed word poured out of the stone.

I gasped. She could hear me! In a rush, I pulled the soul free of the box and clutched it to my chest. A knot formed in my throat as its white light flickered weakly. This was a *person.* How long had she been here? All alone? Trapped, like Juana had been?

"You must bring her back," La Sirena said.

I looked up. "How?"

"You brought back your sister," she said. "Didn't you?"

How did she know that? "But Juana—" My eyebrows pulled together. "I don't really know how she came back."

All I knew was that she'd been transformed into a braid by El Sombrerón, and after I'd spoken to her soul, it had caught fire and she'd become a person again. I didn't know why it worked. I turned back to the curandera's stone. It started to flash with quick, small bursts of white light. Like she knew someone was there. The voice came again: *Ayúdame, ayúdame.*

She needed me. Even if I wasn't sure how to help, I had to try.

Slowly, I pulled my soul stone out of my shirt and pressed it to this stranger's. In my chest, a rumble grew, like a brilliant storm—not the kind that sends hail to ruin crops, but the kind that brings life to the desert. I took a deep breath. When I'd brought Juana back, I'd reached out to her soul the same way I spoke to Coyote's or Lion's.

Hola, curandera. I pushed the words toward the stone in my hand. It felt awkward at first, like talking to myself. But the flickering light became a steady glow in response. *I don't know you, but no one should live trapped like this.*

The light grew brighter. I squeezed my eyes shut. *You can do it! Come back.* I reached out toward her with my soul, and my stone glowed too. I felt the strong, bubbling water of my soul pour over into the moonstone. *You don't have to stay here anymore. I'll help you.*

Suddenly, the stone burst open like a firework.

I dropped it and fell back against the floor. But the stone didn't. It floated in the air and morphed into pure, brilliant light. I shielded my face and peeked between my fingers. The blinding silhouette of a woman pressed outward from all directions, white flashes reflecting across the mural behind her, along with a sweet, desperate gasp.

The brightness finally faded, and a woman stood before me in the aftermath.

She appeared about Mamá's age, with black hair down to her waist, the roots and ends of them stained white. She pressed her hands to her temples, and I realized the gasp had been hers and that she was panting, catching her breath. Slowly, her eyes opened. They were black, but somehow, they caught the light no matter which way she turned. Like stars waited in her irises.

She lowered her hands to her sides. Her dress came to her ankles, covered in painstaking embroidery but torn in several places. Her face was streaked with mud and her sleeves with dried blood, like she'd just come from a battlefield. I probably shouldn't have been surprised. If she was a curandera, she must have been part of the battle of

Tierra del Sol. But it was so surreal that I could only sit there, gaping up at her.

The curandera scanned the interior of the sanctuary, over my head, and stopped on La Sirena's little seawater bath. Her shock morphed into something softer: hope.

"La Sirena?" The woman touched her hair. "I'm back— ¿qué pasó? How—"

"You are back, Metztli." La Sirena nodded toward me. "And it is because you are no longer alone."

The woman lowered her starry eyes to me. I felt silly all of a sudden, sprawled awkwardly on the floor, in my hand-me-down shirt from Juana and ripped, hole-riddled jacket from Papá. I grinned to try to make up for it.

"¡Hola!" I waved. "Um, my name is Cece. I'm glad you're not—er, a stone anymore."

She crouched in front of me, tapping her chin. "So you are the voice who called," she said. "You are the one who listened and *gave*."

She spoke a lot like La Sirena. Maybe it was because they were both so old.

"It has been two hundred years," La Sirena said, answering the woman's unasked question. Her tail made waves in the water. "She is the only curandera since the battle of Tierra del Sol."

The curandera's brows jumped up. "And yet"—she

reached her hand out to help me up—"she has done what we have never known to be possible."

I took her offering, and she pulled me up to stand.

"I am Metztli Valente," she said. "Quickly, curanderita. We must leave. Necesito moonlight."

"Why do you need moonlight?" I followed her to the sanctuary entrance. Then gasped and ran after her. "Wait, you're a *moon* curandera, aren't you?"

She flattened a hand against the silver doors. "Sí, and you are touched of Mother Ocean. So you must be the one to open the doors and let us free." She tapped the entrance. "Speak, and the sanctuary will listen. It was made for such things."

Oh, that made sense. But I still felt awkward as I reached out and tried knocking on the door. Maybe this would work?

"Perdón," I called out to the building. "Um, gracias for keeping us safe, but we'd like to go now."

"Excelente." Metztli's took my hand as the doors started to glow blue. "Now, be ready."

The doors sprang open, and the ocean flooded in. I forced myself not to yelp as the water swept Metztli and me outside. We tumbled in the rush of waves, held together only by Metztli's grip. Then La Sirena cut through the water like a knife after us, grabbed Metztli's free hand, and dragged us both to the surface.

We landed on the beach. I coughed and spluttered, shaking water from my hair. When I looked up, Metztli was standing in the light of the moon.

She had her arms spread and her head craned back as the night poured over her. Staring up at the sky, her eyes filled with so much light that, for a moment, they appeared completely white. The shadows under them disappeared, and she took a long, steady breath in.

And let it out as she gazed down at me.

"She has spoken of all the history left behind," she said, gesturing to the moon. Her nails flashed white with the movement, and I squinted at them. Were they glowing? The way mine did when I controlled water? "You are Cecelia Rios, the one who slayed Rodrigo the Soul Stealer and El Sombrerón. The one who bears criatura souls as the brujas do but who speaks, who listens. Who does not take—who gives. You are the one El Cucuy hunts, and who he hopes will break the seal my sisters set."

I lifted both my eyebrows. "Wait, the Moon told you all of that?" I'd never thought about what a moon curandera's power would be. Could she talk directly to the Moon goddess?

She shook her head. "Yes—and no. The Moon is of the same material as the mind—light. It is brightness; it is intelligence." She tilted her head back to embrace the moon's touch again. "Light has watched all and understood all. It has seen what you are, Cecelia Rios. And it has seen your sister, Juana Rios, who now crawls in a world made for the damned, to retrieve the lost half of her soul."

Dread collected inside me like condensation on a chilled glass. Juana was in Devil's Alley? *Again?* And half of her soul was gone? That had to be why her heart had stopped beating. Did El Sombrerón still have the other half? My mind whirled, and my breath sharpened. My familia. I gripped the front of my soaking shirt, and tears blocked up my throat. My sister was in danger again, and that meant Mamá was probably at home grieving alone. *Again.*

It seemed like the harder I tried to put my familia back together, the more it shattered.

"I have to go after her," I managed to squeak out. Metztli knelt before me as I struggled to push back tears. "But El Cucuy is after me. If I go, I'll have to fight him like El Silbón said." I dropped my hands to my side. What was I going to do? I didn't even know what the curanderas' ancient seal was, let alone how to finish it.

Metztli's brows crushed down. "So my sisters were able to trap him without me, at least." She placed a hand on my shoulder. "Cece, this is why I have returned."

I raised my spinning head. Distant heat moved through

my friends' souls, and footsteps treaded toward us, from up the beach.

Metztli's face was bright and stern. "I will help you finish what we started centuries ago. Before the door to Devil's Alley closes, we will finish the seal and turn the King of Fears, El Cucuy, to stone."

I could only stare at her, wordless, as I sunk under the bigness of it all.

"Cece!" Coyote's voice cried out.

He crashed into the sand next to me and pushed me behind him. Metztli's eyes widened, and something in her expression darkened. Extra worry curled in my heart. She hadn't had a problem with La Sirena, but the old legends said curanderas fought criaturas to protect Naked Man. Would she try to hurt Coyote?

"Who are you?" Coyote glared at her and brought out his claws. "Cece, why did you leave the shed? It's danger-ous!"

"Oh, uh. Funny story—I found the Ocean Sanctuary! Turns out it's not the ruins we found. It's literally *in* the ocean," I explained. Coyote looked baffled. I sent Metztli a trembling grin. "This is my friend, Coyote. He won't hurt you." I looked into his eyes. "Right?"

His stance wilted a little. Metztli, on the other hand, straightened to full height, her mouth thinned, her hair dark against the moon. Ocelot and Kit ran in from the shadows of the cliffside and stopped beside me. But her anger didn't turn on them. It was reserved solely for my best friend.

"Everyone," I said, "this is Metztli. She's the moon curandera from two hundred years ago, who fought in the Battle of Tierra del Sol. I found her soul in the Ocean Sanctuary."

All three of my friends jolted in surprise. The Moon draped Metztli in light, the white ends of her hair drifting in the ocean breeze. She looked beautiful and terrible, her eyes dark and foreboding as she cast a withering glare down at Coyote.

"Great Namer," she said to him. "You, above all creatures of this world, have no right to be here."

10
Juana Rios and the Dungeon

"This way," Jaguar hissed, as we came to a ravine near the castle of El Cucuy.

For the last twelve hours, Jaguar had led the way through the city with the cleverness of a hunter until we reached the outskirts, which was basically a scruffy, lifeless copy of the cerros around Tierra del Sol. Now, we stood at the edge of the creepy fissure in the ground she was beckoning us into.

It was hard to argue with Jaguar's results. But exhausted as I was—I was ready to argue anyway.

"Moon above, where are you taking us?" I crouched at the edge of the sheer drop and pointed behind us, to the southwest, where the tower loomed. "The castle's that way!"

Little Lion perched beside me, frowning. Jaguar had already climbed down several feet into the ravine. But she sighed up at me.

"This path leads to the only unguarded part of El Cucuy's

castle—the dungeon," she said, like she didn't understand why I hadn't already thrown myself down her way.

Lion bristled. "The dungeon? But it's—"

"Your best path inside?" she asked.

"I was going to say 'the worst.'"

"True. But it's your only option." She cocked her head. "Unless you want to be caught?"

Lion sighed. Grumbling and spitting, I eased myself off the edge and slunk into the cavern. The craggy stone wall offered precarious hand and footholds, and my weary legs shook as I crept down several feet. I clenched my gut to ignore the trembling.

"You okay, Juana?" Lion asked as he made his way down close by.

"Of course!" I moved faster.

Jaguar crawled along the wall to my left. "I've never seen you so worried over someone else, *Little* Lion." She shot him a wide, toothy grin. The film on her eyes faded, just for a moment, before she descended into the dark.

"Ugh. When are you going to drop that stupid nickname?" Lion scowled as he plunged into the darkness too. "You're the reason everyone thinks Little Lion is my actual name. It's supposed to be *Black Lion*. Why are you always trying to embarrass me?"

She cackled. "I'm your big sister. That's my job."

"Wait, you think you're his sister?" I joined them in the

total darkness and tried to ignore my discomfort. "I didn't know criaturas thought of each other as . . . familia." More like a pack of rabid wolves or something. That's how it had been in El Cucuy's castle, anyway. I'd once seen El Sombrerón rip a criatura in half just for coming into his open room unannounced.

Little Lion made an aggravated noise in the dark. "Of course we do. Coyote Named us to be familia, remember. Some of us are estranged, but the closer together we were Named, the, uh, I don't know—closer we feel . . . I guess." He seemed reluctant to admit it.

"Coyote Named Little Lion right after me," Jaguar's voice prowled around in the dark, echoing around the ravine so I couldn't pinpoint her location. It made me wish I could hold my knife and climb at the same time. "I was there the moment he was born. So he'll always be *Little* Lion to me."

Lion growled in the dark.

Their sibling banter made me uncomfortable, so I tried to focus on climbing. But as I extended my leg down, my toes scraped something wet and pebbly instead. "What's *that*?"

There was a splash on my right.

"It's just water," Little Lion said, from below me. "Runoff from the dungeon."

Gross. I jumped down and landed next to Little Lion, ankle-deep in a cold, shallow stream of water.

"This way," Jaguar called. Sparks lit up in her direction as she scratched her claws against the stone, indicating where she was in the dark. The brief flash of light illuminated a small tunnel, only big enough for us to crawl into. "The path is narrow and wet. Room enough only to breathe."

"I hate this place," I said, but moved forward anyway. The tunnel was uneven to the touch. I scrunched my nose and crawled inside. Sour water soaked my skirt as Little Lion followed after me.

"There are two rules you must keep in mind once you reach the dungeon," Jaguar said as we moved forward. "One: keep moving. In the dungeon, fears make themselves realities for the vulnerable. Two: you must find the keeper of the dungeon, Bruja Damiana, if you want to escape." Jaguar's crawling made light splashes. "She is the only one who can open the door from the dungeon to the rest of the castle."

I scoffed. "Oh, so we just have to fight the bruja entrusted with guarding the enemies of El Cucuy?" I threw my head back at Lion. "I told you she's not trustworthy."

Jaguar only chuckled. "You mistake her position in the castle. Bruja Damiana was demoted from the higher ranks years ago because she prizes her young criatura over *all* else." She glanced back at me meaningfully.

I paused. "So you're saying, if I threaten her criatura . . . ?"

"Then you can get inside the castle. And reach El Sombrerón at last." She sucked in an eager breath.

Sharp prickles crawled over my skin. I knew why Jaguar was invested in our mission, but something about her still put me on edge. It was probably the glimpses I'd caught of her wearing two different expressions at the same time, like a doll that had dropped stitches in only one side of its face. When I'd pointed it out to Lion earlier, he'd snapped at me about it.

"You don't know what she's gone through," he said. "She has her soul stone, so she's safe. Back off, Juana."

Naturally, I'd yelled at him more for that, and he'd yelled back, and then we'd had to outrun a patrol that we'd attracted because of the noise. Lion was pretty defensive of his so-called sister, it turned out. So I kept my mouth shut about my eerie feeling now. But I made sure not to take my eyes off Jaguar as we moved.

After a damp, sloshy crawl, Jaguar stopped. There was just enough light that I could see a grate made of iron and fire opal barring the rest of the way.

"You will need to be careful from here on," Jaguar said. She slid back around us, leaving me and Little Lion crouched near the grate. "Once you pass this and reach the end of the tunnel, you will be in the dungeon. Remember the two rules."

"Why are you talking like that?" Little Lion reached out to her, but she withdrew in a rush and crawled a few steps back. "You're coming with us, right?"

Jaguar paused. "I can't."

His eyebrows crushed down. "Why not?" he demanded, but slowly, his voice softened instead. "Are you—really going to leave me alone again?"

He sounded younger asking that than he had this whole journey. Jaguar's dark brows pulled together, and light caught on the curve of her soul stone. It swung as she placed her hands on his shoulders.

"Be careful, hermano," she said, hard and deep and insistent. She sounded more alert, more awake, than she had earlier. "You *have* to get to El Sombrerón. But I don't want you to get hurt, Little Lion . . ." Her breath came faster. "Promise me you won't get yourself in trouble again while I'm not around to protect you."

"Then come with us," Lion insisted.

She shook her head, and he scowled.

"So you're going to just run off? Like a coward?" He growled.

There was a hurt beat of silence. Then Jaguar squeezed out, "Coward? I . . . I risked my life for you." A twitch ran through her arms; Lion winced. "Don't try to make me feel guilty for leaving you here," she suddenly snapped, and crawled back again, so shadows disguised her face. "This is your mission, not mine. The least you can do is be grateful for what I *have* done." Her voice faded into something dreamy and distant. "Say, 'Gracias, Jaguar.' You still remember how to thank those you owe, don't you, Lion?"

Lion's face tensed. There was a stiff beat of silence— before his face screwed into a violent scowl. I'd thought he'd glared at me before. But those expressions were barely annoyance compared to the sheer *wrath* gritted in his bared teeth now.

"I didn't *ask you* to risk yourself," he roared. "*You* asked *us* to follow you. I don't owe you anything!"

"We both know that's a lie," she said.

Lion stiffened.

"Go on, now. The keeper of the dungeon is on her patrols; you want to catch her before she leaves."

Little Lion's nostrils flared. "Fine."

He whirled around and grasped the bars with his hands. The fire opal in the bars glowed, and his hands smoked the moment they touched them. I nearly yelped, but he just growled and pressed through the pain until the grate gave way. He released it, shaking.

"We're leaving," he said, gruff and hard and ignoring

the smoking burns on his skin.

"Idiota, what'd you do that for?" I snapped. Lion held his injured hands to his chest. I finished shifting the grate out of his way, and when I glanced back, Jaguar had vanished. Hmph. Coward. "You shouldn't hurt yourself just because you're mad." I clucked my tongue. Little Lion looked up, eyes glistening. "I could have moved the grate—the fire opal doesn't burn me. How are you going to crawl on those hands now?"

Lion shrugged as I fumbled through my bag and found some stray pieces of cloth. I pulled one of his hands over.

"Here. This'll help." I started wrapping a cloth around his reddened palm. "This gato estúpido. Thinks he's indestructible just 'cause he's a criatura."

"I'm a black lion," he insisted.

I rolled my eyes as I knotted the cloth around his blistered hand.

"You know, you're surprisingly naggy when you're not trying to stab things," he grumbled.

I threw the next cloth at him. "Wrap it up yourself, then. Hmph."

I crawled forward. Little Lion followed, silent for a few minutes, before his voice crept back up behind me.

"Jaguar's never said something like that before," he murmured. "I know she's gone through a lot since we last saw each other. But she never demanded I be grateful." His voice caught. "For a second there, she reminded me of . . . Catrina."

I paused. Cece hadn't told me too much about Lion's past as our vile aunt's criatura, but it sounded like she'd been a particularly terrible bruja master. I glanced back to check on him. He'd stopped moving, and his chest shuddered.

"Hey." I softened my voice. "You okay?"

He rubbed his quivering, bandaged hand against his mouth. He shook his head but couldn't speak. The blistering heat in my chest lessened, just a little. I knew that look. Or I'd felt it, at least. Tía Catrina really had done a number on him.

I almost reached out to comfort him. But my skin still crawled at the idea, so I kept my hands to myself and shifted just slightly closer instead. "Hey. Let's talk about something else. Get your mind off that bruja and your jerk sister." I glared down the tunnel. "I thought something was off about Jaguar—I didn't realize it was cowardice. She just wanted to sneak us in to do the stuff she's too spineless to do."

"Stop." Lion shook his head. "Don't talk bad about her. You don't get it. Jaguar's—Jaguar's my Cece."

My insides went quiet. I turned back to him as he cleared his throat and rubbed his nose.

"Jaguar's the one who helped me escape Devil's Alley in my last life." He took a long, steadying breath. "She smuggled me out when I was about six years old, during the criatura months. She protected me, got scars for me, fed me. We stayed together for a while, but one night she went out to hunt for food and . . . never came back." He lowered his hand from his mouth.

Oh. I shifted awkwardly. I had been trying to fire him back up by ragging on Jaguar, but I hadn't realized they were *that* close. Cece-and-me close. I'd just hit another sore spot.

"Do—you think it was a bruja who got her?" I asked, more gently.

"Don't know," he mumbled. After a moment, he started forward again, and we moved together toward the end of the tunnel just up ahead. "It was during Semana de la Cosecha. Anyone would want the royal animal as a prize."

My chest burned. The image of Little Lion, even more of a kid than he was now, waiting alone in the desert for his sister to come back, made me think of Cece's tear-stained, bruised face staring up at me the night El Sombrerón stole me. The way she'd screamed my name like each syllable was tearing her apart.

I winced but forced myself to keep crawling, to outrun the memories. I didn't want to go back there. Never again.

We reached the end of the tunnel quickly. Carefully, we crept out of its confines and, at last, entered the dungeon of El Cucuy.

I stood up in the new, cavernous passageway. To the left, a small river of noxious water flowed into the cramped runoff passage we'd just climbed out of. Now, I stood on a flat, damp stone path that stretched forward before turning and disappearing down another tunnel far ahead. On the left and right side, enormous crystal balls clung likes eggs to the curved walls and floor. Each one was about six feet tall. I grimaced behind my skull mask. The blue torches were bright enough to illuminate the crystal balls' many sharp surfaces, but the flames offered no heat to warm the cold, damp space.

"What are those things?" I scratched at the nearest crystal globe.

"The reason for Jaguar's first rule." Little Lion prowled forward. "El Cucuy's dungeon feeds on people's fears. These are the people who stayed in one place too long. Crystals grow up them and form a spherical cage to trap them inside." He knocked on one of the enclosures and met my gaze. "Let's get moving—before we join them."

11

Cece Rios and the Great Renamer

"We must find my ancient home," Metztli was saying, as we hiked up the beach toward the city, the ocean at our backs. "I have equipment there that will help you grasp the fundamentals. Then, I can show you how to open your own portal to Devil's Alley's cenote, as only an ocean curandera can."

The sun had just bled over the horizon, and only a small group of fishermen was in the area now, ahead of us on the beach. I trailed behind everyone, brushing my left hand against the curved cliff face parallel to our path. From here, I could watch Coyote's silent back, Kit's nervous steps, and Ocelot's easy stride. Metztli was so confident, even though we were planning on entering Devil's Alley and taking on El Cucuy himself. My stomach tangled up as I thought of Juana, lost somewhere in that awful place again. I hoped Little Lion was with her. I gazed up at the red streaks in the sky, so bright and powerful, just like my sister. Even though they didn't get along, Lion had been the one to volunteer to stay behind and watch out for her. They'd at least be safer if they stuck together.

I lowered my head—and ran face-first into one of the fishermen.

The impact sent me spiraling sideways toward the cliff wall. The man jumped to steady me.

"¿Estás bien?" He pulled me up straight before I could hit my head on the rock. "Don't be so clumsy, chica. You could have hurt us both."

"Lo siento, señor." I looked up—and the breath vanished from my lungs.

The man froze. My hand was still in his, and my insides washed cold. For a moment, neither of us said a word.

I checked and double-checked his features. Finally, I whispered, "¿Papá?"

He looked so much older. There was more gray in his hair than I remembered, and the skin on his face sagged around his mouth like it had given up. His eyes were still the same—a hard, unyielding dark brown, with angry black eyebrows hanging low over them. But he wore a colorful thin shirt and wide-brimmed hat like nearly all the men in Costa de los Sueños. He seemed like he belonged here. Like his life in Tierra del Sol had never existed. And neither had we.

Papá pulled his hand away. My heart squeezed tight. Far

off to the side, the men he'd been walking with called out to him, but Papá smiled and waved them on.

"Un momento," he called. "I'll catch up."

He didn't attempt to introduce me. The men turned away, still chatting. And unfortunately, I hadn't realized how far I'd lagged behind because Metztli and the others were at least thirty feet ahead of me already, my friends listening as she planned our next move.

Papá leveled his dark stare down at me. "Cecelia," he said. "What—are—you doing here?"

His low voice made the hairs on my arm stand up. I swallowed as I searched for words. Behind him, Coyote glanced backward, searching for me. His mismatched eyebrows tugged together as he met my gaze across the distance.

I reached out to his soul. *Don't leave me alone*, I begged him.

Coyote stopped and turned our way.

"You should be with your mamá," Papá said, shoving his hands in his shorts pockets. He looked away. "She's all alone now."

A whirl of sharp, icy pain flooded my chest alongside a surge of tears. I struggled to press them back. I couldn't cry, not right here, not now, meeting Papá for the first time since he walked out of our home. It would only give him more reason to look down on me—and feel like he'd made the right choice.

I swallowed as I pulled words up from deep inside. "Mamá's not alone," I said, and I was so relieved it came out with only a slight tremble. "I brought Juana home. I did exactly what I said I would, but you wouldn't know that because—because you *left us*—"

I tried to say more and choked on a lump of tears. Papá looked down at me, brow creased. He sighed out his nose and checked our surroundings, like he was embarrassed I was getting emotional. He used to do that a lot. At fiestas, in front of townspeople on the street, and even alone at home. And as much as that made me want to hide the tears, to preserve some sort of pride, it only made them come more easily.

"Cece," Papá said, "don't make up stories just because you're scared."

My heart crumbled. I don't think he could have said anything that would have hurt worse in that moment. I'd finally done something big, something that proved how strong I was—and he didn't even believe it. My neck and face flushed hot. But I looked up, meeting his gaze even as tears fell out of mine.

"I'm not lying!" I cried, as big, salty drops poured down my cheeks. "Juana's home! I brought her back with the help of my criatura friends."

He still looked doubtful. It only hurt my heart more.

My chin crumpled, and a sob jumped up in my throat. "Why . . . why do you treat me like this?"

Papá looked away, clearly uncomfortable. I gripped my jacket—no, his old jacket—in my hands to try to stop them from trembling. But it didn't work.

"Is that why you left? Because of me?" I asked.

Papá went quiet. He kept looking around, as if for some escape from this conversation—the way he'd left our whole familia behind just so he wouldn't have to deal with me.

"I know I'm not perfect," I whispered. "I tried really hard to be the daughter you wanted, and I guess I'm still not enough, but—Juana really is back, and she misses you." He still had to care about her, right? "She doesn't say it, but I see it whenever she looks at where your boots used to be by the bed." I squeezed my hands together. "Why—didn't you fight for us? Or at least Mamá and Juana? Didn't you . . . love any of us, at all?"

He turned away. "I'm not coming back, Cece," he said, even though I hadn't asked. "That's my last gift to you." He strode off after the distant fishermen.

For a second, all I could hear was my heartbeat, distant and alone. The tears on my cheeks ran cold, and everything inside me felt as tender as a bruise.

"¿Papá?" I stumbled after him, face crumbling, heart aching. "What do you mean?"

He was only a few feet ahead. My chest tightened as I ran toward him.

"We've always loved you! Why won't you even *try* for us?"

He picked up his speed—until Coyote landed in front of him.

Coyote stood deathly still, blocking Papá's way. Papá stumbled back. His frame trembled, just slightly, like he suddenly remembered how Coyote had threatened him when he'd hurt me months ago.

"*Answer her*," Coyote said. His hat sent shadows streaking over his burning gold eyes, and dark colors seeped to the surface of his soul, red and furious. He bared his teeth. "You don't get to run away from your consequences anymore, coward."

My heart snagged somewhere deep inside me. Coyote had been a little off since yesterday, and Metztli's reaction to him hadn't helped. But now, the gray in his soul was dark and deep and sticky. Slowly, almost mechanically, Papá turned to face me. He came to where I'd stopped, nearer the cliffside. His gaze fell to my right eye. I held my breath, legs trembling. I had a small scar there, on my cheekbone, where the skin had torn when he hit me.

"After I slapped you, and before you left, you said you forgave me, Cece. But do you know what your mamá told me before *I* left?" he asked.

I didn't answer. The shadows on his face cut deep.

"She said to forgive someone and to restore them are not the same thing. To forgive and to trust again are not the same." He nodded at the statements. "She was right."

My breath vanished. I stared at anything but his face, but there was no outrunning what he was trying to say: it really was my fault he'd decided to leave. I'd become a bruja, and he couldn't forgive me for it. And he certainly couldn't restore me—couldn't love me as his daughter. So he'd left our whole familia behind.

"Go home, Cece," he said.

I might've been a stranger, the way Papá looked at me as he turned toward the city and his new life. The air inside my lungs iced over. I searched for some way to fix this— anything at all—but there was none. No villain to fight, like when El Sombrerón kidnapped Juana. No soul to heal, because I'd never known how to reach Papá's. My heart plunged, deep down, until it hung like a stone in my gut.

Papá went to stride past Coyote. I sunk to the ground, my whole body trembling with sobs. Coyote's face tensed— hurt, sharp, and angry as he watched me.

Then without warning, he lunged at Papá.

I jumped as he grabbed him by the collar and pinned him against the cliff wall. Coyote's soul flared up in a noxious mix of gray and purple.

"You're just going to *leave her*?" Coyote snarled. "After everything you did? You're not even going to try to fix the holes in her *you* made?" Coyote gripped Papá so tightly, his shirt began to tear at the seams. "You're not just a coward. You're—you're a *monster.*"

Papá scrambled, grasping at Coyote's strong arm where it anchored him. He gagged at the pressure on his throat.

"If you're going to act like a monster," Coyote spat, "you should wear the face of one."

"Coyote!" I called. "Stop!"

But Coyote pressed his second hand against Papá's chest, just over his heart. The place Rodrigo had pulled my soul stone from. Coyote's soul grew darker, so acidic it made me gasp. Papá struggled, but he was no match for the strength of a criatura.

Otherworldly music rose from the ground. A chorus of drums that echoed from nowhere, and stemmed from Coyote's hand over my papá's chest, shook the sand. My breath withered. Coyote's soul tasted like hatred and acid. Purple and white tattoos splintered up Papá's skin, crawling out from where Coyote held him.

I'd seen those markings just once before, when he'd tried to Rename Bruja Bullring.

"No!" I cried, but the sound of drums drowned me out.

Coyote ground Papá's back into the wall. "You, I will Rename Tukákame."

The purple and white tattoos moved faster than they had last time. By the time I'd run halfway to them, they'd completely wrapped around Papá's face, his arms, his hands. Steam rose from his skin. I cried out again, but Coyote didn't even seem to hear me anymore.

"You turned your back on the ocean curandera?" Coyote asked. "Then from now on, water will burn and destroy you."

The strange, sticky music grew thick enough to choke on.

"So you abandoned your familia to feed yourself?" Coyote asked. "Then now, you will feed only on the dead." His eyes flashed, heated and sharp like metal in a forge. "Corpses will be your meals, and death your only familia because you couldn't value what you had."

Coyote bared his teeth. Beneath his touch, Papá's steaming body shrank. His arms thinned until I could see the bones. His skin grew loose and gray, and his eyes glazed over. Papá opened his mouth, but all that came out was a retching, garbled cry.

"Coyote, I said *stop!*" I charged him now, shoving back my fear. "You can't do this! It's wrong!" I yelled. He didn't acknowledge me, like he was purposefully blocking me out. "Is this how you made Alejo into El Silbón?" I demanded. "Is this how you made all the dark criaturas?"

Coyote's gaze finally darted to mine. More tears burned up my throat.

"You told me you made them from darkness," I whispered, as I stumbled into place beside him. "Not people."

"I—I didn't mean to lie. I didn't remember how Renaming worked yet. Or maybe I didn't want to," he said tightly. "But I was still right." He drove Papá harder against the wall. "People like this are made of darkness. I just made their outsides match their insides." He said it hard, with conviction. But there was a small flinch in his face. Just a tiny one, as his soul rippled with confused, gray guilt.

"Don't," I said. "Por favor."

He clenched his jaw and refocused on my misshapen papá, where he writhed against the wall. "He doesn't deserve you, Cece. He had a familia who loves him, and he threw it away just because—because—" His soul swelled with a new wave of burning, blood red. "He has everything I ever wanted, and he treated it like dirt." He squeezed, and Papá's jaw fell open like a skeleton's. "He deserves *this*."

Horror flipped my stomach. "Then—what about me?"

"You haven't done anything wrong," Coyote said, quick and decisive. "You deserve—everything. You're different from other humans."

"No I'm not." My throat tightened so hard that all the muscles in my body shook. A wave of sorrow and guilt crashed over me. "*I'm* the reason Juana got kidnapped, and now she's broken. I was—such a terrible daughter, Papá gave up even trying for us. I make so many mistakes. I—I'm the *problem*." I looked up through a film of tears. My insides felt shaky, wrong. "How are you going to punish me for that?" I reached for his shoulder, to pull him back and stop this, once and for all. "What will you Rename me into, Coyote?"

Before I could touch him, Metztli suddenly stepped between us.

Ocelot and Kit stopped behind me, Ocelot sharp and ready to intervene. And though the moon had set, and the bright sun of day streaked across her, Metztli looked as great and terrible as she had last night. Coyote looked up to meet her haunting gaze.

"I will not let you do this again," she said. Her voice was filled with thunder and the sharp crevices of dusk. "If you will not be reasoned with, then *remember*." She reached in between him and Papá, placing her index finger at the center of Coyote's forehead. "Remember *everything*."

A blinding light flashed between them.

I covered my eyes and fell back against the wall. Coyote let out a sharp cry. A jolt of power pushed my hair back from my face. I righted myself and blinked to clear my vision.

Papá dropped out of Coyote's grip, onto the hard ground. All the changes vanished in an instant—he was all flesh, and human, and alive again. He even winced and clasped his hip from the fall. But on the ground in front of him, hands pressed to his face, entire body shaking, Coyote cringed on his knees. His breaths were wet and shaky, and they sounded like sobs.

I glanced back and forth between him and Papá, my heart stretched in two. How could I help? Should I help? Metztli stood over Coyote's weeping, shuddering body, and offered no comfort.

"What did you do?" I asked her.

There was something cold and removed in her expression when she peered down at Coyote. Like she was fighting back an anger that she herself disagreed with. "I made him remember his last life," she said. "Now he knows exactly how much damage he did, has done, and must, now, make up for at last."

My breath hitched. That sounded like too much for anyone to bear all at once. I knelt by him but looked at Papá, who rubbed his aching hip.

"Are you all right, Papá?" Shaking, I reached out to him.

Papá refused to meet my gaze as he regained his feet. "Cece," he said, voice shaking, once he was upright.

I felt small, like a speck of sand on the wide shore when I spotted tears on his eyelashes.

"It's not what you want, I know," he said. "But leaving is the kindest thing I can do for mi familia." He turned to look at me. I saw myself reflected in his eyes—small and weak and unwanted. "I can't be a proper papá to you. But

I can at least make sure I never hurt you again."

Without another word, Papá left.

He drifted up the cliffside, turned into the city, and vanished among the nameless inhabitants. He didn't look back. Not once. I watched him go and couldn't speak, even as a wound opened up inside my chest, even as I wrestled with his last words, even as I raged and wept on the inside. My soul felt tattered at the edges, like Papá's old jacket, where it still hung like lead on my shoulders.

This was my fault. This knowledge weaseled deep down inside me, staining every fiber of who I was. The kindest thing my Papá could do was leave me behind because I was so undesirable that he couldn't treat me well. I had never been enough for him. I'd always tested his patience. And now, his issues with me meant he'd given up on the rest of my familia too.

"I'm sorry, Cece." Coyote's voice scraped free of his raw, tight throat. He peeled his face out of his hands, tears streaking his cheeks. "I'm so sorry."

12

Juana Rios and the Keeper of the Dungeon

The dungeon was so cold, my breath crystallized on my lips.

I was grateful that the prickling, sharp heat in my chest kept my skin hot. Little Lion and I prowled the thin stone walkway of the dungeon, careful to stay away from the left side where the river of sour water flowed. We passed people-size globes made of crystals on our right scattered across the walls and floor. They were in the place of prison cells, Little Lion said, made to trap inhabitants. But they haunted us like ghosts of failed escapes as we searched for the keeper of the dungeon, and unease crept up the walls around us.

I spotted something tall and dark—horrifyingly familiar—out of the corner of my eye. I whirled around, knife out.

But there was nothing there. Just empty stone walls and crystal prisons.

Had I imagined it?

"What?" Lion asked. "Did you see something?"

I shook it off and grunted. "It was nothing." I adjusted my skull mask so he'd see only its sharp ridges, not the anxiety threatening me beneath. "Where is this bruja anyway?"

My voice came out harder, louder than I'd meant. The anger in the question echoed across the walls.

"Did you hear that?" a voice asked.

Little Lion shot me a look. A few feet ahead, the path curved right into another tunnel. Lion crouched. I flattened myself against the wall. We moved to the corner and peeked around it.

Down the hall stood a tall woman and a child. They were at a fair distance, but the blue torch the woman held lit up her sharp cheekbones and magenta eyes. The sides of her head were shaved, leaving a strip of wild spiky hair down the center of her head, and emphasized the long, sharp structure of her face. She placed her free hand hesitantly on the child's shoulder.

The little girl glanced down the tunnel in our direction, head cocked. But she didn't seem to see us. She had large pink eyes that were somewhere between adorable and bulgy. I raised an eyebrow. Well, that was definitely a criatura. Even her hair was pink, her shoulder-length locks curling up and out on either side of her face like fluffy fins framing her round cheeks.

"Can you see anything, Axolotl?" the bruja's voice carried. "Your eyes are better than mine in the dark."

The bruja looked seconds from falling asleep. Like she'd become part of the drab, dark moss of these haunted halls. This had to be the keeper of the dungeon, Bruja Damiana. Jaguar had been right. She was clearly bottom-rung bruja material.

"Nope! All clear!" the little girl chirped. "Now can we go back up to the castle? I'm hungry, and it's creepy down here."

"You know, axolotls are supposed to like caves." The bruja sounded almost amused.

"But the ones in Devil's Alley *stink*." She made a dramatic gagging sound, really playing it up until the bruja chuckled. "The cenote's the only nice water here. It smells sweet and clear—"

"I've told you, *never* get near the cenote. You know it's dangerous."

Axolotl sighed. This sounded like a tired argument. "I was just sayin'. I don't have to be close to smell it."

Their steps headed our way. "I'll take you up soon," the bruja promised. "I just have to check the south tunnels first."

"Then let's hurry, Mamá!" The little girl sprinted our

way, far ahead of the bruja.

Little Lion and I pulled back out of sight.

"I'll cover Axolotl's mouth just long enough to talk to her." Lion dropped his voice. "If we can get her on our side, she can persuade the bruja—"

The little girl came flying around the corner, her pink hair bouncing. Everything slowed. She turned toward us in the darkness. Lion opened his mouth. Before he could speak, I snagged her from the bruja's line of sight, slapped a hand over her mouth, and flicked my knife up to her neck before she could struggle. The blade glowed a violent orange, and Axolotl froze, whimpering.

Lion gawked at me.

"What are you *doing?*" he hissed. "I said grab her so we can talk, not go full murder-kidnapper."

"We have less than twenty-four hours before the door to Devil's Alley closes," I said. "I'm saving us time, Little Lion."

Axolotl looked up at him. *"Mffle mion?"* My hand muffied her voice.

He rubbed the back of his neck. "Yeah, it's me. Don't worry." He glared up at me. "She's not actually going to hurt you."

Footsteps clacked our way. "Axolotl? Axolotl, where are you?"

I turned away from Lion, and his hope for a promise, just in time to cut off the bruja rounding the corner.

The woman halted in front of me. Her long jacket swung around her narrow, bony frame, so the roses and snakes embroidered down the lapels flashed in the light of her icy-blue torch. The moment her gaze met mine, I made a show of pressing my knife close to Axolotl's face.

"I am Juana Rios, the bride back for her soul." I scowled, hard and relentless, through the empty eyes of my skull mask.

The bruja let out a sharp gasp. I glared, and she went still at the warning.

"If you want me to leave Axolotl alive, you'll lead us out of this dungeon and into the castle, and tell no one we're here." My blade sizzled, and Axolotl flinched. "Got it?"

In an instant, the bruja's face crumbled, like the life might go right out of her as she watched Axolotl quake in my hold. The heat in my chest threatened to turn to smoke and suffocate me. But I locked my jaw so I wouldn't waver.

"I'll do whatever you want," the bruja finally said, lifting both hands in surrender. "Just don't hurt Axolotl. Please."

The way she said the criatura's name reminded me of how Mamá spoke of me and Cece. The smoke thickened inside me, until I was almost choking on it.

"Then move," I said, and jerked my chin toward the way she'd come.

Bruja Damiana turned as directed, still holding her hands up like a prisoner. She checked on Axolotl once over her shoulder. I swallowed and followed her as she led us into the deep, rancid-smelling tunnel.

I dragged Axolotl with me. The little girl stumbled, and Little Lion dove to right her. He flashed me a narrowed, disgusted snarl. The look sunk through my ribs like a knife.

"What?" I hissed, and yanked Axolotl out of his hold, back up to my speed. "Don't look at me like that. Jaguar's the one who said to use her as a hostage."

"Yeah, and I told you I had another plan." Lion didn't try to obscure his withering glare, but he kept his voice low, so Bruja Damiana wouldn't overhear. "It was a better option—"

"This way's faster, so it's better." I frowned. "I don't get what you're mad about."

"Maybe you forgot, but *I'm* a criatura," Lion spat. The bruja led us down a right turn. "So yeah, I have an issue with you terrorizing an innocent kid like she doesn't matter just because she's not human. Look at her face!"

I didn't. I refused. But I could feel the way her legs shook as she tried to keep up with me and the way she craned her head back to avoid the touch of my knife. A distant panic screamed through my mind. My stomach felt sick. But so what if she was scared? I was doing what I had to. I wasn't going to let anything get between me and breaking El Sombrerón.

Strange sounds echoed behind us, and I glanced over my shoulder. The darkness was thick and claustrophobic. But I swore, just for a second, that I saw the edge of a black cloak. By the time I blinked, it was gone again.

Heat traveled like a rash up my chest. Was I seeing things? I couldn't afford to get distracted. I might—get taken advantage of again.

"What?" Lion demanded, voice a bit louder. I swung back around. "What do you keep looking at? What are you searching for, Juana?"

"Nothing," I quickened our pace.

The bruja was only about five feet ahead of us when she stopped at the bottom of a staircase. Water ran down its steps, flickering blue in the light of her torch. The air around the water was sweeter, now. Cleaner. Huh. So the source of the water wasn't poisoned—something about running through the dungeon must make it go sour.

"Be careful as we ascend," the bruja warned. I cut my attention back to her. She stood, lifeless and thin, eyes fixed on Axolotl. "At the top of these steps, you will find the cenote from which this water flows. It is an ancient underground lake—and it is dangerous. Beneath it is a one-way prison that holds the most frightening criaturas in Devil's Alley. Anyone who goes in does not come out." She swallowed, hand shaking on her torch. "We must follow the path around its edges to get to the dungeon exit. So please—don't let Axolotl near the cenote." Her thin, straight brows tugged together.

That gave her an incentive not to push me in, then. I nodded. "Fine." I flicked my knife close to Axolotl's cheek, to remind her who was in charge. Bruja Damiana winced. "Now keep moving."

She hurried up the stairs, but I felt Lion's glare burn through my head. I tried to ignore him as we started climbing.

"You like it, don't you?" Lion demanded in a scathing whisper. "Threatening someone weaker than you. Makes you feel more powerful, huh?"

I rounded on him. Far above us, Bruja Damiana stumbled and dropped her torch. She groaned as the light went out, and we were plunged into darkness. The only light left was a distant speck of dim blue from the top of the stairs, and the burnished glow of my blade.

"I'm not a *bully*," I spat at Lion. "Of course I don't enjoy this!"

"Then what is this all really about?" Lion's eyes caught the light from my knife as he gestured sharply at it, at little

Axolotl, at my skull mask.

"You know what!" I stomped up the steps again. "It's the same reason you're here, gato estúpido: *vengeance*."

Fury straightened Lion's spine. "You think I want to burn down Devil's Alley for *revenge*? I'm trying to save my enslaved familia!" The higher we climbed, the darker it got. "Vengeance isn't interested in healing wounds. I already learned that lesson from your sister." He cut in front of me on the staircase. "But you're so busy trying to save your past self, you can't see that there *is* no saving Juana from two months ago. There's only Juana *now*. And if you're not careful, there will be no saving her soul because it'll already belong to a monster—and I'm not talking about El Sombrerón."

With a shove, Lion broke my hold and yanked Axolotl out of my arms. Tears had pooled in her wide and frightened eyes. He pulled her to him protectively and turned away from me.

My empty chest scratched and squeezed. What right did he have to be so disappointed in me? I wasn't stuck in the past. Or—or if I was, then I had every right to be. Didn't I? What happened to me was wrong. I had the right to change it. I had the *right*.

Lion and Axolotl stepped up into the darkness, and the weak light at the top of the stairs winked out. What? Where'd it go? I listened for footsteps, but their splashing had vanished too. I stumbled forward through the water.

"Hey! Lion?" I called.

He didn't answer. Sharp, needly heat scratched inside my chest. I sprinted up the stairs.

"Lion, don't be a baby! I know you're mad, but . . ." I stumbled on something sharp and caught myself on the wall, panting.

Beyond the sound of my own breath, I listened for Lion's response. There was nothing but the running water—and the sound of a swishing cloak behind me.

I whirled around. The plucking of silver strings rose up in the darkness, haunting the air around me. It was too dense to see in the darkness, but I knew that melody. I'd heard it too many times.

El Sombrerón was near.

I ripped out my knife. The orange glow lit up the walls and waterfall steps but revealed no sign of him. Where was he? My entire body turned into a fire, wild and hot and broiling. No, I couldn't let El Sombrerón get me again. And I couldn't fight on a slippery staircase, where I was at a disadvantage.

A dark laugh rumbled up the steps behind me. I turned and sprinted up the last of the stairs, outrunning the music, and tore into a vast, cave-like space filled with low, azure light.

I skated to a stop at the edge of the cenote. My mind

whirled, trying to catch up to the new surroundings. Lion, Bruja Damiana, and Axolotl were still nowhere in sight. But the underground lake was larger than I'd thought, so wide it could fit the entire town square inside, and the bright blue water so clear, I could see straight down through to a strange film at the bottom. I shook my head. Silver strings and honey-touched music haunted my back. I ripped myself around, my skirt snapping with the speed, and searched the tunnel I'd come from.

"Not there," the velvet voice said from behind me.

My blood ran cold. I turned, inch by inch, to face the cenote again. The distant sound of voices—maybe Lion's? where had he gone?—pulled at me, but I couldn't pay attention to anything else, see anything else. Because rising from the cenote's clear waters was the towering, terrible El Sombrerón.

My knees locked. My feet were so cold and numb, I could have been standing in ice. He lugged his long, inky cloak out the water, and all eight feet of him stretched up to grab at me.

All I wanted to do was run. To crawl away and scream.

So I charged him instead.

"*I hate you!*" I roared, palming a knife in each hand. I leaped off the edge of the cenote, flying toward him over the water, and aimed my knives at his heartless chest. "This time you'll pay! I'll rip you to shreds, you monster—"

The distant voices warped in the air as I careened toward El Sombrerón's dreadful figure. His image shimmered. His hands faded away at the ends. Wait. Something was wrong.

"Juana! Wake up!" Lion's voice shook through me.

Suddenly, everything shattered, like my vision had been made of sharp and fragile glass. My world reassembled into reality. I wasn't charging El Sombrerón—I was falling backward, toward the water, dragging Axolotl with me. When had I grabbed her? Lion hovered above me, in mid-leap, falling with me in an attempt to save me from the cenote. Bruja Damiana had already grabbed Axolotl's hand and tipped over the edge. There was no silver music—just Axolotl's screams and my missing heartbeat. There was no attack—just shards of crystals breaking off from my feet, where my own cell of fears had started to form around me.

Keep moving, Jaguar's warning rang through my mind. *In the dungeon, fears make themselves realities for the vulnerable.*

Lion gripped my wrist as we plunged, all four of us, into the cenote from which no one returned.

13

We followed Metztli up a hill just outside Costa de los Sueños, each soul at my neck tense and quiet. No one had spoken since Metztli had given Coyote back his memories. He'd kept his head bowed most of the way, lingering behind us all. Metztli's expression was sharp and focused as we hiked, but the lights in her eyes weren't as bright as before.

"We will have to be quick," Metztli said. "We're running out of time before the entrance to Devil's Alley closes."

I hung my head. I'd wasted a lot of time back there, trying to get answers out of a papá who hated me. Not to mention causing a fight between my friends on the way. I chewed on my lip as Metztli paused in the grass, her gaze focused on a solitary house ahead of us.

An old adobe house perched on the top of the cliff we'd been climbing, overlooking the sea. It had a broken roof, and vines covered most of the front. Spring had brought bright morning glory blossoms to tangle in the wrought iron bars of the front-facing window. The home reminded me a lot of Metztli—beautiful, but abandoned by time.

"This was my familia's home centuries ago," she said. "If we are lucky, everything we need is still there."

She marched forward. But I found myself glancing at Coyote for the thousandth time that day. He walked at the very back of our group, tailing Ocelot, his eyes downcast. Kit was the only one who seemed to notice me.

"It'll be okay, Cece," he mouthed.

I smiled back at him, because I hoped he was right, even though I was afraid he wasn't.

"My old curandera tools should still be here." Metztli stopped in front of the broken-down door. With a bump of her hip, it gave way and fell inside the house. She strode past it easily.

I went to follow but stole one last glance back at my friends. Coyote, Ocelot, and Kit had all gone to stand by the cliffside. Ocelot rested a hand on Coyote's shoulder. Sad, sluggish colors meandered through their souls. Should I say something to him? But then—what did I say? I didn't know how to fix this for him. I didn't know how to take away his pain, when it was now wrapped up in my own.

"Pain often tells us that we have left something important

undone," Ocelot said to Coyote, and the wind carried her voice my way. She rubbed his shoulder as he bowed his head. "That's why it's important we let ourselves feel it. And why it's important we don't let it overtake us. So we can finish what must be finished, fix what can be fixed, and heal what's left behind."

Ocelot's words lingered on me like the tendrils of a stray cloud. Kit glanced my way again. A small spot of sunny hope filled his stone and warmed my throat. He smiled again, to give me encouragement. Sometimes, I wondered how he did that after everything he'd been through.

I laid my hand over his stone gratefully, turned, and followed Metztli inside. One day, I hoped I could be as brave as Kit Fox.

From the outside, Metztli's house had appeared old and traditional. But inside, it was lined with strange shelves covered in empty glass vials, seashells strung together with cords, lots of tiny rocks, and bowls now filled with only dirt or dust. I approached Metztli on the other side of the main room, where she was rummaging in a large box carved with swirls. A cloud of particles plumed in the air from her movements, and she coughed and batted it away.

"It's still here!" She stood and lifted a dusty glass bottle filled with water. "Behold, Cece!"

"That's weird," I said as I approached. "I thought water

got gross when it's bottled up for too long." I'd learned that the hard way. But this looked fresh and new, even though the ancient glass told a different story.

Metztli shook it lightly, so the water swept around the inside. "That is because it is no ordinary water. It is difficult for curanderas to channel the element of their god without extensive training. Items like this—glass, water, stones, basil—we use them to learn to speak the language of our element." She smiled at me. "Sometimes, we can use them to channel new, extraordinary abilities and produce spells. But you have already done this, have you not, Cece?"

Oh, the Moon must have told her about my spell to hide the house. My heart fluttered. Now that I had Metztli, she could tell me more about how all this curandera stuff worked. Maybe with her help, I'd finally be a good enough curandera to fix things. I squeezed my hands together. And then—maybe I'd be enough to fight off the misery of the people I loved.

"Curanderas can reach even greater power when we combine ours together." Metztli's eyes grew less distant as she held the glass bottle to her chest. "Consuelo taught me that. This was a gift from her. At the beginning of my journey, she made it for me with her very own hands. She said it would help me see the place where truth and love meet." Her brows upturned.

"Wait." I came up to her. "Wasn't Consuelo the ocean curandera? She mentored you?"

"Sí." She ruffled my short hair. "Perhaps it is right, then, that I turn Consuelo's gifts into teachings for you, Curanderita Cece."

I clung on to that promise and tried to fill my chest with something besides the heavy, painful weight that had been bearing down on it since this morning. If I could just focus on this, I wouldn't have to think about everything Papá had said.

A nauseating, gray throb moved in my chest. I winced and glanced out the window, at distant Coyote. He was feeling about as terrible as I was.

"Um, Metztli?" I asked. "C-can you tell me . . . what you made Coyote remember?"

She sighed out her nose—not the way Papá used to, like I was exhausting. But like sorrow had slept in her lungs. She raised her head and tapped the top of the bottle.

"Do you know *how* the gods Named us, Cece?" she asked.

I blinked. "Um. With their—god powers?"

Backlit by the risen sun in the window, Metztli looked faraway and distant, like the moon hanging in a starless sky.

"It is said that gods Named us from What Could Be. Some say What Could Be is the potential for creation.

Some say it is the place where all life waits before it is born. Regardless, we know this is the natural process of all life—to be pulled willingly from What Could Be, to become a soul given mortal flesh. Yet, there is one who was denied its proper Name, and the form that should have followed." She lowered the glass gift in her hands. "This is what Coyote could not, or did not want to, remember: that he pulled El Cucuy from What Could Be—but never gave him his Name."

The information poured over me in a dizzying wave. "But—how could El Cucuy *not* have a Name?" I didn't think you could be *alive* without one.

Metztli brushed more dust away from the glass bottle to reveal a window of pure, clear water. She breathed deeply, holding the glass as she tilted it into the sun. The light caught on the water inside the bottle, and a picture began to form. I drifted closer, lips separating, as the image of a strange, twisted shadow crawled its way in. My breath caught. It was the silhouette of a monstrous criatura. It had backward animal legs, a torso too big for itself, teeth in places where they shouldn't be, and long arms that tangled like parasitic vines. But every few moments, its shape changed slightly, like it had no original state to return to.

"El Cucuy is the one dark criatura who was not Renamed

from another creation," Metztli said simply. My lungs felt starched. *That* was El Cucuy? The amorphous, twisted silhouette rippled and faded a bit. "He is the one being in all Antiguo Amanecer who was pulled from What Could Be, and instead of a Name, was given only Coyote's anger and hatred. El Cucuy is suspended in a limbo of twisted creation. Coyote made the misshapen creature to fix what he thought he could not. He let him loose on the worlds with only one prerogative: to instill order at any cost. That is why El Cucuy seeks to take control of the human world. That is why he will not stop until the seal my sisters sacrificed themselves to create is broken."

"And this"—she looked up at me—"is what I showed Coyote. So he will no longer run from the pain. So he will no longer continue the cycle." She placed the glass bottle in my hands, and I watched the ever-morphing image of El Cucuy with a sharp, held breath. "Coyote is a child in this lifetime. He has a chance to be different from what he was. But only if he chooses it." She placed a hand on my cheek. "You cannot choose it for him, Cece. This, he must do on his own."

But—Coyote was my best friend. Metztli patted the bottle in my hand and walked past me, gathering other things from her ancient home. I'd talked Coyote through his hard times. He'd talked me through mine. Isn't that how you loved people well? By carrying things for them? I glanced out the window. Coyote had his head leaned forward, his hands over his face, in the distance. The position reminded me so much of Papá, I shivered.

I turned away. Coyote had actually reminded me a lot of Papá today. From his anger to his evasion, all I'd wanted to do was cringe away from him. And at the same time, I was afraid that, if I did, he'd finally give up. Just like Papá had.

I'd lost my papá a second time today. I didn't want my best friend to leave me too.

"Do not fear, Cece," Metztli said. I looked up to find her smiling gently. "Now that you have restored me, we will end El Cucuy soon, and set the world aright at last."

Oh, she must have mistaken what my expression was about. I tried to smile back, but I couldn't form one properly. "I—guess." I peered at El Cucuy's picture. "But it's kind of sad, isn't it? It sounds like . . ." I stroked the glass. "It wasn't even his fault."

"It is the only way to end his suffering." Metztli looked sympathetic, but she finished packing tablets and stones, beads and dried plants, inside her bag with knowing precision. "And the suffering of my sisters." She stopped in the door, reaching her steady hand out. "We must break the cycle, Cece."

I hesitated. "But how do we finish the seal?"

She and El Silbón had both talked about it a lot. I checked the bottle of water again, but El Cucuy's silhouette had vanished.

"Once you open the portal to Devil's Alley using your powers, I will fuse my soul into El Cucuy, just as my sisters did long ago," she said.

I jerked my head up. Her face was calm, and grave, and steady.

"That will complete the seal," she said. "Then, El Cucuy will not be simply restricted to Devil's Alley. He will be turned to stone."

My mouth dropped open. El Silbón had told me about how the seal was missing a curandera, which I'd since guessed was Metztli, but I didn't know that was because the seal was literally *made* of their souls.

"Wait—so they had to die? And—and you—?" I stepped forward, gripping my soul necklace.

"It was a spell of ultimate sacrifice. Our last resort." Metztli pressed a hand to the doorframe. The lights in her eyes were faded, almost washed out. "My sisters and I were the last of the curanderas to survive the years of attacks leading up to the battle of Tierra del Sol. By then, we were the only ones standing between El Cucuy's vast army and the end of the world of Naked Man. We were outnumbered. Our powers were not enough on their own. There was only one option left to preserve our people." She closed her eyes. I could almost feel the pain, quiet though it was on her face, stretching out from her soul. "As a moon curandera, I have no physical powers like those of my sisters. But in the wisdom of the moon, I made our plan, a spell that had never been done before. If we combined our abilities, and welded our souls into El Cucuy—my light to his mind, Consuelo's water to his heart, Yollotl's fire to his soul, and Reina's dust to his flesh—we could will him into stone. But El Sombrerón caught me as my sisters started the ritual." Her lips pressed together. "I could not do my part. I failed them, at the last."

I watched Metztli's back. Maybe it was because I'd touched her soul once before, but for a moment, I almost thought I could hear her insides crying out to her sisters: *I'm sorry. I'm so sorry. If only Coyote hadn't done what he did. None of this would have happened in the first place, and I would not have failed you.*

She was still mad at him. The way I was, deep down, at my papá. I could tell she didn't want to be, either. Like she believed in treating him better than her heart was ready to.

"I will not fail them again. Come, Cece." She stretched her hand out to me again. "Though two hundred years late, this time, the curanderas will triumph."

I hesitated as the frightening, twisted image of El Cucuy swam through my mind. Why did the idea of turning him to stone make me sad? I clenched my gut. I'd taken out El Sombrerón and Rodrigo the Soul Stealer; El Cucuy was their boss, the first Dark Saint, who let them do all the terrible things they did. I shouldn't feel bad. But El Cucuy had never had a choice in who he was. I wished we could give it back to him.

Still, if I had to pick between letting him wreak havoc on both the worlds, or turning him to stone—my throat tightened—what else could I do?

Slowly, I crossed to Metztli. I didn't have the heart to take her hand. I just walked into her and buried my face in her shoulder, away from everything. Metztli didn't seem surprised or upset. She just gently stroked her hand through my hair, humming a song I didn't know, as thoughts of Papá, Coyote, El Cucuy, and Metztli's impending sacrifice threatened to crash over and drag me down.

14
Juana Rios and the Court of Fears

Lion and I plummeted deep beneath the clear, icy water of the dungeon's cenote.

I twisted, caught between the heavy cloth of my dress and the pressure of the skull on my face. Little Lion clutched me. I latched on to him in return and tried to swim us to the surface. But just like the bruja had said, something was pulling us down. It was a heavy, invisible, irresistible undertow.

The current won, and we all fell out of the bottom of the water.

I slammed into concrete, and it knocked the wind out of me. Breathless and bruised, I stumbled up, ripping out my knife as Little Lion, Bruja Damiana, and Axolotl all slapped down on the stone floor around me. I turned wildly, scanning our surroundings for danger.

Above our heads, the cenote's water floated, a liquid ceiling suspended by some kind of magic. I stood below it in a large circular room carved out of stone. Something grinded through the air. I turned and found a pair of silver doors extending out from the far side of the wall, like they were bleeding out from the rock. The doors and its frame set in place quickly, and I blinked. Sporadic colors flashed between its cracks, and low groaning sounds poured out of it. What the sunset was that? Where was I? Around the rest of the room, dim, glowing crystals offered blue and lavender light as an escape from the darkness.

Footsteps crunched behind me. I whirled around, knife ready.

A creature unfolded inch by clattering inch into the low, phosphorescent glow of the stones. The light outlined the sharp bones of her skull face and caught in the owl and quetzal feathers of her headdress. Through a wall of pure fire opal bars, I met the hollow eye sockets of the Criatura of Progeny, Stars, and Devouring.

"Tzitzimitl," I breathed.

Confused heat coiled up inside me. Tzitzimitl's name had had a particularly bad taste to our familia after Cece had rescued her. She was why Cece was considered weak. Why no one trusted her. Why Mamá taught me about our opal knives, and why, she said, I had to protect Cece with my life.

But Tzitzimitl was also the reason Cece was alive today. When Rodrigo had stolen her soul out of her chest,

Tzitzimitl had talked her back to life. And Tzitzimitl, of all beings, had been the one to see that Cece's water soul had been strong all along. That still hurt, knowing a criatura had understood my sister better than I did.

"I know that face," Tzitzimitl said, her jaw parting to let out a low voice. "You wear the bones of the Soul Stealer. But beneath, I smell a Rios blessed with fire. Only, there is smoke and heat where light and warmth once lived." She pointed to me through the bars. "Why have you come to the terrible prison of El Cucuy?" The silver moons in her headdress flashed. "Why have you sought out the Court of Fears, Juana Rios?"

Tzitzimitl gestured widely with her bony hands. Dizzy and sick, I turned to better take in my surroundings. Six prison cells were evenly spaced around the walls. Unlike the ones in the tunnels below, these weren't crystals. They were made of pure fire opal bars that glowed lightly even when no one touched them. Inside each prison cell sat a stone throne carved with ancient writing I couldn't read. Two cells were empty. But each of the other four held a dark criatura.

My breath seized in my chest. On the far side of the room sat Atotolin, the Bird King. Mamá had told me stories about him—the dark Criatura of Wind and Fortune. He had long red hair braided down his head, smooth brown skin, and tattoos of feathers lined his bare chest. Behind him, large blue wings sprouted from his back, but they were covered in grime from time in prison. He stared with yellow eyes, the gold mask of a bird's beak secured over his mouth.

"Have you forgotten us, Naked Man? After we fought for you in the battle of Tierra del Sol?" he asked. "Or have you remembered that you should have fought with us, and you've come to join the rebellion?" He gestured to the north end of the room.

In the cell there, another dark criatura perched on his throne. The criatura was a small man, about three feet tall, with a complicated bun tied tight at the top of his head. A glowing red stripe streaked from one of his temples to the other in a thick line. He folded his arms and watched me from his seat. His eyes were a mottled green and brown color, swirled together like paint. I knew this dark criatura too, though his story was so ancient, I'd thought it wasn't even real—Alux, the Guardian of Mother Desert's Bones. It was said that, should you disrespect Mother Desert's lands, he would curse you and your children for seven generations.

"She has not come for us or our cause," Alux said. As he lifted his chin, I caught the long, pointed tips of his ears. "She is here for herself. But something about her is reminiscent of Yollotl, is it not, La Lechuza?"

I swung to face the back of the room. A tall woman hunched in a slant of turquoise light, behind the grate of glowing orange bars. She wore a mask with an old woman's face carved into it, and instead of hair, a cascade of owl feathers draped down her back. La Lechuza—the Owl Witch, Criatura of Widows and Screams. She lifted a finger to tap the chin of her mask. It was long and taloned and clacked against the wood carvings.

"There is, Alux," she agreed. "Yet unlike Yollotl, this one has not learned what her true power is, let alone where it comes from."

I spun wildly as they spoke, trying to keep my eyes on all of them at once. One of the first rules of the Amenazante dance was to always keep your enemy at your front. But there was nowhere safe here to turn my back. I flashed from one terrible criatura figure to the next. If I'd had my heartbeat, it would have been thrashing against my ribs.

I was trapped here, surrounded by *monsters*.

I rounded on Bruja Damiana, where she was helping Axolotl up. "How do we get out of here?" I demanded.

She pulled Axolotl to her chest. "We don't."

"Don't *lie* to me!" My knife flared.

"She is not lying," Tzitzimitl said. I froze, hands shaking on my knife. She steadied her lifeless gaze on me. "There is only one way out from this place now. Though I had never thought to see it for myself." She lifted her jangling finger bone to the doors on the far side of the space. "The silver doors are an ancient legend, so far gone none but the oldest of beings remember. For some reason, Juana Rios, they appeared when you fell here. But what waits on the other side, no one truly knows. It is said the silver doors contain an ever-changing void, the one place in Devil's Alley that El Cucuy cannot control. So they come and go as they please." She tilted her head, and her moon pieces glittered. "However, legends say the doors will take you wherever you need to be—if you do not lose yourself to your fears. Otherwise, it's said you will be lost forever."

Her words buzzed through my skull. Of course the only exit was also a trap. Everything in this place was wretched and cruel, and I was sick of it. Sick of it inventing a thousand new ways to overpower me. I let out a frustrated screech and pulled my hair. Fine, then. I'd go in the void. By sheer force of will, I'd forge my way through it and into the rest of the castle. I couldn't let this place, brujas, criaturas, or El Sombrerón trap me like I was some plaything.

The world smeared, just for a moment, as I charged for the doors, knife blade out. I didn't pause to listen for the groaning, grinding sounds rattling beyond. I didn't hesitate. I pried one of the doors open, roared, and threw myself inside.

El Sombrerón was waiting for me.

Just like before, my entire body went cold. A scream

rattled inside me—only, no, it was chains. Heavy, iron links snaked out from the groaning walls around me and wrapped around my waist. My old scars ached, and I swung my knife at the metal.

"No!" I screamed. "I won't let you trap me, not again, I won't—"

"Juana, stop!"

The image of El Sombrerón shimmered again. I shook my head. The noise of the chains and the corridor dimmed. No way. Was I—hallucinating again? Something warm cupped my cheeks—even though I couldn't see anything touching me at all—and squeezed.

"Wake up, Juana!" Lion's voice boomed.

The image in front of me crumbled. I closed my eyes and shook my head, and when I opened them again—I was still standing in the middle of the circular room. I hadn't taken even one step closer to the silver doors like I'd thought. Instead, I was bent over a cowering Bruja Damiana and Axolotl, my knife plunged into the ground beside Damiana's shoulder, where I'd left a deep, bleeding cut she must have barely dodged.

Damiana had a trembling Axolotl buried in her chest, and pieces of Axolotl's hair scattered around Damiana's wound and my knife. I'd—almost stabbed her. Damiana had protected her. From me.

Horror sunk deep into my bones. These knives were

made for protecting. Not for—this. I ripped it away from her. Sharp crystals were growing up my feet, nearly welding me to the floor. The dark gems surrounded me in a circular base that looked exactly like the start of the fear-made prisons Lion and I had passed on our way here. I struggled to straighten up with my trapped feet. Lion helped me up and held my face, offering an anchor to reality.

"You've got to stay here, Juana," he said, almost violently. His hands shook on my cheeks, as his face struggled against a wave of emotion. "I've been here before, okay? I've lived where you are now. Your tía kept me trapped long after Coyote freed me from her because I was trying to fight what happened. But nothing you do now will change the past. It happened. It hurt. It was awful, and wrong, and *you have to let go*." His jaw trembled. Moisture pooled in his eyes. I started to push him, but he held on. "Don't you get it? The more you try to outrun it, the more power your fears will have over you. If you keep going like this, trying to fight your fears, and the ones who gave them to you, you're going to lose. And you'll lose *you*."

Lion finally released me. The crystals crumbled from my feet as my head echoed with his words. Over Lion's shoulder, over the heads of Bruja Damiana and Axolotl, I caught my reflection in the silver doors across the room. The bones of Rodrigo the Soul Stealer looked back at me.

My hair hung wild around the skull, and my eyes nearly disappeared behind the face of the monster. I was—losing myself, wasn't I? I glanced around, slowly, distantly. The trapped Court of Fears, ancient and frightening dark criaturas, watched me like *I* was the caged animal.

"We did not select our inheritances either, Juana Rios," Tzitzimitl's voice reached for me. I turned, my breathing painful and slow. "We understand how you feel. Each member of the Court of Fears was Renamed by Coyote. Once changed, we became the first of our kind, dark criaturas meant to serve El Cucuy as his loyal inner circle." She stepped up to her bars, so they glowed brighter. "But we chose, instead, to use our powers against El Cucuy. We allied with the curanderas who protected your world." She pointed to my knife, to where it now simmered in my loose grip. "You did not get to choose whether El Sombrerón hunted you. But you choose now, Juana Rios. Will you surrender your bright, protective fire for the smoke and tragedy El Sombrerón has bequeathed you?"

I knew the answer. But I wanted to yell. Scream. Rage again, because it wasn't fair that I had to choose at all. I'd gone through something terrible and was expected to somehow bear it. But a deep, charred grief settled where my heart should have been. My hands shook as I slowly, carefully, sheathed my knife. The Bird King's eyes softened.

La Lechuza nodded. Trembling, I peeled the bone mask off my face. My skin felt new and vulnerable without its armor. But I didn't put it back on. Alux smiled.

I turned with the mask in my hands to face Lion, Bruja Damiana, and Axolotl. Bruja Damiana was busy tying cloth around the wound I'd given her. Axolotl was helping her knot it. My chin quivered.

Slowly, I knelt down and placed the bone mask on the ground in front of them. It was an offering. A relinquishment. The two of them stared at it. Axolotl's curled pose relaxed. Bruja Damiana let out a shivering, relieved breath.

"I-I'm sorry," I stuttered. The apology was difficult, raw, and awkward. "I didn't mean to lose my soul on my way to get it back."

That's what Mamá had been trying to tell me, wasn't it? That's what Lion had been saying on our way here. The charred, scorching edges inside me began to crumble away. And deep down, so deep I was afraid I was imagining it, I felt a touch of nourishing warmth. It seemed so much more fragile than the violent flame that had been keeping me company. But, at the same time, it was somehow more powerful. More meaningful.

Or maybe it was just more *me* than the burning ever was.

15

Cece Rios and the Ocean's Grief

I stood by the ocean, swirling my hands awkwardly for the fifticth time, struggling to summon the portal that would lead us to Devil's Alley—and its king, El Cucuy.

Metztli watched me analytically. Sweat pricked the back of my neck as I made the motions she'd described earlier. "Hand gestures are not necessary," she'd said. "But if you are struggling to connect with your element, sometimes they can help you feel the water again. Opening the portal to Devil's Alley will require you to connect with both the ocean water before you, and the only pure water left in Devil's Alley, which you cannot see. It will require completely uniting your heart with that of Mother Ocean's. Try again, chiquita."

But I'd been at this for hours. Wasting more of our precious, limited time. At first, I'd enjoyed the movements. The natural back-and-forth mimicked the ocean waves I'd already come to love. But now, I just felt like I was doing a bad job of dancing, like when Juana tried to teach me the steps to the Amenazante dance. Except this time, Juana's safety was on the line, and so were all my friends, and Devil's Alley, and my mamá. My hands trembled as my gut wound tight. Papá's disappointed face haunted my every move.

Metztli's brows lowered as I tried to hide the shaking. "Are you all right, curanderita?" She tilted her head and walked behind me, examining my stance.

"Sí, sí! I just—I just don't know why it's not working." I bit my lip. I didn't have *time* to mess up. Semana de la Cosecha would be over sooner rather than later. I had to pull myself together and fix things. I was a curandera now. Why was I still failing?

Metztli rapped her fingers on her arm thoughtfully. "Mija—do you know where an ocean curandera's strength derives from?"

I stared at her. "The . . . ocean?"

She smiled. That eased open at least one of the tense knots in my chest.

"When did your powers begin to show?" she asked me.

She'd asked me that earlier, when she was teaching me about how controlling water was a responsibility and an honor the ocean curanderas did not take lightly. And how curanderas' ability to use their elements depended on making a proper connection to the source of their elements' strengths. Why was she asking again?

"During the Bruja Fights," I said. "I think the first time I noticed was when I came home from the second round. I went to wash the scratch on my arm, and the water glowed."

Metztli always reeled when I told her about the Bruja Fights, and how I'd pretended to be one, and still wore my friends' souls. I guess she'd never seen a curandera dabble in brujería.

But she continued calmly, "And why do you think it happened then?"

I looked down at my arm, at the rip in the sleeve left over from the incident. "Is it because I needed healing?"

Her face softened, but it was clear I wasn't getting something.

"She dove in front of Little Lion to save him," Coyote said, for the first time since Metztli had given him back his memories.

We turned to him, where he stood a few feet behind us with Kit and Ocelot. He froze when I met his gaze. His shoulders hiked up, maybe worried that he didn't have the right to talk yet.

"She, uh . . ." His voice lowered. "She got the wound saving Lion that night."

"Ah," Metztli whispered. "That makes more sense. See, Cecelia?"

The wind over the ocean moaned awkwardly. I scratched my ankle with my foot.

"Um—no?" I mumbled.

She tapped her head like she'd suddenly remembered I didn't live in there with her. "Ah. Understand, Cece, that you must embrace the Ocean goddess's strengths, her love, her devotion, her wide and powerful heart, to connect with her waters."

I scrunched my eyebrows. Was I not doing that? I was here *because* I wanted to rescue Juana and help Metztli save both the worlds. Maybe I just needed to love even harder, so the ocean knew I meant it. I did the gesture Metztli had shown me again. This time, I closed my eyes and focused on Juana and Mamá in my head. Mamá's warm expression. Juana's smile when she wished me happy birthday.

"It's working," Metztli whispered.

I peeked an eye open. The water was glowing. My soul stone lit up in response. A deep, healing breath filled my chest as the waves began to move in a circular motion. It *was* working! I did the motions faster. I could do this. I could save Juana. I could show her how sorry I was that it was my fault El Sombrerón took her. Then, when she was healed, Mamá would be happier too. Then maybe they'd both . . . forgive me.

The light went out of the water. The whirlpool settled back into normal waves.

I dropped my arms to my sides. "What happened? It was working!"

Metztli walked to my side. I braced myself for her disappointment. But she didn't show any. She tilted her head, staring from my hands to the water.

"Interesting," she said. Metztli turned abruptly to Kit, Coyote, and Ocelot, and we all jumped. "She wears your souls, so you each can feel *her* soul as well, can you not?" she asked. My cheeks warmed as they nodded. "What did she feel then?" She pointed from me to the water. "As she lost momentum?"

Ocelot glanced at Coyote. He bowed his head. Kit bit his lip. Why were they so quiet? Were they avoiding me now? My insides squirmed. What had I done wrong?

"She will not like it," Ocelot said to Kit and Coyote. "But if you love her, you must say it."

"Say what?" I begged.

Kit winced. "Cece, your shame is so strong, it . . ." His pale cheeks flushed. "It feels like I'm drowning in it."

Shame? I stared, dumbfounded, as Coyote hesitantly nodded in agreement.

"But—" I started, "I was thinking about how much I loved Juana and Mamá."

"I see." Metztli placed a hand on my shoulder. "You love your familia, and this is good. Love empowers. But shame, Cece, is the opposite, and it robs and poisons where love builds." She nodded. "You need to forgive yourself so your heart has room for love as wide and powerful as the sea once again."

My throat tightened so hard I thought I'd choke, and my soul gave a startling flash. I tried not to cry, but tears stung my eyes, and my chin trembled.

"I don't *understand*," I wailed.

Metztli didn't look upset to see the tears. She brushed them away gently, carefully, without a word.

"And—and *you* don't understand!" The world dissolved into smudges of color. The only thing I could hear was my slamming heartbeat and the steady waves behind me. "My family fell apart because *I* didn't fix it right the first time. My mamá kicked out Papá to protect me, and now he won't even *try* to be better, so Mamá's alone and pretends she's fine, and I can't do *anything* about it!" I sobbed. The truth tightened, sharp and painful, around my chest.

"I thought I could at least help fix my sister because it's my fault she got kidnapped, but I can't even do that right, and now she's back in Devil's Alley doing it herself.

I still can't take care of my familia—and—and—what will they do once they realize it's all my fault?" I wrapped my arms around myself. "They'll hate me as much as—" Fear crawled up my chest and froze up my throat. "As much as everyone else does."

The words echoed down the beach, and the ocean's waves swallowed them.

Metztli, after a moment, crouched down in front of me. "I have seen where this fear lives inside you. The moon remembers all the hateful words people slung at you as you grew up. She knows how even your familia, who loved you, fed the wound." She touched my cheek. "You did not plant its seed, but you must prune the weed." She paused, to let the old proverb sink in.

I'd heard a few older people in Tierra del Sol use that saying before, but it had never landed as powerfully as it did just then.

"Your papá's bad choices are not your fault, Cecelia," she said sternly, so her words reverberated inside me. "Your life is harder now, sí, but tu mamá willingly bears the consequences of keeping you safe because she loves you. And your hermana, I am sure, loves you even as she wrestles with her pain."

Heavy tears blurred my vision. She stroked my hair back.

"This is the great burden of the ocean curanderas, to feel so deeply and so much that you could either drown in the ocean's storms or ride the ocean's waves. Right now, you are sinking under the belief that you are not enough—"

"Because it's true," I barely managed to get out between sobs. "I don't deserve to be a curandera."

"That is where you are wrong, chiquita." Her face softened, round as the moon. "There are many born blessed by the gods as you and I, who can be curanderas and curanderos if they wanted. Being a curandera does not change who you are. It is something you choose. And your bravery, your strength, your love, and determination?" She poked my chest, where my soul swung on the outside. "*That* gives you the ability to fulfill the calling of a curandera. And a curandera like you will stretch as far as the sea in all she can do."

Metztli pulled me to her, and I held her tight, trying to let her words sink deep inside. Footsteps trailed toward me. I peeked out of Metztli's comforting embrace to find Coyote, his gold eyes warm and steady and quiet.

"Cece," Coyote said softly, with warmth and meekness. "You don't need to carry someone's pain in order to be worthy of their love. I don't think your papá left because *you* didn't do enough. I—I think he left because he realized *he* couldn't be enough for all of you." Coyote lowered his head. "I'm not saying it's right, or okay, what he did. But you need to know that it's not your fault."

My bottom lip trembled, and Coyote smiled gently to give me courage.

"Don't carry this for him, Cece. I made El Cucuy to wear my feelings for me, and solve my problems for me, and see how well that worked?" He met my gaze, strong and brilliant and fervent. The shame from inside his soul bled away, dissolved by a powerful pink. "Don't turn yourself into anyone else's El Cucuy, Cece. You'll lose them *and* yourself that way."

I sniffed again as I let the question settle—was I making myself Juana's El Cucuy? Mamá's? Even Papá's? I thought I was just trying to demonstrate my love. But maybe— maybe I was just trying to prove that I was worthy of theirs.

A new surge of tears filled my eyes. Coyote stepped forward across the moonlit sand and pressed his forehead to mine. A cool, raw feeling stilled my soul as he breathed with me.

"You're the one who taught me," he whispered. "That you stand by the people you love, even when you can't carry them. I promise I'm going to do that now. I won't run away like your papá. I'm coming with you to Devil's Alley, and I'm going to set things right."

Tears slipped down my cheeks. My heart slowed to beat

in time with the waves. Metztli continued stroking my hair. Kit Fox came over and nestled his face into the crook of my neck. Ocelot placed a hand on Coyote's head and stared gently down at me.

"We can't heal what you're going through," Kit said. "But we'll love you *through* it, Cece."

My heart bubbled over. My soul's light sparked to life in a bright and turquoise glitter. I squeezed Kit close. I rested my forehead back against Coyote's. And I let myself take in Metztli's and Ocelot's warmth.

They were right. They couldn't take away my feelings of failure, just like I couldn't take away Juana's new fears, or fix Mamá's exhaustion, or make Papá into someone he wasn't. And my friends didn't have to, for me to love them. Which meant I didn't have to fix everything for others to *be* loved. I smiled. The ocean swept up around my feet and left cool, calm bubbles along my toes. At last, the watery places in my soul glowed with a steady, reassured light.

"Gracias, mi familia," I whispered. "Muchas gracias."

Metztli's hand suddenly squeezed my shoulder a bit too hard. "Cecelia, hide your soul stone's light."

Her voice had dropped a pitch. Coyote immediately pulled back, scanning the cliff face for something I couldn't hear. Kit tensed. I scrambled to flatten my hands over my soul, but light still streamed through my fingers. Ocelot crouched in front of us protectively as something moved in the shadows of the cliff.

"I warned you once, little curandera."

El Silbón crept out of the darkness. Under the night sky, his skeletal hands looked like barbed wire, and his white, hollow eyes glowed under the brim of his hat. His rib cage rattled as he growled, an electric, scratchy sound. There was no sign of the human inside him; he was absolutely, one hundred percent, dark criatura.

"And this time . . ." He snapped his long fingers, and the sound echoed impossibly far. Something stirred in the shade of the cliff. "I brought reinforcements."

Nine brujas and their criaturas descended on us all

16
Juana Rios and the Silver Doors

Lion and I huddled together, facing the silver doors inside the Court of Fears. We'd been sitting there awhile, giving Bruja Damiana and Axolotl some space on the other side of the room. I figured it was the least I could do after nearly stabbing them.

It was funny—not a laughing funny, but ironic funny. I never would have thought I'd feel bad for attempting to hurt a bruja or criatura. I peeked over my shoulder, beneath my hat, and watched the way Axolotl curled up on Bruja Damiana's lap. Bruja Damiana rocked her gently, the way Mamá used to do me. I guess there was still more to the world than I understood. How had a woman like that ever become a bruja?

The groans spilling out of the silver doors dragged my attention back their way. It really did sound like the earth itself was mourning in there.

"You okay?" Lion asked quietly beside me.

"For now," I said. "Still don't know how we're getting out of here, though."

Lion curled his lip back at the monstrous noises from beyond the doors. "Yeah. I've never even heard of the legend of the silver doors—or I don't remember it, anyway. I wonder why El Cucuy can't control them. He can transform just about anything in Devil's Alley, since he was Named to rule over it."

Tzitzimitl tilted her head. "You seem to forget, Black Lion, from whose body Devil's Alley was made."

Lion squinted. "You mean Mother Desert? What does that have to do with anything?"

I shook my head to myself, watching the flickering lights at the bottom of the doors. "I can't wait here and do nothing." I gripped my arms. "I can't keep losing myself."

He pulled his knees to his chest. "What are you thinking?"

I stared at the doors. There were more questions than answers about them. They looked heavy and uncertain. Dangerous and frightening. But there was no changing it.

So be it.

"I can't do this on my own," I whispered. I thought it would hurt more to admit, but there was a strange, warm relief in saying it out loud. At least to Lion. I wasn't sure if I was okay with anyone else hearing it yet. "And there's only one way I can think of where I might possibly make it out the other side of those doors." I turned to him. "Will you come with me?"

Lion straightened, and a strange flush spread across his cheeks. I could've laughed at the reaction. But I didn't remember how.

I gestured to the door. "I can't do it alone. So will you help me see reality when I can't? While I'm still—broken?"

Lion met my gaze without hesitation. "I will," he said quietly, so only I could hear.

I hadn't been able to smile for a while. But for the first time since Cece's birthday, I tried. This gato wasn't so bad.

Lion stood and offered me his hand. And for the first time, I took his offering. He pulled me up, and we stood together, facing the doors.

"Okay." I rolled my shoulders. "Let's do this."

"You've seen how meaningless it is to fight this place, haven't you, Juana Rios?"

Lion and I checked over our shoulders. Across the room, holding Axolotl to her chest, Bruja Damiana was smiling at nothing. It was a pained expression, despite the upturned mouth. The kind Mamá used to wear when I was younger, and I came to check on her after she and Papá had fought.

"But you'll still go," the bruja croaked. "Knowing you'll likely die?"

Axolotl's nonexistent eyebrows pulled together, like she heard the strange and lonesome tone in the bruja's voice too. A crackling sound rose from the ground. Crystals were forming between her and the floor, and they moved faster than I'd expected.

Axolotl gasped as the crystals started sticking to her too, crawling onto her from the bruja's body. Bruja Damiana stared out at nothing as Axolotl grabbed the bruja's shirt and shook her.

"¡Mamá!" She gripped the snakes on the woman's embroidered lapels. "Por favor, don't leave me."

The warmth in my chest grew and stretched into a flame that burst into words.

"Hey!" I boomed. "*Wake up!*"

The cenote's water rippled above our heads at the sound. Damiana jumped, and a few crystals broke off. She whipped her head in my direction, bewildered and confused. Axolotl let out a quavering sigh of relief. I took just a few steps closer. Damiana's blinking gaze found me.

"That girl needs you," I said, pointing to Axolotl. "You can't let those crystals get you either, got it?"

Lion squinted at Tzitzimitl. "Hey, why don't the crystal prisons affect you all?" He scanned the Court of Fears and their fire opal cells. "I saw lots of other criaturas trapped on our way in."

"We are already the most frightening things we know," Alux said simply.

"What about El Cucuy?" I asked.

The Bird King cleaned his talons with a chuckle. "We were there at his beginning. Why would we fear what we understand?"

I avoided a smile. The Court of Fears was kind of cool. Damiana wiped her face and laughed too, but it was a thin and scraping thing.

I dropped my arms to my sides. "Bruja Damiana—you can't stay here. You'll get trapped again. You know that." I sighed. She turned away, shoulders heavy. "We're leaving. You should try too."

Axolotl peered up at her, brow puckering. "Can't we go with them?" she asked. "Maybe the doors would let us through."

"Even if we did—there is nowhere left in the worlds for us to go," the bruja whispered. "I have allowed intruders into the castle. And the surface would not have you or me."

"Why?" I asked. "Why don't you think there's an option to go back?"

"I became a bruja as a teenager because I was young and foolish," she said. She covered her face as she sucked in a hard breath. "My familia was hated. My mother, the daughter of a criatura and a human man." Her eyes slid down again. I stiffened. I didn't even know that could happen. Axolotl, hesitantly, wrapped her arms tighter around her. The corner of the bruja's mouth tweaked. "These children come out human, no extra powers. But they are marked somewhere on their body with the image of their criatura parent's soul stone. My mother's was on her face. There was no hiding it." She sighed. "We moved year after year to escape persecution, but we never found a place we could call home. Eventually, my abuelo died. Then my parents. And I was alone." She bowed her head.

My blood boiled inside me, hot like the flames that kept us warm in winter, as the bruja bowed herself over. *Look up*, I thought, as I watched Bruja Damiana. *Raise your head.*

"Grimmer Mother found me after I buried my familia." She didn't meet my eyes, and my chest swelled with the story, and the warmth, and the ferocious hope that she'd *look up* "I was desperate and foolish, so I believed her when she said Devil's Alley could be my home. I did everything she said, but—after years of living here, I couldn't bear it anymore. Not the cruelty, or the castle." Her hand shivered on Axolotl's hair.

So that's how she'd gotten here. She didn't have the killer instinct or love of pain and power that other brujas had. She had just been fed a lie. And desperate and alone, she'd believed it. She didn't belong here. She shouldn't have to bow her head to El Cucuy and accept this dungeon as her only home.

"When I found Axolotl, I took her as my criatura and volunteered to be keeper of the dungeon, to keep her far from the fights." Bruja Damiana shrugged. "There may have been a way for me once. But I've been here so long that you can see from my eyes and fangs I'm a bruja. There's no place in my old human world for me and Axolotl now."

Behind me, the doors moaned and creaked. Blue and yellow and orange lights flickered over the stone floor.

"Listen—I get it," I whispered. I'd never imagined I'd say that to a bruja. But here I was. "It's gutting, trying to push through the weight of the past. And it's scary when you don't know what kind of future you can have. But if you really care about Axolotl, you've got to care about you too." I pointed at her. "Don't give up here, Damiana." The bubble of warmth expanded in my aching chest. "Lift your head and *try*."

Her gaze rose up to meet mine, brilliant and magenta. Her chin trembled, just a little. I suspected no one had said that to her in a long, long time.

"Try," I said again. "You're worth fighting for."

I drew back, nodded to Lion, and together we faced the doors.

"If you do manage to escape—" Bruja Damiana called out to us, and we paused. "Brujo Antonio will be waiting on the first floor. Threaten him, and he'll take you to the crystal lift. It will carry you directly up to El Sombrerón's suite. His room is protected by an impossible puzzle." Her shoulders moved like she'd laugh, even though she didn't. "But I suspect you don't care about 'impossible' anyway."

The small, cozy bubble in my chest swelled. The stretching almost hurt; I still wasn't that used to the warmth. But I held on to it, embraced it, anyway. Because this—this was so much more than I'd hoped for. If we could get through these doors, a direct line to El Sombrerón's suite would save us the time we'd lost. We needed that now that we were only twelve hours from the entrance to Devil's Alley closing.

"Gracias, Bruja Damiana," I said, and I meant every syllable.

I took Lion's hand—his shoulder hitched up in surprise—and we headed to the door. Damiana stayed seated in the center of the Court of Fears, holding Axolotl.

"You ready?" Lion asked as we faced the silver exit.

"No," I said. I could admit it at least. "But let's go."

We pushed open the doors.

The groans disappeared the moment the entrance parted. Freezing-cold air poured from the crack and nearly numbed my fingers. Lion helped me push the heavy metal back all the way, and we stood there, silent, before a veil of nothing.

There was no light, no noise. But the darkness moved and breathed. I reached forward and touched it. My fingers slipped into the shadow, but I couldn't feel it. It was almost like the absence of existence.

My stomach clenched. This was almost worse than the churning, noisy corridor like I'd imagined. This was the absolute unknown.

"There is only one antidote to fear," Tzitzimitl's voice followed us. "Do you know it, Juana Rios?"

I had a feeling I did. I turned to glance back at each member of the Court of Fears. They nodded us forward from their fire opal prisons. Damiana watched us from the ground, squeezing Axolotl. Tzitzimitl tilted her head, listening.

I took a big, fat breath and faced the door again.

"We just have to step forward," I said. I closed my eyes and thought of the castle, of the first floor I barely remembered, of the way back to my soul. Of the heartbeat I missed.

"Let's go," I said.

17

Cece Rios and the Hunted Souls

A mob of eighteen shadows split around El Silbón, and there were so many shapes moving, I couldn't tell who any of the enemies were. Ocelot leaped into the air, ready to plow them through. But five animal criaturas piled her to the ground. She twisted to look back at us as they pinned her shoulders, her head, and her feet against the sand.

"Take them far away, Legend Brother!" she yelled to Coyote. My stomach turned to stone. If Ocelot, the most practiced fighter of all of us, was saying that, we really were outmatched.

But we wouldn't go down without fighting. Coyote and Kit Fox ignored her instruction. Even with Kit's soul full of frightened splotches of screaming white, he rushed forward, reaching for her.

"We won't leave you!" Kit cried.

The wave of brujas and criaturas careened straight for us. Despite being slower than my other friends, Kit evaded capture by slipping through every gap and crack between the brujas and criaturas. My heart leaped as he skated through the sand and slid toward Ocelot.

Coyote slammed a few brujas and criaturas out of his way before leaping over the rest of their heads, taking them by surprise. "Get back, Cece!" He aimed his claws for El Silbón's throat.

El Silbón crouched and swung for Coyote. Coyote barely dodged under the blow and came up in front of him. El Silbón's screeching whistle made everyone cringe.

"Stop it!" I screamed, and ran forward.

Metztli put her arm out to block me. "They're here for you," she said. "Protect their souls and your own."

El Silbón dove on Coyote, aiming a death blow. But Coyote grabbed both his wrists and fought to shove him back. El Silbón wasn't easily thrown off. They grappled, both locked in a battle of strength.

"I bet you regret it now," El Silbón said, voice grainy and sharp. "What you've made me, Great Renamer." He locked his sharp fingers over Coyote's arms and drew pricks of blood.

"You're right." Coyote grunted as he pushed against El Silbón. "I'm sorry I did this to you, El Silbón." Coyote's voice broke, and his soul flickered with a warm, raw orange. Confidence. Something I hadn't felt from him in a long time. "I promise you, I'll figure out how to Name again. And then, I'll give you back yours."

The dark criatura's arms wavered. A low, warbling whistle strained out his throat. Some part of him still wanted that. Some part of him, buried beneath the orders of El Cucuy. But I watched that part lose the battle, and he reared up over Coyote, leveraging his height to crush my friend into the ground.

Coyote's feet sank into the sand, but he didn't give way. He roared as he twisted, fighting to pull the giant off-balance. But El Silbón thrust his leg forward and kicked Coyote so hard in the chest that I heard him gag. My soul rocked with the pain. I gasped and stumbled. With Coyote winded, El Silbón had time to deliver another blow, straight to the face. It was so hard, Coyote flew back into the waiting arms of four animal criaturas. I screamed. They forced him to the ground before he'd even regained his breath.

My friends were absolutely mobbed. Ocelot was biting at anyone who got near enough, twisting her body, trying to slip out and protect Kit. Kit kicked and fought, but he was outmatched. I turned to the ocean, my soul crying out to it. My hands shook, but I moved them in the pattern Metztli taught me. *Por favor*, I reached out to the water. *I have to help them.*

It was low tide, but the waves began to push into the beach. Clouds darkened over the ocean and crawled closer to shore. The edge of the water stretched toward Ocelot and Kit, and the brujas and criaturas fighting to keep them pinned. My heart rushed with the feeling of a storm. The froth of the ocean began to tingle and glow. *¡Sí!* My soul lit up, and light began to catch in my nails. *Help us, por favor!* The waves suddenly roared sideways, with new energy, directly toward my friends. *Free us!*

Out of nowhere, El Silbón swept me up from the sand. Metztli tried to catch me, calling out my name. But he just grabbed her in his free hand. I yelped as he lifted us into the air, and the waves sloshed and lost their momentum.

"No!" I cried.

The water slumped back into its normal tide. I tried to catch my feelings, to reach back out—but El Silbón swung us to face his burning white eyeholes and cackled until the hairs on my arms stood straight up.

"Stop it!" I slammed my fist down on El Silbón's hand. The crackle of a storm formed on the edge of the sea.

"El Silbón!" Metztli thundered. The white in her hair glowed in the moonlight. "Release us and these criaturas now or you will face the wrath of the curanderas!"

"You . . ." El Silbón's voice fizzled through the air. "I remember you."

"As I remember you, Father Killer," she cried. Her nails started to glow. She reached for his head, a single fingertip extended, as she had with Coyote. "You, who sided with El Cucuy and disobeyed your purpose. Did you forget what was given to your leftover heart, El Silbón? You were the Father Killer, Protector of Women and Children, Alleviator of Suffering."

He evaded her glowing touch and squeezed her until she cried out. Her breaths grew quick and shallow.

"Alejo, por favor, stop!" I belted. Heavy clouds swelled above us now, and darkened the beach.

El Silbón reared back and lifted Metztli high to the sky. Even trapped, her face was bright, sharp, clear. She wasn't afraid. But my stomach clenched with terror as El Silbón slammed her to the ground so hard her body bounced— and then went limp, completely knocked out.

"Metztli!" I wriggled in El Silbón's grip. "How could you? She—she—"

"She is a curandera," he said. His hollow stare turned on me. "That alone is against El Cucuy's law." He lifted me so we were face-to-face and clamped my arms hard at my sides. "It is the same for you," he said. "And for your criaturas too."

My gut clenched. No.

Below us, Ocelot had found her feet, but she fought

against nearly ten people every way she turned. Kit was being crushed into the ground. Coyote had thrown three brujas into their own criaturas, and he turned to face me just as El Silbón wrapped his hand around my friends' souls.

"Stop!" Coyote sprang, claws ready, for El Silbón.

I tried to free my hands. I pulled so hard I thought my fingers would snap off in his grip. But El Silbón had me caged, and before either Coyote or I could stop him—he tore my friends' souls free from my neck in one sharp, foul swipe.

If I'd thought it hurt the last time, this was *agony*.

It felt like he'd torn out my heart. Every pump, every laugh, every smile—cut straight out of my chest. My friends and I screamed until we drowned out the sound of the ocean's surf. Coyote convulsed in midair and landed, sprawling, in the sand. Tears poured down my cheeks as I slumped in El Silbón's hands. Below me, Ocelot was on her knees, gasping and shaking. Kit's head lolled on the ground, clearly unconscious. All the rich sounds and colors of who they were, snatched away.

I trembled as my soul flickered violently in the night. But the shuddering emptiness was nothing compared to the pain of watching El Silbón drop their souls one by one into the sand.

The ground swallowed them whole before I could even lift a shaking finger.

"N-no," I said, with patchy, broken breath.

El Silbón's hunting party stepped back from my friends as the sand began to cave in around them, slowly swallowing them down into its gullet. Coyote had told me about this. When you let the ground swallow a living criatura's soul, both the soul and criatura would be transported to Devil's Alley, to the dungeon of El Cucuy's castle. It was El Sombrerón's preferred way to capture criaturas during Semana de la Cosecha.

"Stop!" I screeched, as loud as I could, as the sand sank around them. It hurt to speak. But I'd promised Kit. I'd promised all of them. I wouldn't let them be taken back. "Please, take me instead! Leave my friends alone!"

But the desert was already consuming them back into itself. The brujas all watched, some bored, some delighted, as Ocelot dove through the sand and desperately grabbed Kit. He was still unconscious. She secured him to her and gave me one last look before the ground engulfed the both of them whole. My heart shattered.

"Cece!" Coyote cried. He was scrambling through the sand, the grains already at his neck, when I spotted him. His nose was bleeding, but his eyes flashed as they met mine. "I'll find you, okay? I'll find you!" He extended a hand up to me. "We can still defeat El Cucuy!"

I watched my best friend sink away into the ground, and I burst into tears. My soul's light went out. Everything was terribly silent.

Their absence roared up inside me. My body was still weak, but I pulled myself up to glare at El Silbón. "How could you?" I hissed and gripped his hand. "Fight, El Silbón! You're not just a dark criatura. You don't have to be like this!" I reached out to him desperately.

He threw me into the air. I screamed, somersaulting out of control, before he grabbed me in midair, so I dangled upside down in his vise grip. The blood rushed to my head.

"I am not some animal criatura you can appeal to, Cecelia Rios. I am not one of the elements, who may heed the voice of a curandera." He leaned in so the brim of his hat cast shadows over both of us. "*You keep forgetting what I am. And it will cost you.*"

He reached for my soul. I gasped. He going to try and steal it too?

His fingers clasped down on my turquoise stone. I felt it, like a cold fist in my chest. But this was my soul. I struck out and gripped his hand around my stone. This was my power, and it would not obey him.

For a moment, El Silbón's eyes actually widened as my soul flashed to life.

"You are more than a dark criatura," I declared, squeezing his fingers. "I won't forget, even if you have!"

El Silbón shook beneath my hands. I searched for the human in him again, pushing my soul's light toward him, reaching for any remnant left. Something inside me flickered. I hadn't felt it in a while, buried in guilt and fear as I'd been. But it was cool, and calm, and gentle—and strong. I closed my eyes and listened for the human voice trapped deep inside the dark criatura. The light in my soul pulsed with it, flashing in my nails for a moment, before a ripple of turquoise light rode over El Silbón's skin, up his arm, and seeped into the small, perfectly circular, brown stone swinging around his neck. His soul.

My chest throbbed. But it didn't hurt. Instead, it formed into a sound, a voice, that begged to be heard.

I don't want this, El Silbón's soul whispered to mine. *I want to stop. Someone give me the power to stop.*

My eyes burst open. I wasn't his bruja, and I wasn't touching his soul stone like I had Metztli's, but I'd just heard his soul *speak*. I looked up to find El Silbón's eyes wide and frightened. His hand trembled around me. He'd felt it too.

The brujas around him shifted, some awkward and some angry. "What's taking so long, El Silbón?" one snapped.

The one now carrying Metztli huffed. "Let's get going. I've got cargo, you know."

Suddenly, El Silbón's glare returned, even more ferocious than before. A flood of anger shoved my soul's light back, and he tossed me over his shoulder. I screamed as I fell with a painful clatter into his bag of bones. The top of the bag tightened over my head, and I winced as a rib poked into my side.

"Try as you may, there is no freedom from El Cucuy's laws, curandera!" El Silbón's scratchy voice bled in through the small hole at the top. "You will undo the seal of your forebears"—he started walking, and I yelped as I swung side to side—"or you will die."

"No!" I fought against the bag. "El Silbón, I heard you, I heard you!" But I didn't know how to give him the power he needed to break free. I panted and wrapped my arms around myself to protect my skin from the sharper bones.

"Why didn't you use her soul against her?" One of the brujas snapped. "El Sombrerón would never have been this weak—"

"Only a great fool challenges one who speaks the language of souls. She defeated El Sombrerón with it, remember." He hiked up the bag, and I tipped sideways, crying out. "We will leave her to El Cucuy."

18

Juana Rios and the Amenazante Dance

The world was black-and-white mist. I squeezed Lion's hand as we plowed on. Darkness twisted around my skin, my legs, my arms, my hair. In one breath that felt like a thousand, Lion and I stepped free of the nothingness onto the first floor of El Cucuy's castle.

We stood there, trembling and silent, just for a second. Behind us, the silver doors closed and, before we knew it, vanished into the stone. They left us there, in one of the castle's first-floor rooms. I took a deep, relieved breath as I let the experience bleed out of me. We'd made it. It really worked.

The ceilings of the castle were high and vaulted, with a pattern of black moths carved into the wide expanse. Wait, no. I scowled in disgust. They were *real* moths, crawling on each other's backs, scurrying and clinging to the ceiling's high structure. It made the room rustle with anticipation. Below them, the light from the blue torches glistened off walls made of gray-green pillars of crystal, stacked diagonally on each other to create an opaque barrier.

The room itself was wide, with two different doors set into the walls. One door was all the way across the room, unlabeled and made of metal. It probably led to the rest of the castle. The other door, about ten feet away, had a simple wooden face carved with the word *calabozo*. The entrance to the dungeon, then. And—Lion and I froze—two bodies leaned against it, their backs to us. One of them, about my height but way older and holding a clipboard, grumbled to himself as the Criatura of the Bat crouched silently beside him.

"Damiana's late again," Brujo Antonio snorted to himself. "She's the worst . . ."

Lion and I glanced sideways at each other. And smirked.

We crept up silently behind him as he continued to complain. I eyed his throat, and the soul necklace dangling on it. Lion prepared to pounce. Bat turned and yelped seconds before Lion crushed the brujo's arms to his side.

The brujo spluttered and kicked his legs, but there was no escape from Lion's grip. Bat, his hands jerking with a delayed command, moved to attack Lion. But I was already in position. With an easy flick of my knife, the criatura's soul fell free from the brujo's neck. Brujo Antonio gaped at us as his criatura's eyes lit up.

Criatura of the Bat snatched his soul from the ground and held it to his chest. He eyed both of us, darting from Lion—who was still crushing the brujo—to me and my fire opal knife.

"Take your soul and get out of here." I waved him away. "Just don't tell anyone we're here. Got it?"

The criatura's chin trembled, but he beamed. "¡Gracias!" he kept his voice low as he tied his soul around his neck and scampered away, fleeing out the metal door and probably the castle.

I almost smiled. Good for him.

Then I rounded on the brujo, knife up and burning.

"What are you—" The brujo started but froze as I placed the blade against his throat. He gulped. "Wait. You . . . you're the Bride of El Sombrerón."

"And you're taking us to his suite," I said. "Now."

I headed for the far, metal door. Little Lion dragged the brujo after me.

"There's not a direct way there!" The brujo insisted, as Lion pushed him forward. "You'll have to fight up all the ranks, and the floors are filled with brujas and—"

"We know about the crystal lift," I snapped. He shut up. "You're going to take us to it, and you're going to use it to bring us to El Sombrerón's suite."

"You think you can get in there?" He twisted in Lion's

hold. Lion grabbed at his shirt tighter to control the pathetic squirms. "Only El Cucuy knows how to unlock it!"

Little Lion shoved him forward, so he stumbled into place beside me. The brujo reared back, like he was going to strike. I flicked out my knife and leveled it at his nose. He froze.

"El Sombrerón made a lot of mistakes he's going to pay for. But solving his door's puzzle in front of me because he thought I would never leave that place—that was his worst," I said, voice boiling. Little Lion came up behind us, and the brujo's gaze slid toward him. "Now move it."

Little Lion reached for the door. I glanced his way— only to watch the brujo grab at his neck.

Lion let out a guttural cry.

I leaped back, knife out. The brujo clutched something in Little Lion's shirt. My blood ran steaming hot. I sprinted forward. The brujo yanked Lion's soul necklace over the boy's head and ran with it in his grip.

"And this," the brujo said, evading me with a rancid grin, "is *your* last mistake!"

I roared as I dashed past Lion, knife aimed at the brujo. But something sharp sliced my cheek. I yelped and fell backward, scrambling as I hit the ground. Little Lion stood over me, his claws dripping with my blood. I clutched my face. His usually bright, red eyes were clouded, his entire frame trembling, like he was fighting his own muscles and sinews. Deep, tight pain gritted in his bared teeth.

"Finish her!" The brujo spat, sweat dripping down his chin with effort. "Come on! You're a black lion!"

Little Lion's muscles twitched and jumped, like he was resisting an invisible shove. A fierce fire rushed through my chest. Lion was fighting himself for me. The terrified look in his filmy eyes said it all: he knew he'd lose the battle against the brujo's control. But he was fighting for me anyway.

So I'd better fight for him.

I swirled my dress around, grabbed the knife I'd dropped, and sprinted for the brujo. Little Lion's speed, even slowed by his resistance, was horrifying. He lunged for my head like a bolt of lightning, and I dropped to the ground to barely evade the lethal blow. Lion flipped over me and rolled on the floor, scratching the agate tile as he swung to face me.

I held my knife flat over my face, like a shield. He charged for me so fast, he was a blur. So I closed my eyes. Listened for his movement. The whistle of the wind he made stirred my hair, and I slipped into the Amenazante dance.

I didn't use it the way I had before, as a threatening martial art. This time, I danced the way my instructor had taught me our ancestors used to. "When you per-form the Amenazante dance you must remember its roots. It was once an expression of joy, made of fire itself." I pirouetted left and right, leaping, crouching, and twirl-ing to just barely miss Lion's claws and deadly fangs. "The Amenazante dance is a threat. But it is also a promise of how life can be." Lion's teeth nearly snapped down on me, but I swept into the eighth step, and all he caught was my dress. I watched Lion as the ancient art of my peo-ple strengthened what was left of my soul. Because I was fighting *for* him in every step of the dance I'd once used to frighten criaturas just like him.

With each movement, I came closer to the brujo, dis-tracting him with the performance of our deadly combat.

Then, the moment of truth.

I stopped on the tenth beat, facing the brujo. We were at least six feet apart. But close enough. The brujo smirked. Lion pounced, like I knew he would, for my throat.

For just a second, he was in the air, all claws and teeth. In that second, I had an opening. I gripped my throwing knife between my fingers. I reared back. And watched the brujo's satisfaction fall away as I released it toward him.

He didn't have time to react. My fire opal blade flew across the space and embedded in his arm. Little Lion crashed down on me. My head hit the tile as the brujo screamed.

Lion's teeth flashed, and I crunched my chin down to protect my neck. The fire inside me threatened to turn to smoke and ash again. But Little Lion stopped. Something clattered, and I twisted to see his soul skating across the ground where the wounded brujo had dropped it.

I shoved Lion off me. He was still reeling, but I had to get to his soul before the brujo could. I threw myself across the floor, skating toward it. Clutching his bleeding arm, Brujo Antonio stumbled toward the quartz soul.

I clamped my hand down over it seconds before he could.

Heat flared up my arm, in my veins, mingling with the fire in my chest. Lion's soul. Cece had said it felt something like this. The brujo let out a frustrated yell and dove for me. I whirled around, spinning to my feet, and slipped my other throwing dagger free of my belt. The brujo froze mid grab as I placed the blade to his Adam's apple.

"Step. Back," I hissed. "You're *never* touching his soul again. It doesn't belong to you."

Slowly, the brujo lifted his hands in surrender. He scampered back a few steps as I pressed the blade to his skin. Off to the side, Little Lion climbed to his feet. His legs shook. His whole body, actually. He lifted his exhausted head to me. I kept my blade extended, ready, glaring at the brujo. But I backed myself up to Lion, my fingers locked around his soul.

"Lion," I said, and stopped beside him.

His breathing was ragged. Whatever the brujo had done to him, it clearly hurt. Or—did it always hurt criaturas to be controlled? I'd never asked, never wondered. But his pain was palpable.

"Lo siento," Lion said. His hand shook as he wiped my blood off his claws. "You're bleeding."

Without taking my eyes off the brujo, I extended my hand to Lion. He looked down at his soul in my palm.

"Here," I said. "This is yours. Yours, and no one else's."

Lion's throat jogged. But he hesitated.

"You should probably keep it," he said. His soft expression disappeared as he glared at Antonio again, lip pulled back in a snarl. The brujo flinched. "I should have given it to you earlier. He could use me again to hurt you."

"No. This belongs to you," I said, and pushed my hand toward him again. "It's worth the risk."

Lion took a hard breath before plucking his soul from my hand. He swung the necklace back around his throat, tucking it into his shirt, and laid his hand over it.

"Gracias," he murmured.

I wiped the blood from my cheek, and Lion and I sauntered toward the brujo. With Lion's claws out, and my dagger ready, Brujo Antonio shrunk into himself at our approach. I kicked him into the wall beside the door. He yelped.

Lion brought his claws to his neck. "You saw what I can do," he said. "Now take us to the lift. Or you'll be on the wrong end of it this time."

The brujo was suddenly a lot more compliant.

I held my dagger to Brujo Antonio's spine as we went, and Little Lion prowled ahead of us, eyeing the great hall we stepped into. Far to the right was a pair of huge, wooden doors decorated with iron rivets. The front doors of the castle. The brujo kept his head bowed as I pushed him to the left instead. Above us, the black moths continued their uneasy fluttering. We walked for a while before the brujo lifted a finger.

"There." He pointed to a stripe of lavender crystals embedded into the wall.

I shoved him forward. "Open it," I said.

The brujo placed his hand to the purple crystals. They glowed. He winced as a line on his forehead lit up and sizzled—his Mark of the Binding. He hissed lightly and rubbed it as the crystal wall separated.

"There," he spat. A small rectangular space opened in the wall. "It leads directly to the higher floors. You can get to El Sombrerón's room if you instruct it—"

Little Lion grabbed the back of his shirt and dragged him inside with us. "Great. Drop us off there."

The brujo sputtered as we filed in, and the door shut

in a flurry of reassembling crystals. I flattened the brujo's hand to the purple crystals lining the inside.

"El Sombrerón's room," I said. "Say it."

He pressed his lips together. "El Cucuy will destroy me," he said.

"I'll destroy you right now if you don't," I said. It was a bluff, but he didn't know that. "At least I'll give you time to run before El Cucuy finds out." I kept my pressure on his hand steady. Not painful. Just unyielding.

He paused.

"El Sombrerón's vault," he finally said.

The crystals rippled with dull light again, and the room shot upward.

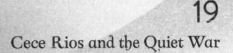

I couldn't see anything inside El Silbón's bag, but I knew we'd arrived in Devil's Alley when an awful smell hit my nose. Juana had said Devil's Alley smelled like spoiled eggs, bad meat, and Papá's socks. I gagged on it, but El Silbón ignored me. In muffled voices, the brujas discussed what El Cucuy would do when he was freed. Bring the surface under his rule. Finally destroy all disobedient criaturas. Snuff out the curanderas forever.

It all turned my stomach, and I clutched myself amid the bones.

"We're here," El Silbón said. The sound of large doors creaked. "Line up, hunting party. El Cucuy's castle will not abide disorderly conduct."

We were already here? But I needed to escape! I had to find Juana and my friends! I needed more time—what could I do?

Metztli's words flooded back into my brain. I'd only

known El Silbón as the Father Killer, but she'd called him the Protector of Women and Children, too. Obviously, that wasn't more important than obeying El Cucuy, but maybe if he didn't think protecting me was in the *way* of obeying his orders . . .

I started coughing and gasping as loud as I could. El Silbón paused, but after a second, kept moving. I could hear the sound of tile under his feet. Next, I gasped so hard it made me choke on my spit for real. El Silbón made a gruff but slightly worried sound. I started pulling at the top of the bag desperately.

"I—can't—breathe—" I squeaked out. I probably wasn't the best actress, but it wasn't hard to pretend. The air tasted so bad here, I really did feel light-headed. I pulled harder on the bag. "Can't . . . breathe . . ."

I gave one last hard pull on the fabric, then stopped and slumped over.

One of the brujas laughed. "You made her sound so powerful, but this will be your easiest kill yet."

El Silbón stopped. "No, she *must* live to face El Cucuy."

With a swing that almost made me yelp, El Silbón pulled his bag around and tugged at the knot. I went slack, letting my eyes glaze over. Hazy light finally shone in above me as El Silbón reached down and pulled me out.

He arranged my arms in his large palm as if I were a

doll. There was a long, tight silence as he and the brujas stared at me.

"Mother Desert forgive me . . . " El Silbón whispered.

I almost felt bad at how heavy his voice sounded. But I couldn't stop pretending or I'd ruin it. Slowly, El Silbón knelt down and rested me gently on the ground. I waited, as my burning eyes started to tear up in the corners. My lungs ached as I held my breath. Come on. Just a few more seconds.

"Will El Cucuy be mad?" a bruja asked.

"Of course he will!" Another snapped. "He'll probably turn us into rocks. What if we just kidnap another human and say it was her?"

Finally, El Silbón turned to face the brujas. "She was the only one who could break his seal, you fools—"

I leaped up and took off down the hallway.

I had no idea where I was going. I rushed down a wide hallway made of diagonally stacked columns of white and gray crystals, across the wide tile floors, taking in the huge, tall ceilings. There were no proper lights, just dim blue torches. I ran and ran, my heart nearly bursting—

—when a woman appeared in my way.

I gasped and stumbled back before I could hit her. She was only a bit taller than me, but with a thin build that made her seem taller. She smiled at me as I froze. She had large round eyes. Instead of glowing some impossible color like most brujas', they were a normal, though dark, brown, framed with thick black eyelashes that swept downward. She wore a long, white dress embroidered with flowers on the hem. It was the kind of thing someone in Tierra del Sol would wear, not a bruja. And her hair was long, sweeping, black, falling in silky waves.

She didn't look anything like the brujas I'd seen. She wasn't even wearing a soul stone. She could've been someone who'd accidentally wandered in here—except that she smiled calmly, the way no normal human could in the castle of El Cucuy.

El Silbón charged up behind me. I squealed and struggled as he scooped me back up and knelt on one knee before the woman.

"Lo siento, Third Dark Saint." He bowed his head so his hat brim came down, and I couldn't see her anymore.

Oh. She was the new third Dark Saint? Would she be as terrifying as Rodrigo had been?

"I lost hold of the curandera," El Silbón continued. "I will place her in the dungeon to await her audience with El Cucuy."

"No, El Silbón," the woman said. She had a gentle voice—sweet, even. "Bruja Damiana has vanished, and there are intruders in the castle." The woman extended her hand. "Leave the curandera in my suite." Her burgundy lips swept up. "I will make sure she meets El Cucuy."

El Silbón hesitated. His fingers tightened around me, and he drew me closer to his chest. I glanced up at him.

"¿Hay algún problema?" The third Dark Saint's expression was suddenly a lot less gentle.

"No. I will do as you wish," El Silbón finally relented, "Catrina, Cager of Souls."

My mind buzzed in the silence as El Silbón took me up a crystal lift to Catrina's floor. If there were intruders in the castle, Juana had to be one of them. How would I find her? My breathing felt shallow and raw. Partially because El Silbón still clasped me in his massive hand, but mostly because I'd just met my tía, Catrina. And I didn't know what she wanted with me.

Tía Catrina was the only reason I'd made it through the Bruja Fights a couple of months ago. Rodrigo the Soul Stealer had said they would have killed me if she hadn't vied to keep me in the tournament. But I never figured out why. Why did the tía who'd never known me, who'd killed my best friend in his last life, who'd tortured Little Lion in his—

Why had she wanted to help *me*?

The flashing purple crystals slowed. I tensed. In front of

us, the doors rolled open to reveal a short foyer and a door covered in moth carvings. They looked like the same ones Grimmer Mother had tattooed on her hands. El Silbón stepped out from the shaft, and the eyes on their wings shifted to stare at us. I held my breath.

"You would have been better off in the dungeon, Cecelia Rios," El Silbón whispered.

He lowered me to the floor and released me slowly, finger by finger. I looked up, searching for the human in him again. Tía Catrina had saved my life once, and El Silbón had been hunting me down for days. But—I felt safer with him.

I grabbed his thumb before he could pull away. "El Silbón," I said. "Please don't leave me."

His hand trembled in my hold.

Suddenly, the door to Catrina's room opened behind me. I turned. Tía Catrina stood there, smiling down at me. A chill flooded my guts.

"I've been waiting, Cece." She grabbed my wool shirt and yanked me inside. I gasped and stumbled past the door, barely catching myself before I fell. She lifted her chin toward El Silbón. "You can go now. I have no need of you."

El Silbón's wide white eyes met mine as she slammed the door shut.

The sound echoed through the large room. Tía Catrina faced me with a calm smile that didn't match the ferocity that she'd just handled me with. I sucked in a cold breath.

She chuckled. "Your shirt's all rumpled. A little clumsy, aren't you?"

My cheeks flushed. *She* was the one who'd rumpled it.

Tía Catrina's room was surprisingly empty. There was a single bed with luscious, velvet blankets and a carved wood frame, a large rug striped with brilliant colors, and huge bookcases set alongside the far wall with a single velvet chair in front of them. That was it.

I squeezed my hands into fists. "Um . . . why am I here?"

She crossed to the bookshelves. "First and foremost, you're here because you killed El Cucuy's second and third Dark Saints, thereby revealing your curandera powers. He now wants you to release him from his seal so he can rule your world as well. Unless"—Tía Catrina pulled a book from her shelf and started flipping through it—"you can end him first. That's why I'm keeping you safe. For now."

I went quiet. Stopping El Cucuy had already been my plan. But Tía Catrina was his third Dark Saint. Why would she want him dead? She gestured me closer. Hesitantly, I drifted near, eyeing her warily.

"Are you waiting for a formal introduction?" There was

a slight note of laughter to her question. "Or perhaps Axochitl never told you she had a sister. Were you confused when you read the note I sent you during the Bruja Fights?"

"I know who you are," I said.

Tía Catrina finally glanced at me over her shoulder. Her smile was pristine and cultivated, like a mosaic someone had set in mortar.

"When criaturas seeking vengeance came back to destroy you, they killed my abuela instead. You took Coyote's life and threw his soul in a well. You were Little Lion's old bruja. I know you, Tía Catrina."

She didn't look worried about the crimes I'd listed. She just pulled another book off the shelf and examined it.

"Yes, I was surprised when you picked up my old friend. I hadn't planned on that." She chuckled as she reshelved some of the other tomes. The book bindings were flaking off, but she let pieces of the covers fall like they were nothing but dead leaves. "I couldn't believe my luck when I first found the Criatura of the Black Lion, such a powerful being, as my first criatura soul." She smiled fondly as she recalled the experience.

My stomach squirmed. Little Lion's memories of the same time had been gut-wrenching.

"He was so good to me back then. Followed me around like a kitten. It would have been pathetic if it hadn't been so cute." She smiled at me. "Is he still in love with me?"

"You *tortured* him," I said. My throat tightened just thinking about the fear, the rage, the desperation in Lion's soul—all wounds she'd left behind. "I've been in his soul, Tía Catrina. I tasted the promises you made and the punishments you gave instead. I felt how much he loved you, and how you used it against him." I marched forward, my soul flashing brighter. Tía Catrina straightened, lifting her chin. "The pain you put him through—don't you care about that at all?"

She stared down at me. Her gaze was so dark. Darker than Rodrigo's had been. Darker than Little Lion's fears. Darker than the well she'd thrown Coyote into after she'd killed him.

Then her mouth spread in a brilliant, stunning smile.

"You've been *in* his soul?" she asked, with sudden girlish enthusiasm. "So you saw the memories? Did you hear his soul's voice?"

The sudden shift sent me stumbling. I stammered for a second, which was apparently all the answer she needed. She dropped her books—I yelped as she did; they were clearly old and probably important—and dragged me to the velvet chair, sweeping my ankles so I fell back into the chair with a thud.

I winced as she loomed over me. Her grin was wild

where it had once been perfect, manicured calm.

"That's what I've been hoping for," she whispered. "Cece, this is how you will end the reign of El Cucuy."

"I don't understand—don't you *serve* El Cucuy?"

She brushed back her hair so I could see a tiny, pale line glowing on her forehead. "I wear the Mark of the Binding," she said. "I can't go against El Cucuy's will. But you, Cece—you have both the power and the freedom that's required."

She reached for my collarbone. I slapped my hands over my soul. She placed hers over mine.

"Haven't you ever wondered how you can hold so many souls, Cece?" she asked.

I hesitated. I had wondered a few times. Back in the Bruja Fights, everyone had been surprised that I could carry so many souls at my age.

"Um, because I'm not trying to control them?" I said, trying to sound more sure than I felt. "I'm not really a bruja, so—"

"Wrong." Tía Catrina leaned in, so I had to cringe back into the velvet seat. "Souls have weight, Cece, whether or not you control them. You can carry as many as you do because you have a higher soul capacity than any I've seen—other than myself. Of course, you would have never discovered it, but by pretending to be a bruja, you stumbled on an art even the curanderas had forgotten: soul language." She placed her fingertips on my forehead. "It is the ability to interact with the world of souls by listening and speaking with them. It might have taken you years to properly use it, but Rodrigo helped you along by pulling your soul out of your body. It made you even more sensitive. It's how you defeated El Sombrerón. Don't you see?"

She beamed, and my eyes widened. I remembered the way I'd pushed my feelings into El Sombrerón, and tattoos had crept up to his soul, and he'd frozen under my influence. But how was that soul language?

"You reached into El Sombrerón, grabbed hold of whatever pathetic piece of him was human, and gave power to it. You reached the sliver of his soul that was sick of his own evil, which stopped him long enough for your group to defeat him. It was messy in application, true. A very rudimentary form of what you could one day do. Nevertheless, you rediscovered a practice so old even curandera writings from the last four hundred years have no record of it." She stood up straight again and gestured to the bookshelves behind me. "But I do."

Reeling, I slowly climbed out of the chair. The titles on the books came into focus. *Cantos de Curanderas; Soul Weight and Criaturas II; Leyendas de Soul Language, Cantos de Criaturas y Curanderas III.* My mouth dropped open.

"*You* have the books of the ancient curanderas?" I breathed.

Dominga del Sol had said that almost all of them had been destroyed. But as I glanced from Catrina's hands to the bookshelf, I could see most of her collection was about curandería. My stomach flipped. How had Catrina thrown them around so flippantly earlier? These tomes were precious.

Tía Catrina's smile grew wider. "That's right," she said. "That's how I realized you could use soul language, and how I knew you were a curandera before *anyone else.*"

I stopped approaching. Her smile held firm, but there was something dry and cracked in her expression now. A pride as bristly as the cerros.

I retreated from the shelf again. Really, I wanted to hug all the books to my chest and run away with them—to share them with Dominga del Sol, Mamá, Juana, and my friends—but Tía Catrina's smile felt like a trap.

"What do you mean?" I asked.

She tilted her head and waved a book at me. "I was different too. No one appreciated the voices I heard . . ." Her brow tightened. Passages from her old journal, about listening to the voices of the desert, came flooding back. "The moment I learned of Tzitzimitl's curse, I knew you were the same as me, with more power waiting inside you than any of the pitiful people in Tierra del Sol could recognize. And, therefore, you were Devil's Alley's best chance." She strode over to me, and I scurried back. "But living with my ignorant hermana, you'd never discover your abilities, let alone develop them into something to rival El Cucuy. I had to do something without revealing myself. I had to force you into an impossible choice."

I pressed my back to the wall as she closed in. A deep, dark dread welled up in my mind.

"What did you do?" I asked.

She smiled. "Do you know how El Sombrerón picks his brides?" She swept a hand toward herself. My gut tightened.

"*You* sent El Sombrerón after Juana?" I burst out.

"It was a roundabout way to help you, I admit. But there's only so much I can do when I wear the Mark of the Binding and live so close to El Cucuy's gaze. I sent you on a journey that would force that power out of you. A power no one in our familia has been able to claim for generations." She smiled. "So really, you should say, 'Gracias, Tía.' It took *so* much tedious work to keep you alive in the Bruja Fights."

And she waited. Like she really expected me to thank her.

"You tortured my sister!" I exploded. "You put my familia through so much pain—"

"Shh, shh. Cece." She waved me down, like I was a toddler. "Try to think, mija. Is it more important to attack me than to break down this corrupt regime? As one of his

Dark Saints, I cannot possibly stand against him, but I can help *you* do so." She reached out to stroke my hair. "I can help you be the hero you were *born* to be."

I slapped her hand away. Hurt creased her face. Guilt knotted in my stomach automatically, and I almost reached out to comfort her—but caught myself at the last second. Because I could only think of what she'd just admitted to. And what she was really after.

"I bet you don't even want to take El Cucuy down to make this place better, do you?" I balled up my fists. "You don't care about the suffering of the criaturas! You probably want El Cucuy dead so—so—"

A chill sunk deep into my bones as a passage from her journal planted roots in my chest.

Soon, I will enter Devil's Alley—
and there, I will be a queen.

"You want to rule Devil's Alley," I whispered. "That's what this is really about, isn't it?"

Catrina paused. Then she smiled and rested her hand on my head. I looked up, stomach sick, as she pushed my black hair back from my forehead.

"Would that be so bad, Cece?" she entreated softly. "If you put me on the throne, I'll finally have the power to set criaturas free from brujas. I could make sure the dark criaturas never hurt humans again. I can give you *peace*." She crouched so we were eye to eye. A look of pity crossed her face. "I know the way you were treated in Tierra del Sol. How they hated the sight of you. How they scoffed, no matter how much you tried to be what they wanted." She tucked a curl behind my ear tenderly, but her words cut deep into the holes that had only just started to heal inside me. "I can give you a home that accepts you. People who love you. Adore you, even. Worship you. Wouldn't that be nice, after everything your town, your mamá, your sister, put you through? Wouldn't that make you happy?" She tapped the tip of my nose.

The hairs on the back of my neck turned to sharp pins. I'd been working on healing my inner wounds, but they felt raw and sore again after everything she said. She smiled, warmly, gently, offering me everything she thought I wanted. And for just a second, it was tempting.

But I shook my head. And her smile fell.

"I know you too, Tía Catrina. I know you've suffered, and Tierra del Sol hurt us both a lot. Sometimes I feel like no one wants or understands me either." I reached out to touch her face, but she withdrew and rose to full height again. "But I also know that I don't want what you want. I don't want to feel better about myself at other people's expense. I just want to love them *and* me. *That* will make me happy."

Tía Catrina stared at me silently. Then she turned to a clock on her wall, sighing as her features cooled. "I should have just stolen you from your mother. Raised you myself. Then maybe you'd be reasonable," she said, almost under her breath.

I gaped. When she looked my way again, her gaze crackled at the edges.

"I'd hoped you'd be willing to end El Cucuy for your friends' sakes, if not out of gratitude. But you're far more judgmental and cruel than my informants said. And useless on top of it." She lifted her chin. "No wonder everyone hates you."

It shouldn't have—I knew she was lying—but her insult only ripped my wounds open further. I winced. My throat tightened. I stammered, trying to find words to push back, but she grabbed my shirt and shoved me against the wall.

"I have another appointment I can't be late for." She spread her hand on a nearby purple crystal. "For now, you can stay in the dungeon. Alone. Like you deserve to be."

"Wait—" I started.

The floor fell out from under me, and I screamed as I plummeted down, down, down into darkness.

20

Juana Rios and Where It Began

Little Lion and I stood in front of El Sombrerón's massive stone door.

It was exactly how I remembered it. The hall around it was cold and quiet, sinister and dim. A large black moth was carved in each of the door's corners, and a skeletal face with a bunch of twisted shapes forming a hat atop its head was emblazoned at the center. Ancient glyphs surrounded the skull, another reminder that Devil's Alley had been left to rot for millennia.

Little Lion stared at me. "You okay?"

I nodded even though I wasn't.

"That brujo's told everyone we're here by now," Lion's voice was gentle but firm. "We should move."

I nodded again. My back was covered in sweat, and my blood felt hot. After all this, it shouldn't be so hard to open the door. I knew how. But now that I was finally standing here, I just wanted to run away.

"I'm not going to let him hold me hostage again," I said aloud, to myself, for myself. "I'll leave this time, of my own free will."

Lion nodded. "He'll be weaker in this life." He reached out for me, then hesitated. "We—you'll get your soul back, Juana."

I took his hand. He jumped, but I squeezed his fingers and stepped forward. My free hand shook openly, and I hated that, but I let it because it was the best I could do right now.

Slowly, I tapped the bottom right moth in the door. It lit up with purple light. I touched three teeth in the skeletal carving at the center. The light filled in the grinning lines. I paused over a glyph at the top left, above the skull.

"It'll be different this time," I said again, and pressed it firmly.

The entire door lit up. There was a grinding noise, and a gust of dust and wind blew out from the frame. Little Lion and I covered our faces as El Sombrerón's suite finally opened.

The room was also just the way I remembered it. The high ceiling, with its infinite number of creepy moths. A red throne where a bed should be, on the far side of the large space, with silver tile beneath. It was boring, really. Not meant for living in, because El Sombrerón didn't really *live.* The only things of note in the room were the two I had the hardest time forgetting. To the right of the throne, shelves covered in soul stones lined the wall. I swallowed. And though I tried to resist, my eyes drew toward a heavy chain on the left.

One end of the chain hooked into the wall. The other end draped across the ground, its shackle open and rusted. My skin pulled cold and tight. I knew that chain like it was an extra bone from my body. I'd worn it for too long.

"It's empty," Little Lion said.

For a second, I thought he was talking about the chain. And I took a looser breath when I remembered it was true. I was free. I could stay free. Just as long as I got my soul back.

But then I realized what Little Lion actually meant: El Sombrerón was nowhere in sight.

"He's not even *here?*" I stomped into the room, searching for where he could be lurking above our heads. Nothing. I balled my hands into fists. Everyone had made such a big deal about how his room was locked and no one could see him, but here the place was, empty. That was just like El Sombrerón. Skipping out just when I'd reached my opportunity for revenge.

"Wait, Juana." Little Lion pointed at my feet. "Look."

I forced my chin down.

A tiny child stood there, craning his head to stare up at me from under the brim of a wide black hat. He wore a cloak so smoky and dark it could have been made of shadows.

I froze.

El Sombrerón—my chest tensed—was a *child*?

"Do I know you?" he asked. His voice was squeaky.

He could've been playing fútbol with any kid in Tierra del Sol, the way he fumbled with his hands and scratched at his shadowy chin. He stepped toward me, scanning and squinting with his large red eyes beneath his sombrero. I stumbled back from him as heat scorched through my ribs.

"Did El Cucuy send you to play with me?" he asked. "I thought he said only he was allowed to play with me until I'm older." He clapped, clearly grateful the rule had been broken.

"No," I said. "I'm not." My mouth went dry. I set my jaw as El Sombrerón tilted his head. "I'm Juana Rios. And—and you—"

Little Lion watched me struggle to speak. I'd planned out what I wanted to say: *You stole me and broke my soul. Now I'm back to* shatter *yours and take back what always was, and always will be,* mine. I'd recited it to myself each night I couldn't sleep. But I couldn't seem to grab hold of the words now.

I'd come here to destroy this criatura. To grab the soul peeking out of his collar and turn it into powder. But a child stared up at me, waiting and confused. His pudgy hands played with his cloak as he waited. And I wondered, even though what he'd done was terrible, horrible, wretched. I wondered, even though I shouldn't have to wonder: What would revenge really get me now?

All the painful, raging heat slowly slipped away from me as I stared down at the once-towering criatura who'd caused me so much pain, now just a small and curious child.

My mouth opened and closed as I struggled for words.

"You stole something from me," I finally whispered.

Little Lion's eyebrows lifted. El Sombrerón tilted his head curiously.

"I'm here to get it back." My voice was thin and scratchy.

"I don't have that much stuffs." He pointed to the shelf at the back of the room. "Is it one of my shinies? El Cucuy said I collected them."

The shelf behind him was comprised of tiny cubes, and in each one sat a soul stone. I drifted a bit closer before stopping short. The souls caught the light of the torches. Gleaming fire opals and rubies. Limestone and coyamito agate souls, striped and solemn. A few moonstone drops, and even the occasional turquoise soul stone, shone silently.

Every single one of them had a scar running through them. I hadn't known what that was before, when I was trapped in this room. But I did now. The scar left behind from where El Sombrerón had broken each of them in half and then forced the soul back together.

A legacy of women stolen from their homes. Trapped, voiceless, forever.

On the centermost shelf, a tiny fragment of fire opal sat all alone. My chest stretched and sparked as I stared at it. I knew without a doubt it was mine.

I pointed at it. "That one," I said. "It belongs to me."

Tiny El Sombrerón turned and looked at it. He toddled over, pulled it off the shelf, and brought it back over. No fight. No fuss. My chest quavered as a warm bubble began to push out the sharp heat from earlier. Finally, El Sombrerón stopped in front of me.

"It's one of my favorites," he said. "But you can play with it for a little while."

The bubble popped, and anger roared through me. "I'm not *borrowing* it," I barked. "It was mine in the first place. You don't get it back."

His shoulders slumped. "But El Cucuy said they belonged to me."

"Well, they *don't*." I raised my voice. He jumped. "You stole them. That doesn't make them yours."

He paused. Then he bowed his head and kicked his booted toe into the tile. "Are you mad at me?" he mumbled.

"Yes," I said. My throat tightened with red-hot tears, because there weren't words for how angry I was, or had been, and probably would always struggle with being. "This is my soul. It's very important to me, and you hurt me a lot when you broke it and took it. What you did was so bad. So—so *awful*, that I can barely think straight because of *how angry I am.*"

El Sombrerón's face crumpled. "Will you stop being mad at me if I give it back to you?" He lifted the small shard of fire opal.

My hands shook as I picked it up. The fire opal immediately began to glow, and it was as warm as a candle's flame in my hands once again. Tears prickled the back of my eyes. I'd missed this feeling. I laughed, just a little, as I pulled it close and savored the warmth.

When I opened my eyes, Lion was smiling. I smiled back. But slowly, his face tightened with something like concern as he glanced from my soul fragment to the place my heart should be beating.

"Can you fix it for her?" Little Lion asked, and El Sombrerón looked at him. "It's supposed to be in her chest. She'll probably be a lot less mad if you put it back."

I released a shivery breath. "Yeah. Fix it," I said. "Put it back."

"Um." El Sombrerón played with his cloak. "I can't."

All the warmth from holding my soul evaporated into rage. I snatched up my knife, and El Sombrerón flinched as I wielded it over him.

"*What do you mean you can't?*" I bellowed, advancing on him. El Sombrerón retreated in a hurry, his little legs scurrying, until he stumbled and fell back against the wall. I had him cornered, and my skin was filled with magma. "You're the one who broke it!"

"I—I don't know how!" He held his arms over his face. "El Cucuy said he'd show me when I'm older."

The blade trembled in my grip. Slowly, Little Lion came up beside me. I felt his gaze as the warmth and the burning fought inside me.

After all this, I was still going to be damaged. Water burned my eyes. I'd spared his life when I could have picked vengeance, and El Sombrerón couldn't even fix what *he'd* destroyed in the first place.

"I hate you." My voice trembled as my throat started to close up. I wanted to strike him as he cowered there beneath me. I wanted to show him what being broken felt like. "Why couldn't you just leave me alone? You did this to me, and now *I* have to live with it!"

El Sombrerón shrank beneath me. I squeezed the knife hilt. It would be easy to just take it out on him. Both worlds would be better off.

But beneath all my broken, sharp edges—beneath the burning coals and ashy fragments left inside my chest—there was still a quiet, warm place that would not give ground. That would not give up.

I let the knife slide through my fingers.

It clanged on the ground beside El Sombrerón. He hugged the corner as I turned away, two steps, three steps, before falling to my knees in the middle of the room. I slammed my fists to the stone ground and sobbed.

"I just wanted to be normal again!" I cried, clutching my soul to my chest. "I—I wanted to be me again . . ."

Little Lion knelt down beside me. He placed a soothing hand on my shoulder. El Sombrerón didn't move from his curled-up place in the corner as I sobbed and screamed and raged so loud, the only noise in the room was my wrath and my pain. It banged from every wall and shook in my bones, and I wailed for everything I'd lost, and everything I was afraid I'd never have again.

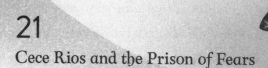

21

Cece Rios and the Prison of Fears

When I woke up, I was screaming.

The terrified sound echoed in the darkness surrounding me. I choked off my scream, gasping for air. I was lying on my side on a cold stone floor. How did I get here? Where was I? I scanned my surroundings, but there was nothing but darkness.

My mind whirled. Tía Catrina had mentioned the dungeon. So that's where I had to be. Oh! El Silbón and the hunting party had sent my friends down here too. Maybe they were nearby.

"Coyote?" I called out. The sound echoed and bounced back to me. I cringed at the volume. My stomach crumpled inward. "K-Kit? Ocelot?"

My whispers roamed around the darkness like flies, buzzing back at me, noisy and disturbing, before eventually flying away. I swallowed. Was I alone? If they were here too, why weren't they answering me? I squeezed my hands into fists, and my heart raced. What if they were ignoring me? What if they were upset because I'd landed them back in Devil's Alley? My breaths came sharp, panicked. What if they—hated me now?

See what you've done? A voice slithered through the darkness. It came from everywhere and nowhere—but it sank straight into my heart. *You're alone after all. You couldn't find your sister, and now your friends have abandoned you because you didn't do enough.*

"I'm sorry!" I bawled. I tried to crawl forward, to search for a way out, but my arms and legs gave way. I collapsed on the ground, wincing at the scrapes on my hands. "Coyote, Kit, Ocelot! I'm sorry—pero, I never meant for this to happen . . ." My breath stuttered and started. "I just wanted . . . to take care of you. I'm sorry I'm not . . ."

That's right, the voice echoed around me. *You're not enough.*

The words scurried around me like spiders. They were paralyzing, sinking into my bones.

And that's why you have to bear this all alone now. You don't deserve their love.

I buried my face in my hands, trembling. My hair stuck to my sweaty forehead. My insides withered like useless, discarded scraps.

You don't deserve more than this. You don't deserve to be a curandera.

My eyes burst open.

I'd heard that before. My skull felt heavy as a stone, but I craned it back to look up all the same. I'd listened to this voice lurking in the back of my head since I was little. I'd used this voice to fuel my determination, so I didn't lose everyone I loved. The darkness surrounding me suddenly seemed—small. I reached out, hand still shaking, and touched something cold. I traced its jagged surface and found myself trapped in some kind of crystal sphere, a prison cutting me off from the light.

You've ended up alone because you're not worth having, the voice insisted again.

But I smiled, just a little, as tenderness softened the panic in my soul. Because this was *my* voice. My fears, and my grief, and the part of me that was afraid I didn't deserve the love I'd found.

In the absolute darkness, my soul flickered back to life around my neck. The turquoise glow caught on the walls around me, and the edges of the dark crystal reflected my own light back to me. I pushed myself off the ground and stood in the orb, with the ceiling only a few inches above my head, and planted my feet even when my knees tried to buckle.

The best thing you could do for your friends is stay here, the darkness said. *Then you could finally stop disappointing them.*

If this was my voice, and my lie, then I knew what to do. Memories of Metztli's tenderness on the beach, of Dominga del Sol's kindness, of Coyote's words and steadfastness, of Kit's and Ocelot's and Lion's friendship poured into me. Images from the last few months, of Juana holding me, of Mamá tenderly apologizing and appreciating me, gathered inside me like bolts of powerful lightning. I cupped my soul between my hands. It brightened, filling the whole space with blue light. I raised my head and looked, searching, into the darkest parts of myself.

"I know we were scared and hurt growing up." I wiped my wet eyes. "I—I know we still are. But we don't need to believe what everyone told us—that we're somehow not lovable. Your friends didn't love you because you saved them. They loved you because you're you. The same way you didn't love them because they helped you save Juana—you loved them, *and* they helped you."

I raised my head to the dark gem ceiling, filling my chest with a great, swelling breath.

"And you know what, me? I love *you* too!" I shouted, and the voice of the prison shriveled back. The light of my soul brightened into a blue star and lit up my reflection in the gem walls. Tears ran down my cheeks as I took in my small and round shape, my large warm eyes, and my short black hair. I watched my soul gleam on the outside—vulnerable, but always, always doing its best. I hiccupped. "I love you just because you are."

The darkness shattered.

Black crystals broke open around me with a mighty crash and clatter. I stood there, shivering, as my soul exploded with bright and brilliant light. The orb finished crumbling in large chunks around me. I laughed and bowed my head as a few crystal shards caught in my hair.

"Cece?"

I looked up, wiping my tears with my jacket sleeve, to find a bruja, her criatura, and four dark criaturas standing around me in a semicircle—and Ocelot and Kit directly in front of me.

I gasped and wiped my running nose. "Ocelot! Kit! You're here!"

I'd thought I was alone. But my friends had been waiting for me just outside my crystal prison. Kit's eyes lit up, and he dove for me. I squeezed him close. My soul bubbled over with warmth and light, and I poured the excess into him. I'd missed the feeling of having his soul so close. I peeked at it, where it hung safely around his neck. Even separated, the sunshine in his soul drifted free and danced around mine.

Huh. I smiled. Maybe—maybe I didn't have to wear my friends' souls to feel them now. Maybe I knew them well enough, could hear them well enough, to feel their souls even when they carried them. Did that have to do with the soul language Tía Catrina had talked about?

"I'm glad you escaped," Kit mumbled, and snuggled his cheek against mine. "I knew you could do it."

"That is the great danger of El Cucuy's dungeon." Ocelot stepped up to us. "You can get trapped here by your fears." Her lips moved with the hint of a smile. "Kit escaped his by thinking of you, Cece." She gestured back at a broken circle of dark crystals nearby.

I gasped and looked at him. He didn't look embarrassed— he just beamed like a mobile sun.

She reached down and patted my head twice. I giggled, even though my throat was still sore from crying.

"I'm proud of you both," she said.

My soul tingled and flashed. A small distance away, a little girl gasped, and I suddenly remembered everyone else in the room. The criatura looked a few years younger than Kit, with pink hair and eyes. She bounced up and down and pulled on the jacket of the tall bruja staring at us. I stiffened. A bruja? Was she going to hurt us? But Ocelot waved me down.

"Cece," she said, and gestured to the whole semicircle of people I realized were staring at me. "This is Bruja Damiana, keeper of the dungeon, and her criatura, Axolotl."

That didn't make me feel any better, but she gestured to the horde of dark criaturas, and my chest loosened as she went on.

"And these are the criaturas she's just released from their cages." Ocelot drew her hand down the line of three dark criaturas. I recognized them vaguely from stories—the Bird King, La Lechuza, and even the ancient Alux. They nodded to me.

"It is good to be reunited," the Bird King rumbled, so his gold mask moved. "We are the Court of Fears, young curandera. We have long been your people's allies."

My mouth dropped wide open as my brain whirled with the info. There was a whole group of dark criaturas who worked with curanderas? Oh, but La Sirena had mentioned the Court of Fears, hadn't she? Ocelot stepped aside to reveal two more people—familiar faces that made my heart jump.

"Tzitzimitl!" I cried, and sprinted forward. "Metztli!"

Tzitzimitl chuckled and squatted so I could wrap her in a hug. It was uncomfortable, because she was made out of bones, but she held me gently. Metztli wrapped her thick arms around both of us.

"Metztli, I'm so glad you're okay!" I said. "Tzitzimitl, I didn't know you were in Devil's Alley! How'd you get trapped in the dungeon?"

It was technically impossible for Tzitzimitl to smile. But

I was pretty sure she was doing it anyway. "You are safe. And I am reunited with the Court of Fears. That is what matters."

"I am grateful to see you unharmed, young Cecelia." Metztli brushed back my hair.

My heart swelled, and I beamed. I pulled back from the two of them to check over the space we stood in, with its six empty fire opal cells and a ceiling made of water—oh, was this the cenote Metztli had talked about? It was beautiful. My eyes stopped on a pair of silver doors on the other side of the room. My brows furrowed as I checked over the crowd again.

"Wait," I said. "Where's Coyote?"

Bruja Damiana cleared her throat. All of us turned to her. She fiddled with the embroidery on the lapel of her jacket and shuffled up to me, Axolotl tiptoeing alongside her.

"Ocean curandera—" she began.

"You can call me Cece," I said.

She paused, clearly surprised, then smiled and nodded. "Cece," she started again. "The last ocean curandera created this cenote"—she gestured to the water above our heads—"to transport El Cucuy to Devil's Alley so they could seal him here. But he has turned it into a prison. There is no way out, except through those silver doors. Coyote went through alone to try to find you. But they are dangerous." She shook her head. "No one can control these doors or where they lead. Whether it will take you where you need to go, or keep your trapped and lost inside it forever, no one knows. No one even knows why the passage exists. It's not worth the risk." She bit her bottom lip.

I stared at the doors. Eerie lights wandered around its doorframe.

"But Coyote's in there," I said. "He's worth it to me."

I crossed to the doors, even as the group called out to me, and flattened my hand against the entrance's silver surface. Moans and groans crawled out from beyond the doors. My toes curled. I meant what I'd said—but fear still curdled my stomach. What was this place, exactly? Considering we were in Devil's Alley, it was bound to be harmful. What if I didn't make it out? The noises from the other side thrummed through my skin, and my soul flashed.

Metztli placed her hand on the door beside mine. I looked up as she scanned its facade, her brows knitted.

"Something about this place seems familiar," Metztli said. "Like a distant memory I cannot quite grasp, perhaps because it does not belong to me." She brushed dust from the door. "What do you feel, Cecelia?"

The thrumming in the door resonated through me. Carefully, I placed my ear against the metal and closed my eyes. I stretched with my soul, like I had with Juana and Metztli, hoping for guidance.

I am the bones of the world. The groans knitted into a voice beyond doors. *I am the dust at the end as I am life at the beginning.*

I gasped. Metztli watched but waited silently as words continued to reach for me.

My son is trapped. Come. Help him. As I will help you.

"Coyote needs our help," I said. "We have to go!"

I grabbed the doorknob, and Bruja Damiana and Ocelot rushed to stop me.

"It's okay! The passage will let us through." I gestured for them to follow. "I know, she just told me. Come on! She wants us to save Coyote."

"Who's 'she'?" Axolotl asked, pink hair bouncing.

Tzitzimitl stepped up beside Metztli. "Remember who Devil's Alley was made from, young ones. Do you think, just because she sacrificed her form, that she does not still love and fight for us?"

I wanted to ask more questions. Was she really implying that I'd just heard the Desert goddess? The way I thought I'd heard Mother Ocean, back when El Silbón found me on the shore? My skin prickled, and my soul brightened beneath my shirt just at the thought.

But my friend needed me right now. So I turned and, together with Metztli, pulled the doors open.

A veil of silent darkness waited for us inside. I took a big, brave breath—and we stepped as a group into the space. I expected to feel the cool of the corridor, as I slid into its shadows. But instead, it felt as if I'd blinked—only with my whole body. One second, I was sliding into the dark. And the next, I was standing in a new room, with new light, with no door—just my friends, the bruja, and the Court of Fears surrounding me.

The room was a wide stone circle, twice as big as the one we'd come from, but Coyote was nowhere in sight.

Kit tapped my shoulder and pointed up. Slowly, I craned my head back.

At the very top of the domed ceiling, high, high above, Coyote hung in a crystal enclosure just like the one I'd been trapped in. Except his was clear as glass. Images of the past swam down from it and displayed across the stone walls around us. And he, curled into a ball, floating upside down, isolated and alone, crumpled under the weight of them.

22

Juana Ríos and the Scarred Soul

"I know what it's like," Lion whispered.

I was still on my knees in the center of El Sombrerón's room, curled over the unfixable fragment of my soul. Far off to the side, El Sombrerón had moved from his corner at the back of the room to one near the front. I turned away from him. Vicious heat and tender warmth battled inside me.

Lion leaned closer to me. "I know it hurts. But nothing El Sombrerón did to it can change the fact that it's *your* soul." He placed his dark hands under mine, as if to help me bear its weight. "This belongs to you. Not him."

His eyes shone, and every word had the firmness that I'd started to appreciate about him.

"Why doesn't it feel like it?" I shook my head. "I feel broken and—powerless—and . . ." I couldn't finish.

"Juana. You have so much power inside you already. A better kind of power than what you were searching for." He guided my hands upward until I placed the soul sliver against my chest. "I don't know if this will work, but . . . but humans are still creatures of the gods, like criaturas. Try and take this piece back into you."

The room fell quiet. Nervous itching rose up my chest. Would that really work?

"But . . . Cece's soul is outside her chest," I mumbled, struggling against the tender call of hope. "If that was possible, wouldn't she have done it?"

"She's never tried." Lion shrugged. "And—you know, it's different to have your whole soul outside your chest." He tapped his through his shirt. "Yours is in two pieces. Don't you think it wants to be whole?"

I was almost more scared to try and it not work. But I took a steadying breath. Trying was always better than counting yourself out. I'd counted out all the best parts of myself for too long. I had to believe in a path forward for myself again, even if I didn't see it.

That's what hope is. Not knowing, and trying anyway.

I took longer, deeper breaths, feeling for the empty places in my chest. Trying to imagine what it had been like when my whole soul had still been there. The shard in my hand warmed against my skin so subtly, I thought my palm was just getting sweaty. Then a rosy, gold light began to glow between my fingers. I gasped.

And that's when I felt it.

A heartbeat.

I flattened my hand tighter to my chest, and a whisper, like the crackling of a distant fire, grew in my ears.

Please, I begged the Sun god. *I know it can't all be perfect. But let me be whole.*

Light flashed, and a sharp, quick pain shot through my skin. I dropped my hands and coughed as the discomfort wore down into my flesh and bones. An open wound filled with light glimmered along my ribs.

I had been trying everything I could to avoid pain. And this hurt deeply, like knives in my bones, like a hand tearing through my chest to reach my heart. But even as tears poured down my face . . .

It was worth it.

The two pieces snapped back together, and I cried out. For a moment, my veins felt on fire. My toes tingled, like they'd been waiting for the blood to come back to them. And the painful, burned parts of me crumbled away. The light died down, and the pain dissipated.

But it didn't all disappear. As I took what felt like my first full breath in months, a tiny stitch caught in my chest. I winced. Little Lion watched me, eyes still shining with moisture.

"It worked," he breathed.

"It feels like . . ." I rubbed my chest. "A scar."

"It'll hurt sometimes." Lion reached out with his soul in his palm and flipped it over so I could see the four lines carved through its back. He brushed his thumb over them. "But you'd be surprised how beautiful life can still be, even with scars."

When Lion smiled, he looked like he was born to be happy. And that made me feel like I could be, too.

"Come here, gato!" I threw my arms around him in a hug and buried my nose in the side of his hair. It felt so good to hug this unexpected friend of mine—and to actually be able to enjoy it. Lion wrapped his arms around me in return, awkwardly at first, but he melted into my hold soon enough. The dam burst, and for the first time in weeks, tears of joy poured out of my eyes.

I was finally back together. I had my whole soul, and it was scarred, but it was all mine. Warmth bubbled up in my chest and expanded until my entire body felt tingly and rosy. No burning, no scorching. Just a strength like sunlight, like courage.

I lifted my head from Lion's hair, and as I breathed in, I knew I was ready. Ready to face a world that was unsafe—and be okay. I slowly pulled back to look at Lion. I thumped my chest once, and my heart kept beating in response.

"Well." I cleared my throat. "You've held up your part of

our deal. So now it's my turn. Let's go rescue your familia or whatever." I offered my hand. Lion took it, and I helped him up. "Your plan better not be as dumb as mine."

Lion snickered. We turned toward the door, more confidence in our steps—only to find someone standing there, smirking at us as she gripped El Sombrerón by the collar.

"It's good to see you, sobrina," she said.

El Sombrerón screamed.

23

Cece Rios and the Lost Boy

Coyote looked so alone in his crystal cage, hanging like a chandelier from the stone ceiling. I held my breath as I watched my best friend slip away, isolated from us, with only the worst of his last life's memories for company.

They played out on the walls around us. Coyote roaring as he stood in a tall, domed building—before he ripped a hole in Mother Desert. The building broke in half and Devil's Alley rose up in the wound. Coyote helping the curanderas build their sanctuaries—and then abandoning them in a rage. Coyote grabbing a young, frightened man at a gravesite—and twisting him until he wore the face of El Silbón. But I also watched the way he'd raised his criatura familia. I watched him love them. I watched him lose them. First, to humans. Then again and again, to brujas.

Sorrow settled like rain on my skin. I think I finally understood my friend now, in a way I hadn't before. Coyote hadn't just been the Great Namer. He'd been the first of a nation. I watched the criaturas of the past gather around their oldest brother, making demands, begging for relief. I watched his young confusion harden into a cynical wrath as he tried to solve unending problems. I watched him grow lonelier and lonelier, even with his familia around. Because he felt responsible for making a perfect world for them. An impossible task.

I'm sorry, Coyote's soul cried out across the bleak room. *I don't know how to fix it all. I tried, but nothing ever worked. What if I can't make up for what I've done?*

My heart ached for him across the painful distance.

"This is my fault," Metztli said as she scanned the images of his past. "He's just a child. I shouldn't have given him only his worst memories. He doesn't remember the good things because I—I—"

"Because you were still angry," I whispered, and her face tightened in remorse. "And you wanted him to feel the way you did when the curanderas had to fight El Cucuy alone."

Her bottom lip trembled. "Sí," she admitted, forthright and honest. "Consuelo always taught me that justice must hold hands with mercy. How easily I forget." Metztli lifted a hand to Coyote's faraway crystal prison. "How do we save him now?"

Bruja Damiana stepped closer. "The dungeon's crystal

prisons can only be broken by the prisoner. If it helps, his crystals haven't darkened yet. It means he's still fighting." She bit her lip. "But I'm afraid with this much pain in his past, if the crystals darken all the way—there may be no bringing him back. Ever."

The adults debated the best way to help Coyote break his prison. Kit Fox came to stand with me as their voices faded into the background. We watched our friend, and the veins of darkness creeping up through the base of his crystal prison.

"You know," Kit whispered to me. "I was the first criatura stolen by a bruja."

I looked at him, a knot of horror in my throat.

"Coyote rescued me," he said, and his ears wilted back against his head. "I was the reason for the first war between Coyote and Naked Man. The bruja who'd stolen my soul was hiding out in a normal town. Coyote raided every single house, terrifying humans in his search for me."

The memories, as if called from Kit's description, started to form across the walls. The darkness stopped spreading across Coyote's crystal prison. Kit's soul swelled with a million colors that vibrated in the air and resonated in my soul.

"I know it's hard to remember the good things when you've seen a lot of bad," he cried up to Coyote. Everyone hushed. "But that doesn't mean the good isn't still there!"

Kit plastered a hand to his chest, over his soul. "You saved my life! You were *always* there trying to protect us. And we saw! But you ran away before you could see that we'd be there for you too." His cheeks and nose flushed pink. "You don't have to do it alone this time, Legend Brother."

Far above, the scene of their past continued playing, with an older Coyote picking up a weak Kit Fox. He held him close, carrying his bruised body out of the bruja's house. Near me, Kit's furry ears perked up as the dark veins in Coyote's crystal retreated. I gasped.

"That's it!" I whirled around to Metztli, to the Court of Fears, to Ocelot. "You all knew him! You have to remind him he's still worth saving."

I knew that would be hard for the Court of Fears. I looked from Tzitzimitl to the Bird King to La Lechuza to Alux. They had been remade by an angry Coyote who'd given up hope. Who'd offered only a twisted justice when he thought mercy would never work.

But Ocelot strode forward. She joined us under Coyote's prison, her mouth stern and flat. I held my breath. Was she angry? What would she say?

"Do you remember?" Ocelot craned her head back to him. "You brought me with you to meet with Naked Man, to make peace. You told me criaturas and humans were both creations of the gods, so we should try to act as one great familia."

Images appeared of Coyote and a band of criaturas, including a young and brighter Ocelot, speaking with tribe delegates across a fire. Ocelot growled at something a human said. Then, one pulled a weapon on her.

"When they turned on us, you protected me."

Coyote dove in front of her and took the blow instead.

"Afterward, I was bitter and angry. But you kept trying to make peace with Naked Man and soften my heart to them. Even once you disappeared, that persistent example stayed with me. It is how I one day fell in love with my human husband. And the reason I got to have the most wonderful daughter in all the worlds."

Pictures bloomed on the walls of Ocelot standing with the man I'd seen in her memories. She held him close, and they both wore bright, wide smiles. Between them, holding both of their hands, a little girl with short dark hair beamed—and a birthmark resembling Ocelot's soul stone shone on her right cheek.

My heart jogged, and I squeezed my soul in my hand. Damiana stared, fixated, hanging on Ocelot's every word. Her eyes filled with the tears Ocelot wouldn't let out.

"This time," Ocelot said. Her voice rose in a raw, swelling tone I'd never heard. "We will fight for you too, Legend Brother."

Her words settled inside me like starlight. Then Metztli

strode up. She craned her head back, face softened, the way she'd looked at me back at the beach.

"Coyote, let me tell you the beauty of your beginning. When you were first made, Mother Desert formed you out of What Could Be and elements from the four gods."

The crystal swirled, and Mother Desert stood above a sleeping Coyote. She was so similar to her depiction in the Ocean Sanctuary, with legs as strong as mountains, and hair that rolled down in great, black waves that turned to verdant forests.

"From Sun, her dear brother, she plucked a drop of light to house your soul. From Moon, her dear sister, she gathered moonbeams and braided them into a bright mind. And from her loving hermana Ocean, she drew water that formed into a powerful heart. She placed the brilliant gifts of her brother and sisters inside a body made from her dust. And with her voice, she Named you. You were made from every good thing. You were the pattern from which all life was made."

The picture changed above. And my blood rippled, my soul flashed, my fingers tingled, and my mind sharpened as I watched the images of the four gods wrapping their arms around Coyote, just before they sacrificed themselves for a world that could be his home.

A crack broke through the crystal. It was just one. But it was hope.

I palmed my soul stone and lifted it as far as I could over my head. I felt the distant colors of his soul stretch for mine. I closed my eyes and stretched, pushed, reached my light out to him.

"You saw that I was strong when I didn't know I was yet. You stood by me when I didn't think I was worth standing by," I whispered the words, but they echoed in the room like thunder. "None of us can take away the pain of your last life. But we will love you as you wrestle with it. You're so much more than the weights bearing down on you."

My papá hadn't seen that for Mamá or Juana or me. He hadn't been interested in wrestling with his pain for us. But for all Coyote's mistakes, he'd done everything he could for his familia. He'd sacrificed for hundreds of years before the pain whittled away at his hope, and he'd finally broken under the pressure. But I knew my friend. I opened my eyes as cracks broke through the crystal dome above. And I knew what he was made of.

The crystal prison split open, and Coyote fell free.

We all dove for him. Ocelot caught the brunt of his weight, but we all crashed together into a pile on the floor. I pressed close to Coyote. Kit laughed in delight, brushing crystals from his hair. Coyote's body was limp. But slowly, his eyes batted open in a daze that melted away as he saw us. His soul swung around his neck, and when he gazed up at me from where I had wrapped him in a hug—I could taste new colors there.

A bright, sharp turquoise—a more honest sorrow—had replaced the depressed navy blue and hopeless gray that had haunted him for so long. He looked from me to Kit to Ocelot. And his eyes lit up as they filled with moisture.

"Gracias," he said, with a hard and difficult swallow. "Gracias, Cece, Ocelot, Kit." Coyote wiped his cheeks as Metztli crouched in front of us. "Gracias."

I rested my forehead against Coyote's. "You did it. You freed yourself, Coyote!"

I reached for his soul with mine, even as they hung separate, around our own necks. His soul started to glow beneath his shirt. Coyote squeezed my hands. His cheeks were streaked with tears, but he raised his head to meet my gaze.

"And now," he said, "I'm going to free my familia too." He faced Metztli. "That includes El Cucuy."

Everyone froze. My stomach flipped.

But he smiled, and it was stalwart and clear and ready. "I know how it sounds. But por favor—give me a chance to offer him the Name he should have had all along."

24
Juana Rios and the Cager of Souls

My mind churned as the woman in the doorway kicked El Sombrerón to the ground. She held his soul in her hand, rolling the smooth, dark stone in her fingers. The moment our eyes met, her smirk widened.

"I've waited years to get inside this room," she said, her voice honey sweet. She had long, silky hair and wore a flowing white dress. But the bloodstains on her hem betrayed the illusion of gentleness. "Gracias, Juana." Her gaze slid to Lion. "It's nice to see you again, too, Little Lion. I hope you've been doing well."

Beside me, Lion flared up. His shoulders set, and his lip curled back in a snarl that shook the room. It was a wordless, seething rage—the kind that melts metal.

She just kept smiling. "Seems you couldn't help but be drawn to the Rios familia again, hmm?"

Lion's face twisted. He stepped forward once, opening his mouth to shout. But something changed in the air. A sort of pressure, like a hot wind skating past me from where Tía Catrina narrowed her eyes. Lion's voice caught. His tongue twisted. And something terrible shook through his body.

Throughout our adventure, Little Lion had been as steady, and sometimes as sharp, as obsidian. But obsidian is also brittle. And at that moment, I found out what obsidian looks like when it shatters. Lion seized up as if Catrina had wrapped her fingers around his heart and squeezed. His eyes widened; his entire body shook like his world had been pulled out from under him. A film covered his eyes, the same way it had when Brujo Antonio had controlled him. Only, Lion still safely wore his soul. And Tía Catrina stood nearly ten feet away, framed by the door.

But Catrina's gaze stayed fixed on him, too intentional to be a coincidence. It didn't make sense, and I didn't know how, but I knew she was messing with Lion's soul, even from a distance.

I planted myself in front of him and spread my arms to block him from view. "Stop hurting him!" I said, so loud my voice echoed.

She finally broke her stare. Lion gasped behind me, like she'd released his lungs from a vise grip, but he couldn't seem to find words just yet.

"Juana," Tía Catrina said, her tone gently chastising. "Is

that any way to speak to your tía? Cece at least tried to be polite." She clucked her tongue, and El Sombrerón moved mechanically to meet her at the doorjamb.

A punch moved through my gut. Cece was here? But I didn't rise to the bait. I wouldn't lose my head this time.

She hummed a laugh. "You should be more grateful. I even sent someone to help you through the city." She tilted her head. "Jaguar! Tell my niece not to be so unkind."

Slowly, Jaguar stepped into view. Her dark skin caught the light, and her glassy eyes found us. She stopped beside Tía Catrina, her braids rustling. Her shoulders were up by her ears, though. And she seemed afraid to take up the space she stood in. Tía Catrina rested a hand on her shoulder proudly.

"But she had her soul stone!" I said.

"Points for observation, mi sobrina." Catrina smiled and tugged Jaguar's collar down. Jaguar was still wearing the necklace. "You may think I'm a villain, but I've *always* cherished my criaturas." She tried to peek at Lion around me, and I shifted to keep him from view. "In fact, I know them so well, I can speak to their souls even without holding them. You probably haven't heard of that ability," she said, with a smirk. "It's called soul language. After a little bit of trust training at the beginning, I let my criaturas keep their soul stones. Because, after a while, they carry my voice inside them. Everywhere. They. Go." Catrina patted Jaguar's soul stone through her shirt.

My stomach twisted upside down. Heat and bile climbed up my chest. I'd never heard of "soul language." I didn't know how it was possible to control a soul from a distance like that. But I knew it was too similar to what El Sombrerón did to me. She was breaking the souls of criaturas with this soul language, so no matter what happened, no matter where they went, her commands haunted them. The same way my soul carried the scar of what El Sombrerón had done.

"Soul language is a valuable tool," Catrina said. "Initially, it can take some time to embed your voice into a criatura's soul, but the effects are long-lasting."

Her smile widened. Little Lion's breath dried up in a painful hitch. So she was able to use their connection from his last life on his soul now? My blood boiled, heat rising up my throat. This woman was—she was—

"You can pretend like this makes you special all you want," I exploded. Catrina jumped at my sudden outburst. I stomped up to her, so we were nearly nose to nose. She reared back with disgust, and I didn't flinch at it. "But I see you for what you are, Tía Catrina. You're nothing but a pathetic *parasite*."

Disdain festered on her face. She either didn't realize, or

didn't care, that her calm mask was slipping.

"You're just like your mother," she hissed.

I sneered back. "That's a compliment."

"Fine." She summoned a stiff smile. "Have whatever opinion of me you want. You were necessary to get into El Sombrerón's room, but you're not important anymore."

Jaguar suddenly leaped forward and shoved me away. The blow wasn't aimed to wound, but it sent me stumbling as Catrina stepped out into the hallway. El Sombrerón followed, but his movements were delayed, mechanical, while Jaguar came easily. With a flourish undermined slightly by a pained tremble in her hands, Catrina looped El Sombrerón's soul around her neck and tucked it into her dress collar. My heart clenched.

"You sent Jaguar to help us because you needed me to open this room," I said. "It was for El Sombrerón's soul, right?" I stabbed a finger at him. "What do you want with it, cucaracha?"

"A bit slow, aren't you?" she asked, with a self-satisfied smile. Sparks flew through my blood. "Who do you think told El Sombrerón you were the most beautiful girl in Tierra del Sol?"

My heart skipped one of its newfound beats. She nodded.

"And why, do you think? Perhaps to awaken the only

power that could stand up to El Cucuy—your devoted little hermana," she said. "She's such a predictable chiquita.
My favorite thing about her. And she's played her part well
again, following you down here. Now that I have El Som
brerón's soul, I only have to wait until she kills El Cucuy
so I can get my hands on his next." Her hand shook slightly
around his soul stone. Was she having trouble carrying it?
Her smile swiped up like a knife on one side, wide and
sharp and cutting.

My brain felt like mole sauce. But I scoffed.

"So let me get this straight," I said. "You ruined your
familia's lives so you can rule some crummy hole in the
ground?"

"Oh, I'll rule far, far more than that." She snapped her
fingers. "But, fortunately, you're not needed for those
plans."

El Sombrerón raised a hand, and the door began to close.

"No!" I sprinted forward.

But the exit was shutting fast. I wouldn't make it. So I
took a deep breath. Grabbed the throwing knife at my belt,
aimed, and flung it through the air. Tía Catrina gasped as
the blade whizzed past her criaturas—and lodged in her
arm.

I heard her cry out just as El Sombrerón sealed the door
shut.

I crashed into the stone as it locked into place. "No!" My shoulder blazed with pain, but I kicked and slammed my fists against it. I was locked in El Sombrerón's suite *again*. "No, no, no . . ."

I had to escape. I'd wounded Tía Catrina, but that meant nothing if I couldn't get out of here. If Cece was already on her way to fight El Cucuy, I had to get there first. I rubbed my hands down my face. Sure, I'd tried every way out of this room before and had never made it. But I wasn't chained this time. I had Little Lion with me now—

Holy sunset, Lion.

I turned around. Little Lion stood stiff and frozen in the exact same spot he'd been all this time, his entire body shaking, staring at the door like he could still see Tía Catrina. I rushed to him.

"Hey, hey," I whispered. "Are you okay?"

He didn't respond. His mouth moved, like he was trying to talk, but nothing came out. I wrapped my arms around him. He shuddered like a newly born animal. Angry, resolute heat roared up my chest. And right then, I promised myself I would never let that woman do this to him again.

Lion finally took a full breath. "Sorry," he said, voice paper-thin. "I—I should have grabbed the door. Now we're trapped."

"None of this is your fault." I rested my cheek on his

spiky hair. "It's Tía Catrina's." I rubbed soothing circles on his back, the way I used to for Cece when she'd had a bad dream. "We're going to make it out of this."

My confidence stemmed from the warmth in my chest. I looked at the window on the other side of the room, next to the wall of shelves littered with souls from past brides.

"We're going to make it out of this—and . . ." A new thought sparked. "And maybe we won't be the only ones."

25

Cece Rios and the Name of Devil's Alley

Coyote crawled along the stone floor of the dungeon room. He was searching for something, I could tell. But from here, it just looked like he was getting his hands really dirty.

"Um, so, does anyone know how to get out of here?" I asked. "We probably need to escape if you're going to give El Cucuy his Name. How are you planning on doing that, by the way?"

Coyote let out a breathy chuckle. Tzitzimitl and the other Court of Fears watched him from a distance. They hadn't said much. But they didn't watch Coyote with resentment, like I'd expected. Instead, they watched him curiously, like they were trying to understand him for the first time.

"I remembered something," Coyote said. "Or more like, figured out something while you were all reaching out to me." He crawled to the far wall, and placed his left hand against it. "You hear us, Cece," he said. He closed his eyes and turned his head, like he was listening for something in the walls, too. "You listen to our voices, both out loud, and in our souls. Metztli called it soul language. It's not the same thing as Naming, but it's related." He took a long, deep breath. "All this time, I was so busy trying to remake things, I forgot to listen to what they already were . . ."

The cavern rumbled. The ceiling above us shivered, and the crystal lights on the wall blinked out for a second. Coyote's eyebrows pulled together.

"She's in pain," he said. His voice was low and respectful.

"Who?" I asked and tiptoed over.

He pressed both hands to the stone. "Devil's Alley. She's grieving." His face softened as he listened to a song none of us could hear. "I Named her from Mother Desert. She was meant to protect the criaturas, to offer solace and shelter. And she's been coerced into the opposite." He frowned, but there was no anger in the expression. His soul swelled across the space with the sunny orange of determination. Confidence. Vindication.

"She doesn't have the strength to save herself." He started tapping his hands against the wall. The vibrations echoed in the stone, each one transforming into a mighty drumbeat. "But I do. And I *will*."

I gasped in awe as Coyote drew back his arms—and then thrust them into the wall.

The wall gave way, like it had been dying for relief.

A staircase wrapped itself out of the stone. Each step slid into place, fanning out in an upward spiral. I peeked around Coyote's shoulder as the stairs disappeared into the darkness above. His smile was gentle, his soul softened at the edges with pink, as he looked at us.

"This way." He gestured forward. "Devil's Alley wants us to free her, and our familia. She was never meant to be a cage."

Bruja Damiana stepped up, her hand shaking where she held Axolotl's. "Is it finally happening?" she whispered. "You're . . . really going to stop El Cucuy? Set us all free?"

"Sí." Coyote nodded firmly. "And you're a part of that now. Right . . . ?" He waited for her name.

"Bruja Damiana," she said. Axolotl cuddled into her side. "I–I'm Bruja Damiana, Great Namer."

Coyote reached out to her. "Do you want to leave now, Damiana?"

She held her head a bit higher when he said her name like that, without the "bruja" title.

"Sí," she said. Her voice almost broke, but a spark of life came back into her eyes. My soul tingled. "Sí, I will stand with you! Let's go!"

Damiana led the charge up the stairs with a laughing Axolotl. Ocelot and Kit Fox went next, glancing back at me with a powerful resilience I wanted to dance in like rain. But the Court of Fears lingered behind. Coyote met their watchful gazes. His mismatched eyebrows pulled together hard as he waited for what they would say.

"We look forward to knowing who you've chosen to be in this lifetime," Tzitzimitl said, and offered her bone fingers.

Coyote's smile wobbled as he took her hand and shook it. "I'll make it up to you," he whispered. He scanned down the line of them, from patient Tzitzimitl and silent Bird King to evaluative Alux and waiting La Lechuza.

"After you see to El Cucuy," Alux spoke up, pinning Coyote with a sharp stare. "That must be the first priority, Great Namer."

Coyote nodded. "As you wish."

Smiles flickered across the four dark criaturas' faces. Tzitzimitl glanced my way, and I beamed at her. It was a difficult and brave thing to offer: forgiveness *and* a willingness to restore. Tzitzimitl led the Court of Fears up the stairs, and then, it was just me and Coyote.

He knelt to the ground, to the stone, in front of the stairs. I padded closer, silently, as he scooped the dust that had fallen from the walls into his hands. It slipped through his fingers like elegant waterfalls.

"I'm sorry, Mother Desert." He squeezed his eyes shut. The remorse didn't taint his soul like the shame had. It lit up the crevices of who he was and drove the grays and navy blues away. "I misused your voice. You were always creation and compassion, a beautiful home for What Could Be." He held the dust to his chest, where it smeared on the worn, red fabric of his shirt like a manifesto. "I'll strive to be all the best of what you gave me. I'll use your power well this time."

Coyote slowly looked up. I smiled at him as I stepped onto the first stair and offered him a hand.

"Are you ready?" I asked.

He leaped up, his soul surging with words even before his hands touched mine. *Sí.* I heard his soul say. *We'll do it together. And this time, I won't give up.*

The staircase brought us to the second-from-the-top floor of El Cucuy's castle. Above us, the moths on the ceiling rustled their papery wings, crawling over each other frantically, like our arrival had spooked them.

"Tu hermana should be on this floor," Damiana said, pointing at a large, stone door down the hall. She'd caught me up on Juana and Lion's plan. "But—the door to El Sombrerón's suite is closed."

That wasn't a good sign. But I sprinted for the door, ignoring the strange markings on the walls, the moths overhead, and the staircase at the other end of the hall that must lead up to El Cucuy's floor. I had to make sure Juana was okay—

Suddenly, the window next to me shattered.

Coyote lunged and covered my eyes with his arm as glass sprayed through the hallway. I yelped, and an annoyed, frustrated grunt followed the crash. Coyote dropped his arm as a brown hand reached in from outside, wrapped in fabric, and broke the rest of the stained glass out of the window.

"Okay!" a familiar voice said from outside. "Be careful with my bag, Lion, there are souls in there." A head of wavy black hair peeked inside. "Let's get inside before the fire opal burns you even more."

Juana's stare met mine through the newly broken window. Her mouth dropped open.

"Juana!" I beamed and raced forward.

"Cece!" Juana, looking the least graceful I'd ever seen, stumbled into the hallway. Little Lion came crawling in behind her, her bag on his back, his cheeks flushed. I laughed and threw open my arms. They were beat up, but they were safe and alive!

Juana caught me in a hug and spun me around the hall.

I squealed and squeezed her tight. Tears filled my whole soul. My sister was safe. I rested my head against her chest, cuddling closer to her warmth. A sound knocked against my ear.

I pulled back. "Juana," I breathed. "Your heartbeat!"

She smiled down at me. She looked tired, but it finally seemed like the good kind of tired.

"That's right! I've got my soul back. The whole thing." She tapped her chest.

This had been one of the hardest days in my life. But seeing my sister smile and my friend empowered again— that also made it one of the best.

I turned to check on Little Lion and found him scowling at his hands as he blew on them. Oh! Was there fire opal on the castle exterior? Why had they been out there? Fortunately, the burns on his hands were already healing. I sighed in relief.

Coyote and Kit sped over to him. "Little Lion!"

Lion growled as they buried him in an aggressive hug.

"We saw each other *just* a couple of days ago. Ech. Stop." Lion's muffled voice mumbled out from between them. But despite all the protest, he hugged them both in return.

Juana grabbed my face. "Wait, we don't have time for this." Her strong brows lowered. "We need to get out of here." She looked over my head and hesitated. The Court of Fears and Damiana stared at her. "Our crazy tía just stole El Sombrerón's soul and wants you to help her kill El Cucuy so she can rule the world. Also, the door to Devil's Alley closes in about an hour. We have to leave *now*."

My heart stumbled. "You met Tía Catrina?" Did she know about what Catrina had done to her?

Juana went to answer, but Coyote stepped out of his group hug to face her.

"We can't leave yet," he said. He stood tall and resolute. Completely sure. "We have to free Devil's Alley."

"Coyote's right," I said. "And we have a way to stop El Cucuy without killing him!" I looked to Metztli, who smiled and nodded. "That means Tía Catrina won't get her way, so it'll be all right, Juana."

"But—it's so dangerous—" She looked at our steady expressions. After a second, she sighed and gestured us forward. "I guess I did promise Lion I'd help him save his familia. Fine. On to El Cucuy, then."

I hesitated at the expression on her face. It looked like she was wrestling with two different feelings. But after a moment, she smiled at me.

"Don't worry, Cece," she said, in a softer voice than she'd used in months. "I know you can do this. If anyone can stop him, it's you and your friends."

My heart surged with warmth. My big sister believed in me.

Juana chuckled as we all turned and faced the stairs to El

Cucuy. She drifted toward the back of the group, to stand with Lion. Her confidence filled my chest, and I raised a fist.

"Then let's go!" I cried.

And we all charged forward.

When we arrived on El Cucuy's floor, El Silbón was the only thing standing between us and the throne room.

We stood silent. His long, clawed hands scraped the ground as he strode toward us, stopping just a few feet shy of our group. La Lechuza and Tzitzimitl stepped toward the front. Ocelot pulled Kit closer to her. Damiana clutched Axolotl. I froze, staring up at the man turned dark criatura.

"Are you going to try to stop us, El Silbón?" Metztli asked.

His white eyeholes looked sad. "I cannot disobey El Cucuy's will." Slowly, he lifted his sombrero. The cool torches on the wall lit up his gaunt face and bald head—and a thin, pale line scratched into his forehead, where it glowed softly. Dread and sorrow swept through my stomach.

"The Mark of the Binding?" I whispered. "I didn't know El Cucuy put it on criaturas."

"Just those closest to him," Bruja Damiana whispered. She touched her own forehead, nodding to herself. "After the Court of Fears rebelled, he instituted it to ensure absolute loyalty."

The Court of Fears looked at one another. I glanced up at El Silbón apprehensively. But slowly, he stretched his clawed hand out to me. His face crinkled with something like a smile.

"Fortunately," he said, "there are times when his orders have loopholes. And this time, he's ordered only that I bring you to him. Not that I keep anyone else out."

El Silbón didn't have true freedom. But he was doing what he could with what he had. I took his hand, and he led us to the doors at the end of the hall. There, he hung his head and gave me one last meaningful look.

"Be careful, Cece," he whispered.

He withdrew, slipping away from our group. Everyone moved past me, huddling around the door. Metztli was saying something, but I couldn't hear her. Coyote and I looked at each other. I squeezed my shirt in my hands. He nodded.

I turned back around and pushed to the back of our group, searching for El Silbón. But when I stopped in front of him, he was no longer stretched tall and grotesque. He stood there before me, small again, back in his original form. Was it because he'd completed his mission? He held his father's bones in his bag, his face blotted out, his human expression completely hidden. Big feelings bubbled up in my soul, but for the first time in a long time, I was at a loss for words.

"You remind me of my daughter sometimes," he said, in that electric voice. He chuckled, just once. "Look at that sad face. You're not worrying about me, are you, chiquita? You're the one who has to fight El Cucuy."

"Can't you come with us?" I whispered. "Damiana has a mark, but she's coming."

El Silbón sighed. "Sí, and she's lucky she's so low in ranking that El Cucuy hasn't given her orders in years. He probably doesn't even remember she's a weapon in his arsenal. But if he gives her a direct order, she will still have to obey." He patted his chest. "Me? I hold the fourth-highest rank in Devil's Alley." His hand lowered. "I . . . am one of his most-used tools. And I already have my next order. I have to get going soon."

Coyote stumbled into place beside me. "Then—then let me give you your Name back." His eyes shone. "You never deserved this form, Alejo."

El Silbón stared at us—or I thought he did, since it was hard to tell without his face being visible. "I've waited a long time to hear that." He scratched his ear. "Ay. Such bad timing. You know as well as I that you need to reserve that power for El Cucuy. It will take all you have." He faced me. "Let me ask this instead. Will you come back for me?"

Tears welled up inside me. "I promise, Alejo."

His chuckle scratched the air. Gently, he tipped his sombrero and ushered me forward.

"Go, then, curanderita," he whispered. "Go help the Great Namer set right a thousand years of sorrow."

26
Juana Rios and the Last Fight

I lingered behind as Cece led her friends up the stairs to fight El Cucuy. She had a plan for him. And even though some part of me prickled at the idea of Cece facing the king of Devil's Alley at all, she was strong. I knew she could do it.

So I had to do my part and make sure Tía Catrina didn't interfere. I pulled my knife out, turned from the stairs, and hunted down the tiny drops of blood Catrina had left behind on the hallway tiles, from the wound I'd given her.

The crimson splotches made a trail. I followed them until they stopped in front of a tiny opening in a dead-end, crystal wall.

Tía Catrina's wound hadn't suddenly closed here, that was for sure. I peered closer. There was a thin crack in the wall, between slabs of crystal. Hmm. I pressed my blade into the opening and wiggled it. The crack widened. I wedged the blade deeper and pushed until the wall suddenly rolled back, revealing a twisting, turning set of narrow, shadowed stairs.

Aha. A secret passage.

"Wait, Juana!" a voice rang out behind me.

I whirled around to find Lion running toward me. He was raring to go, even with my bag and its precious contents draped over his shoulders. His black eyebrows lowered as he stopped in front of me.

"You're going to find Catrina, right? To make sure she doesn't pull something while Cece's fighting El Cucuy?" His hands shook slightly, but he spoke with confidence. "Then I'm coming too."

I put my hands on my hips. "Oh no you're not. Last time you saw her, you completely froze." It came out harsher than I meant. Lion bristled, and I softened my voice. "What I mean is—she really hurt you. You shouldn't have to face her again."

"But that's why I need to," Lion insisted, even though his arms trembled. I went still, silent. He swallowed. "I've *got* to be able to . . ."

Tinges of melting sorrow moved in my chest. I knew what he meant. I sighed and stepped forward, placing my hands on his shoulders.

"You don't have to prove anything to her," I said, in the gentlest voice I had. "You've saved my butt a lot lately. But now I'm going to protect you. Plus, Cece and Coyote need all the help they can get going against El Cucuy. That's why you came down to Devil's Alley, right? Go free your familia, kid." I stepped back and pointed down the hall.

"I'm not a kid," he mumbled, but he didn't follow as I turned into the secret passage.

I smiled over my shoulder. "The second I'm done with Tía Catrina, I'm coming to help you. Don't lose in the meantime, okay? You've got to keep that bag safe." I nodded toward it and the hundreds of small stones now stuffed inside. They were heavy, but Lion carried them well. "We're going to set them free too. Okay?"

Lion mumbled an ambivalent response. I sent him one last smile before disappearing up the passage.

The stairway was cold and stuffy, with only one torch hanging on the wall halfway up the narrow, suffocating space. I grabbed it on my way past. The blue flame's light spread over the crystal walls and lit up the door at the top of the stairs. I sucked in a steadying breath.

I had to face the fact that, as much as I wanted to be the biggest, scariest thing in any room—I was human. I was fast, and I was a fighter, but I was just human. Tía Catrina was a bruja with criaturas under her control. And one of them had captured and shattered me once.

I gripped the cold, silver handle. This might not go well.

I'd definitely get hurt again. But that was okay. I knew what I was fighting for now. I was fighting for Cece. I was fighting for Lion. And I was fighting to make sure that no one else, human or criatura, would go through what I had.

So I turned the knob and kicked in the door.

Tía Catrina stood by a large, stained glass, half-moon window on the far side of the empty room. She glanced over her shoulder. The cool torches lit her calm expression. I readied my hunter's knife.

She smirked. "Made it out already? You must have wanted to stay a captive months ago, if you were able to break out so easily this time."

Sharp heat flooded my chest. Oh, she was good. Manipulation was her rice and beans. I took a deep breath and let the sharp heat cool to a steady warmth. I stepped forward and glanced around the room. Jaguar and El Sombrerón were nowhere in sight.

I gripped my knife tighter. "Where are your criaturas, Tía Catrina?" I smiled. "Did you send them on another errand?"

Her brows lifted, and suddenly, yellow light poured through the window behind her. I flinched, just a bit. As I came closer, I spotted a grand room down below us, where a giant, bleak, stone throne stood beyond the glass.

"No way," I muttered.

Tía Catrina smiled. "I have a timetable to keep, Juana. As you can see—" She gestured to the room far below, and the distant people wandering inside. And up in the beams lining the ceiling of the room, El Sombrerón and Jaguar crouched, bearing down over the throne room. "I have a show to watch."

Of course she'd find a safe place to observe everything, away from the actual fighting.

I spotted Cece's tiny form far below. El Cucuy wasn't there yet. Or I didn't see him, at least. So that gave me some time.

I glanced at the arm Catrina kept limp at her side. Blood stained her long, white sleeve. She'd bandaged the wound with a haphazardly tied piece of cloth. Tía Catrina caught my stare, and her features tightened, just a fraction.

"What have you come here for? You have your soul," she said. "And the door to your human world closes soon."

I didn't bother answering. I started toward her, knife ready.

"So serious," she said, but her breathing quickened. "Are you're planning to kill me, Juana? How will you justify that to yourself?"

Tía Catrina was the kind of person who only asked questions to open up cracks of doubt. Or because she hoped to tie you up with your answers. So I didn't give her any. Instead, I surged forward and grabbed her dress. She kept silent, even as I slammed her against the window. But for the first time, Tía Catrina's eyes flickered with fear.

"I'm not going to kill you." I placed my blade at her collarbone. "I'm going to take away your criaturas." I tucked the knife under the necklace strap still hanging around her neck. El Sombrerón's soul. "Let's see how you fare when you have no one left to *use*."

I tugged to cut it—and she kneed me in my ribs before I could.

I coughed and stumbled. Catrina fled, twisting away, but I was hot on her heels. I followed Catrina's every move as she tried to escape, aiming my slashes at the necklace around her throat. She dodged back, careful, quick, like a scorpion's tail, her long hair swinging. My blade grew brighter and brighter as I struck forward. I feinted and slashed for her necklace again. She lunged back, and I caught the ends of her hair instead. She took the opening.

Her foot struck me square in the chest, hitting the bruise she'd already delivered. I fell backward. My hunter's knife clattered to the floor as I struggled to breathe.

"You're as tenacious as your mother, I'll give you that," Catrina panted, brushing her hair back. She made for the door, hugging her wounded arm. "But all the passion in the world can't defeat the third Dark Saint. I have been planning this since before you were *born*."

"I don't need to defeat you. I just have to distract you."

I scooped up the knife and charged to tackle her. But she dodged me again. "You can't control your criaturas if you can't focus, can you?"

Her face flashed with frustration—and a hint of panic.

So I was right. I'd noticed how exhausted she'd looked when she took El Sombrerón's soul. He was the second-most powerful criatura in existence. So even if she was powerful enough to control him, he had to be draining most of her focus and energy. Even without controlling Jaguar too, she had to be near her limit.

Tía Catrina was still quick, but her fatigue was showing. I swept my knife at her, and it cut the collar of her dress. No blood, but another layer of fear crept into her face. I could tell she hated being afraid as much as I had been. But I wouldn't give her reprieve. I twirled around and caught the sleeve of her already wounded arm. Just the fabric. But it was enough to start unwinding her like the thread of her shorn clothes.

"Just like Axochitl," she spat. She scrambled around me, glancing back at the window. Checking on her criaturas. Her good hand clutched at a soul stone. "Thinking you can bully your way into getting whatever you want."

"That's hilarious coming from you!" I sliced again, but she evaded, clinging to the soul. "You sure you don't want to call your criaturas?"

Tía Catrina scowled. I twisted around, to meet her when she stepped left, and grabbed her arm. She tried to yank back, but I locked my leg around hers, and we were suddenly grappling. I tried to get my knife to her neck. I'd bite the necklace off if I had to.

"You think you're going to win this, Juana?" she spat. "Your mother will be so proud of you then, huh? You're two of a kind, thinking you're better than everyone else."

I forced my foot down, so we both nearly toppled sideways. My stomach lurched, but I used all my weight to hold her immobile. Our gazes clashed: her stony rage and my unyielding fire.

"This isn't about pride," I said, voice low so it rumbled in the air between us. "It's about power, and making sure people like you don't get it."

I ripped my hands out of her grip. Brought the knife up, so close she had nowhere to run. Her eyes widened. I sliced it across the necklace strap at her throat, and Tía Catrina winced as the necklace fell free.

I wrenched it out of her dress and leaped back. Finally! Now, I just had to keep it out of her grip and—I froze. The light from the window traced the soul as I held it up. Jaguar's andesite stone rotated slowly as it dangled from my hand.

My stomach turned hot and sick. Jaguar and El Sombrerón still crouched on the beam, both focused and ready.

Crap. Tía Catrina had swapped El Sombrerón's necklace for Jaguar's, knowing it wouldn't matter if I freed her. Where had she hidden El Sombrerón's?

I turned back around—just in time for Tía Catrina to punch me in the face with what was supposed to be her bad arm.

The blow cracked through my nose. Jaguar's soul spiraled out of my hand and skated across the room. Blood dripped down my face, the pain reverberating all the way into my soul. I landed on the floor with a painful slap.

"You have skill and drive, Juana, but you're impatient like your mother." Tía Catrina stepped on my stomach.

While I was gasping and grunting, she pulled the bandage off her bad arm and rolled up the sleeve beneath. The wound I'd left her with was gone. I struggled to shove her off, but she pressed her weight down on my diaphragm, and I could barely breathe.

Tía Catrina considered me calmly. "Sucking power from criaturas isn't my preference, as it was Rodrigo's, but it has its benefits. Healing wounds, for one." She kicked my side and strode away.

I searched for my knife, still gasping, still struggling. It lay near Tía Catrina. I moved to crawl toward it, but she kicked it away, and it skidded to the other side of the room.

"Power," Catrina whispered, "isn't something you understand. You've always had it, just like your mother. You can't appreciate what it means. But you will, once it's all mine. As it should be." Her smile was wide and wild.

A rumble shook the room from below.

Cece was in danger.

When I looked up, Tía Catrina was holding a fire opal knife. Not my hunter's knife. The throwing knife I'd wounded her with earlier. It didn't glow in her hands, but it was sharp, and it caught the light. I knew how much damage it could do.

"Adiós, chiquita," her voice slithered.

I raised my arm to block the incoming blow.

And the window exploded in a vicious rain of glass.

Little Lion burst in, nearly flying through the broken colored frame. Tía Catrina stumbled back. He landed in front of her and bit down on the fire opal knife she held. It steamed, but he swung around, kicked out his foot, and sent Tía Catrina skating across the tile floor in a heap of bloodstained white clothes.

He spat out the knife. "Juana, are you okay? Can you move?" He pulled my bag off and set it down safely.

I waved him off. "I—told you—to stay behind!" I wheezed.

"You're not my bruja." He flashed me a grin over his

shoulder. "You can't tell me what to do!"

A fragile laugh burst from my mouth. This kid.

He turned back to Tía Catrina, who was scrambling up against the opposite wall. Her hair hung over her face in streaks as she glared at us. Lion's legs shook. I could see the tremor travel all the way up his back. That strange pressure moved through the air, and I reached out to him as he struggled to stay standing.

"Lion?" I called. His back shook, and his breathing quickened. He shook his head, grunting, as Catrina began to sweat. I grabbed the back of his shirt. "Hey. Just remember what you told me. It's awful, and it hurt, but what power she had over you lives in the past. You're Lion today." I struggled as I found my feet and grabbed his shoulder. "And Lion today isn't alone."

Lion's chest rose and fell hard. But slowly, he lifted his fists in a fighter's pose, and his stance readied again, cementing into something firm and strong. He met Catrina's gaze over the distance with a sharp, clear glare.

"Right," he said.

I gripped my last throwing knife. Tía Catrina placed a hand over her ribs. Was that where she was keeping El Sombrerón's soul?

More terrible crashing, creaking sounds echoed below. I forced myself not to take my eyes off Tía Catrina.

"Don't worry," Lion said. "Cece and Coyote have got this."

I had to hope Lion was right. I flipped my knife, picked up my aching feet, and charged ahead at Tía Catrina. She couldn't hide El Sombrerón's soul forever. She flattened her back to the wall as Lion and I aimed for her.

The sound of breaking glass resounded behind us. We swung around. Jaguar pounced—and sent me flying into a wall.

The blow splintered like heat and glass through my skull, and I slumped to the ground. Little Lion cried out my name. But he didn't have time to help me. Or stop Tía Catrina, as she ran for the door. Jaguar had turned on him next.

The two criaturas grappled with each other. I panted as darkness creeped into the edges of my vision. But I started crawling forward. Jaguar was older than Lion, and stronger, but he gritted his teeth and shoved her back.

"Wake up, Jaguar!" he yelled. Sweat streaked his face. "Fight her!"

Tía Catrina scooped up Jaguar's soul, where it had fallen earlier, and glanced back at Lion as she reached the door. Disgust filled the lines of her face. My head was pounding so hard, I thought I'd throw up. But I pulled my last throwing knife free from my belt. *Por favor*, I prayed. *Just a few more seconds of strength.*

The knife trembled in my hand as I aimed. My nails reflected the amber light from the blade, and my chest swelled with something powerful. My hand steadied. And I let my ancestor's weapon fly.

Tía Catrina recoiled, but she was too slow. The blade flared bright and brilliant before it lodged in her leg, just above the knee.

Her scream was drowned out by an explosion below us. She collapsed to the floor, hand plastered to what had to be El Sombrerón's soul beneath her dress. She shot a withering glare my way.

"Wherever you go," I hissed out, crawling toward her with my vision blurring. "Whatever you do to me. We will stop you. However long it takes."

Trembling and panting, Catrina rose and forced the door open. She sent me one last glare before limping away into the hidden passage. I tried to go after her, but the world was turning black and blue, and it swallowed me with all the pain of a bruise.

"Juana!" Lion cried.

His footsteps rattled toward me, and I sunk into unconsciousness.

27

Cece and the King of Devil's Alley

"What will you do if he will not receive a Name?" La Lechuza asked as we stood before the doors of El Cucuy.

Coyote's brows pulled, tight and hurt, together. "Then we fight. But I hope you'll fight with me, first, to save him. If he'll let himself be saved."

"We stand with you," Ocelot said to Coyote. "Court of Fears, I hope we can rely on you to be the primary attackers. Damiana and I must focus on keeping our younger friends safe, since Damiana cannot directly oppose El Cucuy due to her Mark of the Binding." She ruffled Kit's hair. He looked embarrassed but clearly pleased. Bruja Damiana nodded and squeezed Axolotl close.

"Yes indeed," Tzitzimitl spoke for the Court of Fears. She gestured to the doors. "Quickly, now. He expects us."

I took a breath and looked at Coyote. He offered a confident smile. Together, we planted our hands on the doors, pushed them open, and entered the royal hall of El Cucuy.

It was a lot of empty space. The ceiling loomed far overhead, crossed with large beams and stone chandeliers swinging between them. Far in front of us, at the center of the room, sat a stone throne so large it would have fit all of us at once. But it was empty.

"Curanderas," a voice echoed out of the walls. I jumped. "You have returned. And you come banded with the disloyal and the dregs."

I watched in horror as an iridescent, inky substance, thick like oil, climbed up through the cracks in the stone throne. Coyote pulled me a few steps back as the sticky liquid coagulated into a derelict creature with legs that bent backward like a deer's, and arms like wild tree roots. Its shadow towered over all of us as it reared back, and its head sloshed into a firm, bald shape with two, large eyes.

My breath froze in my mouth. The eyes weren't placed where most creatures' were. They slashed diagonally across his entire face, leaving no space for a mouth. The two irises spiraled until they focused on us. The top one was a freezing cold blue. The bottom, violent red. Sharp teeth framed each eye instead of eyelashes, and they ground together when he blinked down at us.

I couldn't speak. Couldn't breathe. I'd seen his image once before, but El Cucuy, the first Dark Saint, King of Devil's Alley, was far more terrible in person.

His entire body shone like he was made of oil, with iridescent rainbows on the edges of his skin. Mist flowed behind him like a cloak, and when he took a single step down from his throne, the entire floor shook.

"Cecelia, the new ocean curandera. The stones have spoken of you." He took another step. The room shuddered as he crouched to look at me. "The brujas have spoken of you. The land has spoken of you. Have you come to undo the curanderas' seal? Or will I have to twist your soul until you oblige?"

My feet turned to lead. This close, I could only stare at him, tracing down his monstrous eyes to a string of blue, red, and orange tattoos ringed around his neck. Beside me, Metztli gasped and covered her mouth.

"See, then," El Cucuy said, tracing his throat with twisty fingers, "your mentor remembers these well, does she not?"

Metztli's breath seized. And suddenly, noise burst through the air. I winced as sounds crawled around the room, hissing, whispering. Coyote grabbed my arm.

"Cece?" he asked. "What's wrong?"

He didn't hear it? His ears were more sensitive than mine—so it had to be soul language, right? I squinted as the disturbing frequencies echoed around my head. They were insistent, like people talking over each other. No, wait, that was exactly it. They weren't just noises; they were *voices*.

There were three. I craned my head as the mist around El Cucuy whipped my hair back. The world flickered and distorted. And for just a second, I saw the orange, blue, and red tattoos stretch into the filmy, transparent figures of three women, each holding him by the throat.

"The last curanderas," I whispered. "I can see their souls."

Ocelot glared up at the king of Devil's Alley. Coyote's eyes widened.

As El Cucuy moved, the flickering image of the women faded away, though the bright tattoos lingered on his neck.

"So you have learned to speak the language of souls," he said.

The entire room shuddered at his voice, and even my bones got goose bumps.

"Yet it means little." He stretched over us. The stones in the room began to shake. I trembled as the floor itself roared. Coyote turned a glare on El Cucuy. "For I was given to make order. And you, Cecelia of Four Souls, will undo what your predecessors have done. You will release me." His eyes stretched wide across his face, as he loomed down on us. "Or I will break you."

My knees quaked. I couldn't give in to it, I knew, but fear lined my skin, and my throat felt like it was going to collapse. The souls around El Cucuy's neck turned my stomach as he closed in on me.

Coyote stepped between us. El Cucuy hesitated.

"Legend Brother," El Cucuy said, and the room's light brightened. I gripped the back of Coyote's shirt. "You have come in your infancy to behold your greatest creation," El Cucuy said. "Are you proud of me?" He stretched his arms wide, and the bricks trembled in the walls. "See the order I placed on chaos, as you desired. See how I have molded this world. Witness me."

Coyote's soul shuddered with streaks of blue grief, but a resolute orange remained.

"I witness you," Coyote said. "And I'm sorry."

El Cucuy lowered his hands slowly. His sideways eyes locked on Coyote.

"I shouldn't have made you the way I did," Coyote said, louder this time. He straightened to his full height, spreading his arms to block me. "Every other criatura, I made from What Could Be and gave a Name to form them. But I withheld yours. And what I gave you instead was my hatred and disappointment. I made you for what I wanted, and for what I was too angry to carry."

El Cucuy's red eye bulged. Around us, the torch lights began to dim. The mist that hung around his wiry body expanded into clouds of smoke. Ocelot stepped up beside me on my left, Tzitzimitl on Metztli's right.

Moisture caught in Coyote's eyes as he beheld the ruler of Devil's Alley. "But I can fix that now," he cried again, so loud the room echoed with it. "Let me give you your true Name."

Coyote stepped closer to him. El Cucuy waited, staring, his silence brimming with something dark. Coyote reached up for El Cucuy's soul, a jade chunk that swung on a silver chain. I held my breath.

El Cucuy lashed out and seized Coyote by his face.

"Coyote!" I surged forward, but Ocelot yanked me back. Tzitzimitl, the Bird King, La Lechuza, and Alux rushed for El Cucuy, Metztli at their head.

"Stop!" she cried. "In the name of the four gods, release him!"

El Cucuy lifted my best friend far over our heads. Coyote struggled, his claws scratching at El Cucuy's massive, five-jointed hand.

"Don't hurt him!" I screamed so hard my lungs burned.

The Court of Fears soared up to him defiantly. The Bird King and La Lechuza swooped down and slashed. The Bird King's talons left gashes so deep I could see all the way through El Cucuy's inky mass. La Lechuza screeched as she sliced through his head. His diagonal eyes swam around to avoid her blow, but his head split like sliced fruit—until the pieces stitched themselves back together.

Beneath them both, Alux ran up, dodging the vine-like limbs winding off his body with a dexterity that would have made Juana jealous. Tzitzimitl bolstered him at the last second, so he could place a hand to El Cucuy's inky body. A patch in the shape of his hand turned to stone. The shell-like substance began to spread, encasing El Cucuy's chest. Tzitzimitl placed her bones on the patch next, as the Bird King and La Lechuza continued to tear El Cucuy's body into gelatinous pieces. La Lechuza nearly freed Coyote, but El Cucuy slammed her out of the air. Tzitzimitl's headdress glowed, and the stone shell Alux was encasing him with lit up. Moonlight thrummed across it, and El Cucuy's inky body steamed when the light touched him.

Metztli sprinted forward and whispered something, her nails flashing as she aimed for the tattoos around El Cucuy's neck. They were trying to finish the seal! The moonlight grew nearly blinding, and El Cucuy's skin dripped and melted around the growing stone shell. Metztli leaped on Tzitzimitl's back and reached for his neck. The steam turned to smoke and choked the air.

El Cucuy's twisted eyes swiveled down to the Court of Fears. His chest jogged once, with a sound almost like a laugh. And his entire body rippled as he let out a deep, wrenching roar.

The stone shattered off him like an egg's shell. It blasted

Metztli away, and he batted the Court of Fears across the room with his free arm. They cried out, scattered like toys. I escaped Ocelot's hold and dove for Metztli and Tzitzimitl, where they crashed into the ground. Ocelot snatched Kit, where he'd run up to help, and leaped away as El Cucuy nearly reached to do the same to her.

Damiana was nursing the Bird King and Alux, pressing Axolotl far behind her. Sweat dotted her face. Coyote's muffled voice cried out from El Cucuy's closed grip.

"I am El Cucuy. The king of Devil's Alley, Keeper of the Desert's Children, the Hunter of Disobedience." El Cucuy rose on his backward knees and stood so tall his head nearly scraped the wooden beams far overhead. I trembled as he stepped toward us, and darkness sprouted from his feet. It lifted into the air as smoke, joining the mists that clung to him, until everything disappeared in a storm so thick I couldn't see my own hands.

"I am the one who owns." El Cucuy's voice rumbled through the vast, untamable nothing. "I will be so forever."

Something hit the ground beside me. I yelped, but when I reached out to find out what it was, Coyote came up under my fingers.

"Coyote?" I whispered. "Coyote, are you okay?"

"Still breathing . . ." he squeezed out.

Oh thank the Sun and Ocean. I put my forehead to his

shoulder, quivering. Footsteps like earthquakes shook the room. A giant foot cut through the darkness toward us. Coyote and I both screamed as it sent us flying.

Someone caught us. I coughed, and Ocelot's voice came above us: "It seems we must all fight."

Wings beat on either side of her, and I jumped as La Lechuza's shriek and the Bird King's sharp cry echoed in the mists. The rattling of bones and terrible shouts pierced the vastness. Tzitzimitl? A distant, flickering white light almost interrupted the darkness. Metztli.

Ocelot placed us on the ground. "Stay here," she said. "Be safe."

She ran into the fray.

I listened to the sounds of people fighting, and my heart broke. Fear and guilt piled inside me like rocks, and my insides felt frozen over. Someone else whizzed past in the darkness, their scream fading in the distance. I hugged myself, heart slamming. I had to fix this. I had to make sure no one else got hurt. I had to—

Silence suddenly bloomed in my chest. Everything fell still. I raised my head in the darkness as I saw Metztli's nails flicker with light. That was right. My power came from love and listening. It came from moving forward and caring. I couldn't let guilt and shame and fear hold me hostage. Slowly, I stood.

I closed my eyes and let the darkness swell around me. My soul's cool, steady temperature soaked into my hands as I gripped it close. I couldn't summon water. I didn't control it. But water listened to me, cared about me. I scrunched my eyebrows as I searched for any that could reach me here in Devil's Alley.

My senses stretched, and I felt something rumble far below the fight. It was different from the chaos of the battle. It was powerful, steady, listening: water. Floors and floors down, in the deep pits beneath the tower. It was clear, and pure, and it recognized the call of an ocean curandera. I felt it rise toward me, reaching for my reaching. My soul brightened between my fingers.

Streams of water burst through the tile. My heart surged. I shot my hand forward, into the dark, where I couldn't see and the water could.

Ayúdame, I pleaded. The water streamed ahead. The mighty rush of the clean water hit something. Droplets hung on my short hair. *Por favor, help my friends! Save them from El Cucuy!*

"You're doing it, Cece," Coyote gasped as he sat up. "You're doing it!"

There was less screaming, now, though I heard a few groans. Water pooled around my feet and glowed where it touched me. People brushed past me and Coyote as the water pulled them free from El Cucuy. I pressed my soul forward, pleading. The water rose around us—and suddenly bombarded El Cucuy where he loomed in the dark.

The roar of the water was deafening. But it didn't stop the hand that suddenly ripped me off the ground.

I screamed but held tight to my soul. The giant hand swung me around so hard I thought my head would pop off my neck. And when El Cucuy slammed me, finally, into the ground, I lost all my breath. The water splashed up on either side of me and began to seep away.

"*Enough!*" El Cucuy roared.

The darkness vanished in a wave of vicious wind. Everything fell silent.

I lifted my head from the damp tile, trembling. Everyone seemed awake and alive. The remnants of the water pulled my friends out of El Cucuy's reach before dribbling away into the cracks between the tiles, returning to the cenote far below. But we were scattered like dust to the floor. Every bone in my body ached. I tried to breathe, but my muscles were pulled so tight I couldn't remember how.

El Cucuy marched toward us across the agate tiles. His steps were the only noise left in the room. More eyes opened sideways across his body as the images of the curanderas swung around his neck, beside his soul stone. All his eyes—red and blue, purple and gold, brown and yellow—turned to me.

I looked at my friends. Ocelot held Kit in her shadow as she nursed a bleeding wound. Tzitzimitl sheltered Metztli's bruised body with chipped bones. The Bird King, La Lechuza, and Alux lay sprawled across the opposite side of the room. Wait—where was Little Lion? And Juana? I searched, but both of them were missing. My heart quickened.

Finally, I turned my head to my left. Coyote met my stare with an exhausted one of his own.

He didn't say anything. But his soul whispered to me, *Our plan didn't work.*

I nodded. He reached a hand shakily toward me. I took it.

"Cecelia the Curandera, the Bruja, Speaker of Souls," El Cucuy's voice rumbled through the stone and shuddered in my gut. "You have brought your army and my Namer. You have wielded powers long forgotten. But watch, now, how easily I who was made to bring order to monsters— watch as I fulfill my role."

But I was too tired to move. Coyote and I stared at each other, our hands clasped, our souls reaching across the space to meet one another, as El Cucuy stopped in front of us. I blinked through sweat and blood. Coyote's brows tugged together through a cut he'd gotten on his forehead. Beneath the behemoth, as we lay helplessly, our souls met in the silence. And in that sacred place, we spoke without ever opening our mouths.

Do you remember when you said I could listen to souls? I asked.

Somehow, it connected perfectly to Coyote's soul, as he asked at the exact same time, *Do you remember the way I spoke to Devil's Alley, and remembered what she was meant to be?*

Do you remember how curanderas need each other to make their powers stronger? we both weaved together.

El Cucuy had stood there for only a second, maybe even less. But we'd said it all, we'd connected it all, in the same moment.

El Cucuy bent down, his arms stretching into a web over us. Coyote lifted his head. I rose to my knees. We reached our free hands out to touch El Cucuy's chest, where the jade soul stone waited.

He wasn't scared to let us touch it this time. He probably thought we'd try to control him, the way a bruja would, and fail against his power. We pressed our fingertips to the stone as El Cucuy stretched out the web of shadows and bone and darkness all the way across the room, to consume all of us at once.

Where Coyote and I touched El Cucuy, blue and white tattoos bloomed across his skin.

And the world vanished in a wave of white smoke.

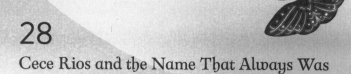

28
Cece Rios and the Name That Always Was

I stood in a white void, alone except for a hovering energy dancing around my hands like stars, and three women who watched me from a distance.

I knew who they were without a word. The curanderas of the past stood there, focused, quiet, the edges of their bodies fading gently into the white void. I hesitated. But they nodded and smiled. The one standing in the middle, draped in bright colors, with long gray hair pulled into a braid, gestured me to keep moving. Consuelo. The last ocean curandera.

Go on, Cecelia, she said without opening her mouth, in a tender voice that echoed.

There was only peace in this place. But their souls were fused into El Cucuy, so whatever happened to him would affect them. I had to ask: *What will happen to you?*

We will be free, she said. *At last.*

It was their blessing. Consuelo's eyes gleamed with tears

as she gestured again, and her soft smile drove me on.

I took a step forward, and suddenly, the white shifted and folded around me. I stumbled as a maze rose out of the ground. But I wasn't scared. I could feel Coyote's warmth in my hands, his power to Name bobbing around my fingers as dots of light. His voice floated through me: *We can do this. Together.*

I moved into the maze, and stretched out my voice to search for El Cucuy's.

What are you really? I reached through all the white nothing and confusing gray walls. The maze was intricate, careful, but tangled. It was order without heart; all the structure with none of the beauty.

I pushed forward, and Coyote's presence shook the walls as I wound through the maze. I tried again: *I know you're here. What do you want to be? What Name do you choose?*

Coyote's power drifted around me, glowing bright. *I won't remake you,* he promised.

I can't do it for you, I whispered into the airy world of El Cucuy's soul.

But we will help you do it, we said together.

I stopped before a dead end. There was a large stone door covered in rusted locks and latches. I placed my hand to its surface. Coyote's warmth filled the stone. It didn't open. So we waited together for a while, listening.

Slowly, the entrance began to unbolt itself. I watched the heavy iron padlocks and hinges fall off. They hit the ground in a rain of metal. I knocked on the door, and it fell open with a muffled crash. But the sound wasn't frightening.

Finally, I walked into the center of the maze.

There was a cenote there, in the very middle, dark and calm and cool. And standing at its edge, looking down into it, was a man. He wore an animal pelt as a cloak, except instead of fur, it had iridescent feathers. He turned to look at me from beneath a crown in the shape of a snake.

This. I stared at him, as a light and airy wind moved around us. Beneath everything, this was El Cucuy's What Could Be.

I stepped forward. He turned toward me, and his long, straight black hair fell to his waist like a curtain. I reached out to him. Coyote's power covered my fingers like constellations, glowing bright and ready.

The man hesitated. Like he was afraid I'd pull away at the last second.

I smiled up at him. *It's okay*, I said.

Trembling, the man placed his hands in mine.

It's real, Coyote promised. Bright blue and white light encircled us. *I won't withhold this from you anymore. Your Name is, and always has been . . .*

★ ★ ★

My eyes burst open in the real world. Every inch of my body hurt. Coyote and I still lay strewn on the floor, holding hands. We looked at each other, something important and powerful thrumming through us. Slowly, we craned our heads to back look at where El Cucuy had stood.

I smiled. No. El Cucuy wasn't his name anymore.

Standing there above us, trembling and staring at his new smooth, brown hands, was the criatura Quetzalcoatl.

29

Juana Rios and the Flight

The world came back to me in spots. I blinked wildly, cling-ing onto the light, until it rearranged into a moth-covered ceiling.

"You're awake?"

I lifted my head. I was resting on Little Lion piggyback style, and I was clearly too tall for this short kid. But he was strong enough to carry me, spitting out my hair whenever it dangled in his face.

"What happened?" I asked, as I tried to slip off him. My head spun, and I nearly fell sideways.

Little Lion grunted and tottered left and right until I slumped back onto his shoulder. "Yeesh, stop! You have a head injury. Even *you* have to rest, loca." He shook his head and trudged on. My bag, still filled with the brides' souls, thumped against his knee. "The throne room is just ahead. I think they won."

"What about us?" I glanced forward.

"Eh." Lion frowned awkwardly. "Well, Catrina ran away. El Sombrerón and Jaguar ran after her. Seems like you scared her into hiding." He adjusted me as we closed in on the end of the hall. "Not surprising, I guess. You're kind of terrifying."

I slapped his arm. He smirked as he stepped up to the doors.

"Hey," I said. "Help me stand, kid."

"I'm only *two* years younger than you," he grumbled, and stopped at the entrance. "And no. You're just going to flop like a fish again."

"If you carry me in like this, Cece's going to worry." I kept slapping his arm. Little Lion sighed. "Come on. Help me stand."

He relented. My head swam, but I managed to get to my feet and stay there. Lion put his hand on my back to support me, just in case. It felt weird, but I'd do worse to stop Cece from freaking out.

"She better be okay," I whispered, and we shoved the doors apart together.

Cece was *not* okay.

My stomach spiraled with fire as I saw my baby sister sprawled on the ground. Her shirt was ripped, and she looked like she couldn't move. She held on to Coyote's hand, who lay next to her. All her friends and allies were strewn across the floor like someone had spat them out on the tile. Bruja Damiana was near the back, clinging to both Axolotl and Kit Fox.

I scanned viciously, searching for who I had to fight next. And my eyes stopped on a man standing in front of Cece and Coyote.

He was—beautiful. I hated to say it. But he had long, straight hair that fell to his waist, even longer than mine had been before El Sombrerón cut it. And his skin was a smooth, deep brown, with a mole near his warm eyes and thick lashes. As I watched, he fell to his knees, and his cloak of rainbow feathers pooled around him. The snake crown he wore on his head clanged to the floor.

Lion and I blinked.

"Is that El Cucuy?" I murmured out the corner of my mouth.

He was way prettier than I'd imagined.

Lion snorted. "No." He squinted as the man pulled a jade stone out of his magnificent clothes. "I don't know who that is."

"Gracias," the gorgeous man said, as we neared Cece and Coyote. "Muchas gracias." He lifted his head to peer at them both. "Legend Brother. Curandera."

Had they done something for him? Lion helped me kneel down by Cece. Tears were absolutely gushing from her face. I almost wanted to laugh. What was it now? She grabbed my hands.

"Juana," she wheezed out. "You're okay!"

I laughed, glancing from her to the new guy and back. "Hey, chiquita, I'm your big sister. Of course I'm okay." I tried not to appear as dizzy as I felt while I cleaned her face with my sleeve. Her nose was running and everything.

"So—who's the new guy?" I asked.

"El Cucuy. No, sorry—his real name is—" she began.

"My last puzzle piece."

We all looked up. Lion froze beside me, where he was helping Coyote. The man before us craned his head back as well, still weak and shaking. Tía Catrina stood just behind him, and her hand was already wrapped around his jade soul stone.

"No!" I roared, and charged forward. But my head swam just two steps in.

Fortunately, Lion was faster than all of us. He pounced for her in seconds, claws aimed at her hand. Her face darkened—and the man sent a gust of wind crashing into Lion's gut. Catrina grinned.

Lion flew back. I spread my arms and caught him, so we both skated back to Cece and Coyote. Lion winced.

Tía Catrina's face was streaked with dust and sweat. But her burgundy smile cut through it as her hand shook around the man's stone. He rose beside her, jerky and awkward. His brown eyes kept going in and out of focus.

"Run," he said.

I grabbed the back of Cece's jacket. "You said that was El Cucuy?"

She was shaking. Clearly exhausted from a battle, and now scared on top of it. But she nodded. "Quetzalcoatl now. But he's just as powerful."

I tugged her upward. "In that case, yeah, we should run."

"Semana de la Cosecha ends in less than two minutes," Tía Catrina said. She was panting, her whole body shaking under the weight of the criatura souls. Quetzalcoatl hunched over. He spread his cloak, and the feathers started to glow. "You won't make it to the entrance now," Catrina said. "Bienvenidos—you're all subjects of the new queen of Devil's Alley."

She beamed as tiny El Sombrerón stepped out from behind her. On her other side, Jaguar slinked into view. Her head was bowed. Lion tensed.

"Jaguar," he said, like his heart was aching. "Come on."

She looked away.

Ugly sweat poured down Tía Catrina's face, and shadows pulled at the skin beneath her eyes. Jaguar was wearing her own soul stone again, but controlling both El Sombrerón and El Cucuy had to be nearly breaking Catrina. It was shocking she could control them at all. I helped Cece stand upright.

"How fast can we get to the entrance, Lion?" I asked.

He shook his head. "It'd be an hour, at least." He adjusted my bag on his shoulder, freeing up room to run.

"Wait," Cece murmured under her breath. My vision spun for a second, but I stayed standing. "The cenote."

"I just need one more soul for my collection," Tía Catrina called out. We looked up. She pointed at Coyote, and he jerked back.

"Get him," Catrina said.

El Sombrerón, Jaguar, and Quetzalcoatl launched toward him.

Little Lion, still the fastest, grabbed Coyote and yanked him toward the exit. I lifted Cece in my arms and sprinted after him. She yelped as Tía Catrina's criaturas chased after us. The world spun as I reached the door, and I nearly toppled sideways—but a pair of bony hands pulled me up.

Tzitzimitl held me, and behind us, the Bird King had stopped El Sombrerón. The two were wrestling.

"We must move quickly!" Tzitzimitl said. "What was your plan, Cece?"

Another person I didn't recognize ran up beside me, but this one seemed human. She threw her white and black hair over her shoulder. "You must be thinking as I do, Cecelia," she said. "Can you transport us to the surface using the cenote?"

Cece's eyes brightened. "¡Sí! I can do it this time, I know it!"

"Then run!" the woman cried, and pulled me forward.

I wasn't sure how I did it, but I dashed out the door. Ahead of us, Lion carried Coyote piggyback, my bag slamming against his leg as he ran. At one point I nearly tipped over, but Bruja Damiana pulled me upright. We kept running. Axolotl rode on the bruja's back, checking on our hunters' progress.

"I want that power to Name, Coyote!" Tía Catrina's voice echoed shrilly after us. Far behind us, Quetzalcoatl struck the ground, and the castle's floor began to crumble. "You've never been able to live up to it. You need someone to save you from yourself."

The floor under us collapsed completely.

I screamed as we plummeted. Cece clung to me, screaming even louder, as we plunged down through the broken floors of the tower. La Lechuza wound her arms around us, and we looked up to find her wings spreading to control the fall. Coyote, Lion, Kit Fox, Ocelot, and the Court of Fears rained down around us along with hunks of stones and tile, and dozens of dead moths and purple crystals. Bruja Damiana held Axolotl to her, and the Bird King grabbed them both. But there was nowhere to go.

The tower was dissolving. High above us, Tía Catrina's dark criaturas followed our path.

Far, far below, our only chance waited—

The cenote. I squeezed Cece as we plunged straight toward it. She closed her eyes. Took a deep breath. Her nails started to glow blue. Her soul shone brilliantly through her shirt. The water beneath us started to swirl. It bubbled with light. Could she really do this?

I smiled. Of course she could. She was my sister, with a soul as strong as water.

We crashed into the cenote and sunk deep into the pure, wild cold.

My automatic urge was to try to swim. But instead of being dragged down to the Court of Fears again, a current pulled us into a whirlpool instead. The water swung us in tight circles. My lungs ached to breathe. But the water still whipped us down, down, down . . .

Before spitting us out into the desert.

I gasped for air as I lay spread-eagled on the ground. The sweet smell of the cerros poured into my nose. My head swam as I sat up, but smears of blue sky and cactus and familiar, beautiful scrub danced in my vision. I closed my eyes for just a minute and listened.

No panic. No screams. No crumbling tower.

We were at the base of Iztacpopo, in a particularly large puddle leftover from what must have been a spring rainstorm. An awkward, shaky laugh rose in my chest. Holy sunset! We were home. I let myself giggle until my stomach hurt.

Cece lifted her head from the muddy edge of the puddle. "Did we make it?" She swung upward, stumbling. "Is everyone here?"

People started raising their hands. Cece counted them as I laughed harder and harder. We were free. I wiped my hands down my face as Cece sighed in relief. "Everyone made it," she said, as my laughter slowly died down. "Everyone except . . . Quetzalcoatl."

I stood up and tugged her into a hug.

"You're safe." I clutched Cece close. "We're safe. Your friends are safe. I have my soul back, and—well, we didn't win, exactly." I held her and savored the warmth in my chest. "But we have each other."

Cece's eyes were misty, and her chin trembled. But as she glanced around at her friends, at Coyote, shaking his hair dry, at Lion, wringing water out of my bag, at Kit, at Ocelot, and the freed Court of Fears, her lips wobbled into a smile. She buried her face in my shoulder. I brushed my hand over her coarse, dark hair. Slowly, one by one, our criatura allies rose and wiped themselves off. Bruja Damiana sobbed as she held Axolotl to her chest.

"We actually did it." Damiana wiped her cheeks. "I almost . . . almost didn't believe."

Tzitzimitl placed a skeletal hand on her back. "In part, thanks to you, Damiana."

Damiana's chest jogged, and she bowed her head as the Court of Fears came around her to hold her and little Axolotl.

"That was wild!" Axolotl laughed like we hadn't just been in a race for our lives. Damiana choked on something between another sob and a snicker. Tzitzimitl chuckled.

Behind them, Coyote stared off at the volcano.

"The door is closed," he said. "We're safe. For nine months, at least." He sighed. "But Quetzalcoatl is at the mercy of that bruja. And what'll we do when the door opens?"

Little Lion threw an arm over his shoulder. "We've got nine whole months to plan the takedown of an evil queen and the most powerful criaturas in the world. That should be plenty of time. Don't you think?"

They paused. And started snickering.

Soon enough, everyone was laughing, even Damiana through her tears. I wasn't sure whether it was because we had all just narrowly escaped a fate worse than death, or if all our hearts were dancing with a sort of bittersweet, sort of grateful, sort of manic cocktail of emotions. But either way, dark criatura, animal criatura, human, curandera, and bruja alike, we were all hugging each other and laughing.

Because at least we had this. We were alive. We were free.

The sun's warm rays set over us and traced us in golden light. The water shone with it as we splashed and laughed. And I wiped away happy tears, rejoicing in my human world and non-human companions, with an audacious confidence in the future I hadn't felt in a long time.

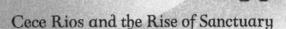

30

Cece Rios and the Rise of Sanctuary

"Are you sure Mamá is here?" I whispered.

Our entire group had wandered carefully through the quiet streets of Tierra del Sol beneath the night sky and arrived at the back door of the Sun Sanctuary. I held a hand up to the door but I didn't quite have the guts to knock. I'd just survived a terrifying ordeal, but I was probably more nervous wandering through Tierra del Sol with a former bruja, *four* dark criaturas, all my animal criatura friends, and another curandera in tow. I had jumped at every sound as we slipped through the sleepy streets, even though we never ran into anyone.

Coyote smiled mischievously at me from the bottom step. "Sí, Cece," he said. "I can smell her. And hear her." He tilted his head. "She sounds exhausted."

Mamá had every reason to be. I took in a deep breath and turned to the door again. Juana sighed.

"Cece," she said. "Come on. It's just Mamá."

"In the *Sun Sanctuary*," I spluttered. "What if one of the priestesses finds us?"

Juana rolled her eyes, brushed past Coyote—though more gently than usual—and stopped beside me. "Then let's go in together. Huh?" Her face softened.

I smiled. We both reached up and knocked at the same time. I held my breath in the silence after.

Coyote straightened and gestured back to the others. "There's someone else in there with her. Quick, quick—"

They all dashed out of sight as the door opened, and golden candlelight poured out.

Mamá and Dominga del Sol stood together in the doorframe.

Mamá looked so tired. Bags hung under her eyes, and her hair was a mess, half in and half out of a sloppy bun resting over her wide shoulders. Behind her, the counters of the laundry room were absolutely strewn with Dominga del Sol's curandera writings.

"Cece!" Mamá ran forward and pulled me to her chest. I squeezed her back. "Juana! ¡Mis hijas!" Mamá pulled Juana in to cuddle beside me. "Do you know what you've done to my heart? Híjole, the Sun gave me two troublemakers . . ." She shuddered. "Las quiero mucho. I thought I'd lost you both again . . ." Two delicate tears traced her cheeks.

"Lo siento, Mamá," I snuggled close to her. "We keep scaring you."

Behind her, Dominga del Sol laughed a sweet, tender laugh. "You have no idea, chiquitas. Tu Mamá has been in here every day scouring my curandera lore to try to save you." She smiled.

I grinned. To think that it wasn't so long ago that Mamá wouldn't even speak to Dominga del Sol. It was a beautiful thing to watch Mamá's heart soften. To see her choose what had always been waiting inside her.

Juana nuzzled into Mamá like she wanted to make a home in her arms. "Lo siento, Mamá. But we're okay. See?" She straightened and gestured to her heart. Mamá hesitated, then leaned in and pressed her ear to Juana's chest.

I waited. Juana grinned at me over Mamá's head. We both giggled as Mamá gasped and straightened up.

"Your heart! It's beating, mija! ¡Qué bueno! Thank the Sun, oh . . ." She cupped Juana's cheeks. Her chin trembled like she'd sob—but then she pulled back and swatted us both. "What were *you thinking*? Cece, you were supposed to come back and tell me what you found! And you, Juana, especially you, without a heartbeat—" She cupped Juana's cheeks again and pulled her in close. Juana looked sheepish. "You left without a word, and with our knives! What were you thinking? Where did you . . . go . . . ?" Her gaze finally shifted behind us.

The Court of Fears stood there, lit with striking shadows from the candles inside. Bruja Damiana stood with them. Mamá's mouth dropped open.

"Dark criaturas," she whispered. "A bruja?"

Axolotl peered out of Damiana's coat, and the woman gave a weak, hesitant smile that accidentally showed off her fangs. Coyote, Kit Fox, Little Lion, and Ocelot poked their heads out from behind the court. Mamá sighed, like seeing my friends put her at ease. Coyote waved to her. She waved back. Axolotl smiled as Mamá did.

"Mijo," she called to Coyote, scanning the court more carefully. "Who are . . ." She stopped on Tzitzimitl. "Oh."

Tzitzimitl nodded. "Señora Rios."

"Tzitzimitl," Mamá said, and her voice was soft and fond now. She even smiled. "I have no idea why you're all here. But I bet it will be a legend of its own." She laughed.

Metztli stepped forward. Her long white-and-black hair streamed behind her in the wind. Mamá scanned her ancient clothing, her bare feet, and her light-dotted eyes.

"It can't be," Mamá breathed.

Dominga del Sol clasped her knobby hands together. "But it *is*. Isn't it?"

"I am Metztli de la Luna," Metztli said, placing a hand on my shoulders.

I grinned awkwardly up at Mamá's shocked expression.

"Señora Rios, su hija rescued me from where I had been trapped for two hundred years. I mean to train your daughter in all the powers she has chosen."

Mamá shook her head and laughed. It was a wet laugh. Tender and fragile and bold all at once.

"After all the time I wasted being afraid," she whispered. She pinched my cheeks gently, and my heart warmed all the way through. "Mi mamá was right," she said, and released me. "Mamá was right."

Thinking of the abuela I never knew, but who'd drawn close to the old teachings of the curanderas, made me smile. If she'd been here today, I bet Abuela Etapalli would have been as happy as Dominga del Sol was now.

"My dear," Dominga del Sol reached for Metztli. "I have hoped for this day, when the curanderas would return to the Sun Sanctuary they made. Por favor, will you come inside?"

Metztli took her hand with a smile. "I feared we would not be welcomed into our old home." She stepped up and scanned the interior of the sanctuary. "It is good to be here again." She brushed her hand along the stone walls reverently, as if even the laundry and mess were something precious. She turned to face Dominga del Sol and Mamá. "We have much to discuss." She looked beyond me, to the Court of Fears. "Por favor, amigos—let us explain what lies before us. Come, enter our home."

Alux stepped forward first. "I have missed this place as well."

We all filed inside, and Coyote and I grinned at each

other as Metztli and the dark criaturas began to catch Mamá and Dominga del Sol up on everything that happened. I led him over to the laundry pile, and we nestled into it together. It was nice to relax like that again.

The adults and Court of Fears chatted over the old, patchy writings of the curanderas. But off to the side, I saw Mamá take Tzitzimitl's hand and say something to her. I was too far away to hear, but I was pretty sure it was a thank-you.

And in Mamá's warm face, in Tzitzimitl's gracious nod, in Damiana's hopeful eyes, in Metztli's careful teaching—I saw the beginning of something priceless. A new world we were going to need. I took a deep breath and let the moment settle inside me.

"One of you wake me up if I sleep too long," Juana said as she plonked down beside me. She leaned her head on my left shoulder. "I have a head injury. Did I mention that?"

"You do?" I would have checked her, but she was too heavy for me to move with her leaning on my shoulder.

Little Lion came over as Ocelot joined the adults. Juana's bag jingled oddly as he set it down next to us. "That's because she decided she was a one-woman show all of a sudden." He folded his arms as he sat next to her. "And she calls me estúpido." He flicked a sock onto her. Juana tried to frown, but a smile bloomed anyway. Her eyes fell closed. I watched the exhaustion and pain bleed away from her face, and I rested my cheek gently on top of her head.

Kit came bouncing over. I opened my arms and he nestled down on my lap.

"Thanks, Cece," he said.

"Thank you, Kit." I soaked in his and Juana's and Coyote's warmth.

Kit's soul was filled with sunshine. He smiled, and finally, seemed totally content and safe. He closed his eyes and let himself rest.

Soon enough, most of my friends drifted to sleep as the adults (and Axolotl, who Damiana held in her arms) continued to talk. Kit dozed peacefully in my lap. Little Lion fell against Juana and conked out. And Juana cuddled peacefully with me as she slept. My eyelids grew heavy, but my heart was so full I wanted to stay awake to enjoy it all.

Coyote leaned his head gently against mine. I could feel his smile against my cheek.

"It's not perfect," he said, as we stared at the meeting of curandera, bruja, human, and criatura in front of us. "But it's better. Gracias, Cece. None of this could have happened without you."

"Or you. Or Juana. Or Lion and Kit and Ocelot, and— well, everyone. We did it together." I lifted a hand and gently rested it over his soul, where it hung around his neck. All the hope I could hear from a distance rushed into my chest as a powerful, steady pink and a dedicated orange. "It takes all of us to make something like this." I smiled as my heart melted into a waterfall. "Thank you, Coyote," I said. "Thanks for being brave, and letting 'better' be enough."

His hand laid over mine, where it still cupped his soul. And together, we rested with our familia. My dreams drifted to Quetzalcoatl and El Silbón, and my hopes and love reached out to them. As the world floated into rest and reprieve, I could almost see them in my mind's eye.

Don't worry, I whispered to them there. *We won't leave you alone for long.*

Acknowledgments

To my editor, Stephanie, and the whole HarperChildren's team, who gave me the opportunity to continue Cece's story. Stephanie, your anime third eye is a treasure, and so is your enhancing, guiding editorial hand. Thank you!

To my agent, Serene, who works with me so well. Thank you for offering the advice I need, always championing me, and working hard to help me prosper. I'm grateful to have you as my ally and agent during this wild, amazing publishing journey.

To my mom, the one who reminds me where the real war is and where the light truly comes from. Thank you for being my first editor. For being my first coach. For loving me. Thank you for choosing love. Thank you for being exactly who you are. I love you, and I always, always will.

To my abuelo. Thank you for fighting for the light inside of you, for offering me advice, for reaching toward greater heights with grace. I will be grateful to you throughout eternity.

To my nanny and grandad. Grandad, I miss you, and I love you. I like to think you're still proud of me, and that if you were here, we'd be two currant buns right now. Nanny, I love you and your fairies so much. Thank you for carrying magic with you and for sharing it so generously with me all my life.

To Laura, whose insight and deep, abiding dedication to growth and love give me and my work room to grow. Thank you for sharing your thoughts, time, and hard work with me. And most important of all, thank you for being my friend. You are the sister of my soul.

To the 5th Wind group. Thank you for your support and comradery. I'm glad to know you.

To my sister's wildly absurd albino African frogs. You had absolutely nothing to do with the creation of this book, but I feel I should thank you just for existing.

And thank you to all of *Cece Rios and the Desert of Souls*'s supporters. Thank you, everyone who read it. Thank you, anyone who mentioned it favorably to a friend, who reviewed it, who suggested others read it, who put it on a best-of list, who nominated it for an award, or even those who cherished it quietly in their hearts. Thank you, lovely readers. You are largely the reason I have the chance to continue my chiquita's story. And I'm grateful for that opportunity.

And of course, last but never least, thank you to He who made me, my loving God. Thank you for my voice, my words. Thank you for where I stand now. Thank you for the difficulties and triumphs that brought me here, that you have carried me through, that you taught me to pass through, in equal measure. Thank you for every ounce of what I've been through, and who I am, and the most important gift of all: You.

Glossary

adiós—Goodbye.

alux (singular), aluxes (plural)—Pronounced "ah-loosh" or "ah-loosh-es," these magical beings are only about three feet tall and have a powerful connection to nature. The original Mayan legends describe aluxes as fierce but mischievous beings who bring either good or bad luck depending on how you treat them. In Cece's world, Alux is a dark criatura.

amigos—Friends.

atotolin—A colorful bird in Mexico, known as the king of the birds, hunted to prove a warrior's prowess and to obtain good fortune. In Cece's world, Atotolin is the first name of the Bird King, a dark criatura.

axolotl—A type of endangered salamander native to Mexico pronounced "ah-sho-loh-tl." In Cece's world, Axolotl is also an animal criatura.

ayúdame—Help me.

bienvenidos—Welcome.

Costa de los Sueños—Coast of Dreams.

curanderita—Little curandera.

¿Estás bien?—Are you okay?

estúpida/estúpido—Stupid.

exactamente—Exactly.

excelente—Excellent.

feliz cumpleaños—Happy birthday.

fútbol—Football; also called soccer in the United States.

gato—Cat.

¿Hay algún problema?—Is there a problem?

hermana/hermano—Sister/brother.

híjole—An exclamation used to express surprise, similar to "wow!" or "yeesh!"

hola—Hello.

La Sirena—The mermaid or the siren. La Sirena is a character generally associated with la lotería, a game of chance sometimes referred to as "Mexican bingo," which became popular in Mexico during the early 1800s. In Cece's world, La Sirena is a dark criatura.

las quiero mucho—I love you very much.

loca/loco—Crazy.

Metztli—The Náhuatl name of the goddess of the moon, pronounced approximately "mets-tlee."

mole—A wide variety of sauces used in traditional Mexican dishes, comes from the original Náhuatl word "molli."

necesito—I need.

no puedo creerlo—I can't believe it.

¡Qué bueno!—How good. Used to express general satisfaction, much like, "That's great!" "That's nice!" or "Excellent!"

¿Qué paso?—What happened?

Quetzalcoatl—The feathered serpent. This powerful deity's role in Aztec religion and tradition evolved with the people, but he was generally known as the god of winds and rain, and he was said to be an important part of creating the world and its people.

Semana de la Cosecha—Week of the Reaping or Week of the Harvest. In Cece's world, this is the week before the door to Devil's Alley closes.

Tukákame—This ancient Huichol legend is like a cross between a demon and a zombie, with a skeleton body and a hunger for human flesh. Though the details depend on who tells the story, most agree that water burns Tukákame, so he avoids it at all costs, and he has a flock of skeleton birds for pets known as "the birds of death."

vamos—Let's go.

Yollotl—This Náhuatl name means "heart" and is pronounced "Yoh-loh-tl."